Three O'Clock's Dark Night

Books by dusty bunker:

The Number Mysteries:

> *One Deadly Rhyme*
>
> *The Two-Timing Corpse*
>
> *Three O'Clock's Dark Night*

Numerology and the Divine Triangle

Numerology and Your Future

Numerology, Astrology, and Dreams

Birthday Numerology

Dream Cycles

Quintiles and Tredeciles: The Geometry of the Goddess

Three O'Clock's
Dark Night

❀

The Number Mysteries

dusty bunker

iUniverse, Inc.
New York Lincoln Shanghai

Three O'Clock's Dark Night
The Number Mysteries

iUniverse, Inc.

For information address:
iUniverse, Inc.
2021 Pine Lake Road, Suite 100
Lincoln, NE 68512
www.iuniverse.com

Any resemblance to persons living or dead is purely coincidental.

ISBN: 0-595-32735-4

Printed in the United States of America

For Skip

Acknowledgements

❀

Thanks go to Joan Hansen, my sounding board and supporter.

And to Sharon Allen, whose dependability, insights, and strict Catholic upbringing served me well. What a difference a wandering or missing comma makes.

In a real dark night of the soul
it is always three o'clock in the morning.

—F. Scott Fitzgerald, *The Crack-up*

Prologue

❀

Richard Howard Brennan was a walking dead man. He wondered when he would make it official. What he didn't know was that someone would do it for him.

He hunched over his beer mug at the stained bar in Iggy's Den where he'd been beaten up numerous times. If this wasn't Hell he thought, rubbing blood-shot eyes, it was the pit next door. But he really didn't care how much he got hammered because he figured he deserved the abuse. He was the one behind the wheel the night of the accident. And now she was gone.

Brennan's head dropped to his chest. He drew a breath so deep it seemed to come from the bottom of his soul. As a moan escaped his lips, he closed his eyes against the pain.

Smoke roiled beneath the low ceiling of the cinder block bar. Cue balls rumbling on nearby pool tables underscored the curses that erupted from throats tight with anger and resentment and despair. From the jukebox, Clint Black's voice wailed about a lost love. The words pierced Brennan's heart like the Devil's poisoned pitchfork.

He clasped his fingers behind his neck and moaned again.

Suddenly, a hand clapped hard on his back. He jolted forward.

"Hey, *dick*! Heard Benny's after you. You owe him money, too?"

There was no mistaking the deep timbre of that voice. In a happier time, Brennan could have imagined an affable Sam Elliott with the distinctive bushy moustache gracing his top lip, his head tipped to one side, a twinkle in his eyes, his hand extended in an invitation to buy you a beer at the town's only saloon. But this was not a happy time. And the velvety voice had a razor edge to it that could slice to the bone.

Slowly Richard Brennan lifted his head and turned to his right, squinting through the haze at the barrel-chested man.

"Christ, Quinn. You practically knocked me off the stool."

1

In place of the trademark moustache, Quentin "Quinn" Stevens had a thick curly beard that festooned halfway down his chest. One gold tooth glistened amongst stark white stalactites behind sneering lips. He wore a blue bandana tied around his head and a black leather vest studded with badges and buttons and one large safety pin. Dirty jeans hung below his burgeoning belly and tattoos decorated his huge biceps. He smelled of beer and bad cologne.

"You'll be lucky if that's all I do to you," Quinn growled in that ironically soothing voice. "You having a good time spending my money on suds?" The sneer faded into the black web of his beard. "Listen, *dickey-boy*. I don't care how much you owe or who you owe it to. I'll knock you from here to Sunday if you don't pay me the fifty bucks you borrowed two weeks ago." His eyes turned flinty as he leaned close to Brennan's ear. "You don't want to see me mad, man. I can think of things to do to you that you can't even imagine."

Quinn straightened up and clapped Brennan's shoulder again, this time hard enough to send Brennan's face flying into his beer mug.

Sputtering, Brennan lifted his head with a grimace. He wiped a figure eight pattern over his face and cleaned his hand on his shirtfront. With both hands, he raked back his greasy hair.

In the streaked mirror behind the bar, Brennan could just make out a red outline curved around the outer edge of his left eye and halfway over his eyebrow. He could also see the mountain of flesh looming behind him. A cold shiver ran down his spine.

"I'll have it for you tomorrow, Quinn, honest."

Quinn's eyes were heavy with hate.

"Tomorrow, I promise," Brennan pleaded. "I'll meet you here about this time. Okay?" He coughed smoke and foam out of his lungs. "Really."

Quinn stared at him for a long moment, and then said with terrifying Sam Elliott softness, "You'd better be here tomorrow night, Brennan, unless you plan on crawling the rest of your life." He gave Brennan a look that caused prickles to run down his arms and vibrate at his fingertips. Quinn Stevens moved off toward the restrooms and disappeared through the door marked HOGS.

At the same moment, two women emerged from the SOWS quarters. Brennan massaged his fingertips with his thumbs as he gazed at the jugs on the brunette. He wondered why women went to the bathroom in pairs. *Sort of like boarding the Ark*, he thought, and snuffed.

But the joke was short-lived. He looked down at his trembling fingers, then touched at the spot between his eyes. He'd been avoiding Quinn successfully up until tonight. Quinn was bad enough. He could handle this threat, even if it was from the big biker. But now, according to Stevens, Benny Madden was after him too. Jesus Christ! He was in deeper shit than he thought.

The cold shiver again. Richard Brennan knew he had to disappear.

An hour later, Quinn Stevens straddled his Harley in the gravel parking lot outside the bar, the place known unaffectionately by the residents of Georgetown, New Hampshire, as the Pigpen. He stared at the blinking neon sign that read IGGY'S DEN. A large cutout resembling the letter P was duct-taped beside the word IGGY'S so that the sign read PIGGY'S DEN. This year's high school seniors had already performed their annual spring ritual.

However, the history of the Pigpen was not on Quinn's mind this night as he sat on his Harley in the filtered yellow light from the bar's one plate glass window, his right hand under his leather jacket idly stroking a spot above his heart. He stared at the sign but he didn't see it. He didn't feel the cold. He didn't hear the peepers in the boggy lowland behind the bar or the traffic zooming out on Route 125. He didn't see the Full Flower Moon that celebrated the life that burst forth during this month of May. There was no celebration in his heart.

There was only the pain.

His mind was on the memory of her.

It was when he'd gone to the Mall of New Hampshire on his Hog to pick up some Garth Brooks CD's that he'd seen her standing in front of Mrs. Field's Cookies counter. His heart had almost stopped. He'd felt as if he were in a time warp, a sort of suspended animation, that limbo where there is no sense of sound or movement. There had been only her.

She'd been wearing a pink sweater and blue jeans, and her blond hair had fallen in soft curls to her shoulders. She and her friends had been munching chocolate chip cookies, licking the chocolate from their fingers, and laughing at whatever girls laugh at.

He'd been cleaner cut then, still in leather and chains, but about twenty-five pounds lighter. He'd known that a lot of women were attracted to his bad boy sexuality, and he'd used his animal magnetism successfully on more than one occasion.

After more than two years, the scene was still vivid in his mind.

He watched her.

She sucked at the chocolate on her thumb, glanced at him, then looked away. He leaned against a wall, more to support his weak knees than to look cool. He watched to see if she'd look again. If she did, she was interested.

She tipped her head to one side as if trying to peek at him without being noticed. A lock of hair fell over one eye. She used her forefinger to tuck that loose strand behind one ear.

To Quinn, she looked like an angel with only a brief passport into this life. Liquid heat pulsed through his veins. His heart beat so hard against his chest that he thought everyone passing by could hear it.

It was then that she looked at him again.

His heart stopped.

Quinn Stevens would never forget how his body had gone electric. At that moment, he had fallen in love with Lynda Johanssen.

CHAPTER 1

❀

SATURDAY 5:32 A.M.

Nick stood in the doorway peering at his watch. "What are you doing, Sam? It's five-thirty in the morning."

On the sun porch of their Cape Cod home, Samantha's hands paused over her split keyboard. She grabbed the green sponge roller from her bangs, hid it between the two small spider plants next to her computer and fluffed her bangs. "Haiku," she called over her shoulder.

"Gesundheit," Nick replied. He did a jaw-breaking yawn and scrubbed his face with both hands.

"What?" Sam asked.

They exchanged puzzled looks until Sam realized his mistake. "No, Nick. I didn't say 'ah-choo', I said, 'haiku.'"

Nick leaned against the doorframe. He smiled and stuck his hands in his jean pockets. "Is that contagious?"

Sam smiled back. "Not unless you read it."

Nick gazed through the wall of windows that faced into their backyard, breathing in deeply, sloughing off sleep. The baseboard crackled with incoming heat. A lone bird sang to the lifting morning.

Sam stifled a companion yawn and tugged at the neck of her red plaid nightshirt, one of three purchased some years ago during a desperate foray into the bowels of the mall. These were added to a wardrobe comprised mostly of sweats and tee shirts. She hated to shop and usually waited until she was threadbare to venture into the department stores.

For a brief moment she contemplated the pitfalls of continuing the conversation then, in customary fashion, threw caution to the wind.

"A haiku is an unrhymed Japanese poem," she explained. "It refers, in some manner, to the seasons of the year. The poem is conveyed in three lines, using seventeen syllables: five, seven and five. It's a good mental exercise because each word must be chosen carefully. One has to be spare with her words."

"No one has ever accused you of that," Nick said. His right dimple deepened as his eyes caressed her. After twenty-six years, she still loved that look.

She tipped her head at him. "Tread lightly, big boy." Her eyes took in his six foot one inches. She was amazed that his dark hair hadn't yet shown signs of his age.

"I guess I'd better," he said, "since I've convinced you to go camping with me, even if it's only down to Pottle's Pond for two nights. You know, you might really like it." He grinned, as if that would convince her how much fun it was going to be.

Sam leaned back in her swivel chair and folded her hands across her belly bulge. She sniffed. "Yeah, maybe."

She looked down at the cellophane evidence from the package of Ring Dings she had just eaten and thought about the thirty pounds she wanted to lose. That thought segued to her doubts about preparing meals in a motor home and the notion that camping was not that much fun no matter how you looked at it. But at least they'd be inside a heated camper, not lying on the cold ground. Even though it was May, the nights could still be chilly in New Hampshire.

"Want to hear my haiku?" Sam asked.

"Sure," Nick said, settling into the stuffed green rocker in the corner by the ficus plant. He crossed his ankles. "Achoo away."

Sam read her verse.

Nick nodded.

"Do you get it?" she asked.

"Yeah." He frowned. "I think." He rocked as he gazed at the matching red chair on the other side of the corner table. "Well, I'm not sure."

Sam leaned forward. Her eyes lit up. "You know that life is a progression that can be understood through the language of numbers. Numbers are the alphabet and geometry forms the words."

Nick tapped the arm of the chair. "Right. Figures measure things whereas numbers represent qualities."

Sam nodded. "Correct. Numbers indicate qualities, characteristics and also progressive cycles. So, as I was saying, the progression of life can be understood through numbers. Number one is the point, the energy, the beginning. Two is the two points connected by a line. These two points represent the opposing forces in nature: up and down, light and dark, dry and wet, male and female."

"You and me," Nick said.

Sam hesitated, stared at him.

Nick lifted his eyebrows and said, "What? I'm listening."

Somewhat placated, she went on. "It's in the next step, number three, that the opposing forces marry and begin the process of creation. You know the common expression: 'things happen in threes'?"

Nick did. He shuffled his feet. He examined a leaf on the ficus. He pondered his fingernails. Sam waited until he looked back at her.

She knew he'd heard all this before, but she was so caught up in the magic of her world that she couldn't stop the flow of words. "The triangle symbolizes number three. It's the first shape that can be constructed with straight lines; therefore the triangle is considered the first perfect geometric form. It's the pattern for the creation of life that occurs with the passage of time: like past, present, future; beginning, middle, end; and maiden, mother, crone.

"Now, the triangle is bursting with energy. It's the life spirit seeking a container. You'll notice that three is the spiritual family, the trinity in most religions around the world."

"Father, Son, and Holy Ghost," Nick said dutifully.

"Exactly. Although the Holy Ghost is the Mother. The early Christian fathers eliminated Mary from the Trinity, but the people wouldn't let go of her. They needed a Mother figure. I mean, how can you have a son without a mother?"

Nick laid back against the chair, resigned to the inevitable.

"Anyway, the next step in the progression of numbers is four, the square, the second perfect form that can be constructed with straight lines. Symbolically, squares represent matter, things that have form."

"The four corners of the earth," Nick yawned again.

"Yes. Even though we know that the earth has no corners, we are motivated subconsciously to use the symbology of four when speaking of earthly matters. Therefore, when I wrote 'Form, cast out of time,' I was referring to the form, the square, that results from the passage of time, the triangle. And that form is the human body, the home that is animated by the Sacred Light or the soul."

Nick leaned forward and stretched while he scratched his head and lower back simultaneously.

Undeterred, Sam went on. "Seven is considered the spiritual number in metaphysical literature. Curiously, if you place the triangle over the square, you have a stylized drawing of a home, another symbol for the human body. See? Three—the triangle, plus four—the square, equals seven—the triangle and the square."

Nick settled his head against the back of his chair. His eyelids opened and closed in slow motion, but were leaning toward the lower elevation.

"So," Sam was in a state of euphoria, "although my haiku is about the birth of the human being, it's also a metaphor for Spring and eternal rebirth. So, listen again.

> "Form, cast out of time,
> is home for the Sacred Light.
> Kneel. A child is born."

Sam glowed as she looked to Nick for a response.
She waited.
Finally, she said, "Nick?"
Nick blinked, opened his eyes, pulled himself upright, and stared at his wife. "Interesting."
Sam's lips tightened.
When he was once again alert and the obligatory moments had passed, he said, "I know you'll like camping, Sam. We're leaving around 4:00 tomorrow afternoon. Don't forget."
Through narrowed eyes, she regarded her husband. She thought about turning his socks inside out, or eating that last piece of silken chocolate pie he had set aside in the refrigerator for himself, or maybe…hiding his L.L. Bean catalog. Yeah! That's what she'd do.
"*Cool it!*" she told herself as she slumped back into her chair. She massaged the spot between her eyes. Just when she thought she had resigned herself to his short attention span, something like this would pop up and bam! she'd be primed for battle.
She grumbled at Nick, "How could I forget about camping? You've been reminding me all week."
The heat climbed her chest and on to her cheeks and forehead. The heat of the battle. She tried to convince herself she was not menopausal.
Nick stood and stretched, looking into the backyard once again. His body showed lean in his blue jeans and New Hampshire wildlife tee shirt. "Guess I should take down the bird feeder and clean it today," he said.
Sam grabbed a tissue from the box on her desk. She took a swipe at her forehead and, before Nick looked over, dropped the tissue into the wastebasket at her feet.
"You got any plans for the weekend?" he asked as he turned toward her.
She nodded. "Mom and I are going to the Water Street Bookstore in Exeter this afternoon. Dan Brown is speaking about his latest book, The Da Vinci Code. Remember, I took one of his books to the Vandalay mansion last year."

"Oh, yeah."

Sam didn't think he remembered, but she wasn't going to push the point. "His books are *interesting*. I'm sure he's got some *interesting* things to say about his research on this new one."

Oblivious to the gibe, Nick asked, "Are the girls going with you?"

"No." Sam sighed. "Sadie's going to the mall with Medra, and Caroline's watching the Inn for Mom."

"What does Sadie need now?"

"Sadie doesn't *need* anything. But if you're asking what she wants, now that's a question you would be able to answer."

Nick chuckled. Both daughters had inherited his taste for the finer things in life.

"Okey dokey, my girl," Nick said, rubbing his hands in anticipation. "Get that gorgeous body into some sweatpants. We're going to The Bog for breakfast."

Sam finally smiled at her husband, and shook her head. *How do you fault a man like this?*

CHAPTER 2

❈

SATURDAY 10:59 A.M.

Richard Brennan was holed up in the CircleTo Motel in Portsmouth, New Hampshire. His money was running out.

He sat in his underwear, with his head in his hands, on the edge of the rumpled bed. The blinds were pulled tight against the late morning sun. The only light in the room came from the bluish glare of the television screen; the sound was muted. Although the room was clean, it had that dead air odor that comes from enclosed spaces with stationary windows.

Brennan didn't dare go back to his apartment. Both Benny and Quinn Stevens knew where he lived.

The bookie and the biker. B&B, he thought, almost hysterically. *They wouldn't think anything of serving me up for breakfast and putting me to bed permanently.*

His mouth went dry. He rubbed his hands hard over his face and grimaced as his fingers met the bruised flesh around his eye, the result of his encounter with a beer mug at the Pigpen. Regardless of what Quinn Stevens said, he *could* imagine what the big biker would do to him.

Brennan knew he had to think his situation through with a clear mind. He dropped his hands on his knees and stared at his feet. *Concentrate,* he told himself. He heard the high-pitched squeal of a big rig's brakes on Route 1 as the truck approached the Portsmouth Circle. The sound caused his shoulders to lift as a shiver ran across his back and up to his head, tickling the fine hairs on the back of his neck.

As the vibration from the truck rumbled under his feet, he looked down at the ragged nail on his big toe. He thought about trimming it, but he didn't have any clippers with him.

A slow breath escaped his body.

He stared vacantly at the toe as if it were a disembodied member that had no physical connection to him. His thoughts slipped into the past, as they did so often these days. He recalled the countless times he had sat at the foot of his mother's wheelchair and washed her feet in the peeling yellow plastic basin and carefully clipped her toenails. Then he'd touch up her nail polish with Pretty in Pink, the color she favored. She took pride in her feet even though she hadn't been able to use them since Brennan was eight years old.

He struggled to suppress his resentment. It wasn't his mother's fault that she'd contracted muscular dystrophy and destroyed his childhood.

For minutes he sat slack-jawed as vignettes of his life swirled around in his brain, spinning into a maelstrom that pulled him deeper into despair. He couldn't stop the images—his crippled mother, loosing Lynda, his addiction to gambling and now drinking, stealing from the Frazettas who had been so good to him, Claudio Frazetta's suicide, big Quinn Stevens who hated his guts, Benny the Bookie who hated no one but got his due one way or another.

At the thought of Benny, he moaned.

He'd heard about the kinds of things that happened to Benny's slow-pay and no-pay customers, and it wasn't pretty. Scuttlebutt had it that a few of those hapless souls had ended up walking the bottom of the Merrimack River in a pair of formfitting cement shoes. The question of which man's execution style you would prefer—the bookie or the biker—was like choosing between being pulled apart by wild stallions or sliding down a twenty-foot razor.

Brennan's body went slack. He swung his head back and forth like a tired pendulum on an expiring grandfather clock. He was thirty-eight years old, broke, and in debt to some really bad people. He had no job, no friends, and the most important person in his world…he swallowed hard. He wouldn't think about her. He fell back on the bed. He was at rock bottom.

Suddenly, there was a sharp rap at the door.

Brennan leaped off the mattress and crouched into the blind corner beside the bed. The rap at the door came again, this time more insistent. He barely heard the sound above the blood pounding in his ears.

"Maid service," a female voice called out. She knocked a third time, waited a few seconds, and then began to rattle a key in the door.

Even though he had flipped the security lock, Brennan darted around the corner of the bathroom and fell against the wall beside the door. He looked to see if the lock was secure. It was.

"I told you, no maid service," he croaked. "Please!"

"Sorry, sir," the woman said. "I'm taking over for the regular maid who's sick. I didn't know."

"Don't you see the Do Not Disturb sign on the door knob?!"

"No, sir. There's no sign here."

"Well, there should be. Please. Just leave me alone!"

She was lying! He knew she was lying! She was waiting for him to open the door and then she'd blow him away in a hail of gunfire. No. That would make too much noise. She probably had a silencer on her gun.

She had to be a hit woman! Brennan recalled that Kathleen Turner played the role of a hit woman. In the movies, killers often pretended to be service personnel in order to gain access to their victims. But he wasn't a fool. He wasn't going to be taken in by that transparent ruse.

He waited. Fear rose like bile in his throat. A sheen broke out on his upper lip.

Then he remembered he hadn't found a Do Not Disturb sign in his room when he'd signed in and he'd asked the night clerk to bring one and hang it on the doorknob. *Maybe that idiot forgot*, Brennan thought. He prayed he was right.

He listened, his ear tight against the wall, staring at the doorknob, waiting for the maid impersonator to break down the door. He knew a woman could do that. He had seen some women wrestlers who could take on Arnold Schwarzenneger.

Brennan was barely breathing. Beads of sweat now peppered his forehead. From under his armpits, trickles ran down his side. He could smell the fear oozing from the pores in his body. His mind was so frozen that rational thought congealed into a block of ice in his brain, sending waves of pain through his head. All he could see was the deadly black hole of the silencer pointed at his forehead, and behind it the sneering face of the hit woman, laughing as she pulled the trigger and blew away his face and his pathetic life.

A few seconds later, a cart rumbled down the hallway to the next room. He listened, trying to control his raspy breath. After a long minute, he thought that maybe the woman really was a replacement. He swiped the sweat from his forehead and brushed the back of his hand against his shorts. He had to get hold of his imagination.

He stumbled back to the bed, curled into the fetal position, and pulled the covers over his head. He had to get some sleep.

Richard Brennan was scared out of his wits. His heart was hammering against his ribs. Taking deep breaths, he tried to calm himself. His eyelids fluttered as he relaxed into the softness of the bed. He hugged his chest tighter. Somehow the warmth of the blanket made him feel safer.

Mentally he retraced his steps, as he had so many times that morning, to convince himself that he hadn't been followed and to keep from going insane.

Knowing that he shouldn't use his own vehicle, and using the excuse that his beat-up Bronco needed repairs and he had an appointment for a job interview that morning, he wheedled the loan of his neighbor's old Dodge with the promise of twenty bucks—which he had no intention of coughing up. Not one to turn down easy money, his neighbor agreed.

After packing a few things into a duffle bag, and with a glance up and down the street, he climbed into the Dodge. He headed to the nearest parking garage where he switched license plates with another vehicle. He then drove to Portsmouth and parked the car behind the CircleTo Motel where it wouldn't be visible from Route 1.

His neighbor, who'd had run-ins with the police, would be furious, but he probably wouldn't report his car missing just yet, if at all. The Dodge was a clunker and not worth the hassle. And as far as the stolen license plates went, sometimes a car was left in a parking garage for days. Even if the owner did pick up his vehicle the same day he'd parked it, he probably wouldn't notice the switched plates for a while.

Brennan rolled over on his back and bunched the covers against his chest. No one could possibly know where he was. He figured he'd be safe for a week, a week in which he could figure out what he was going to do.

Of course, that pitted-faced night clerk could be a problem. Besides having a rotten memory, he seemed the nosey type.

Brennan scowled as he tried to remember the guy's name. After a moment, he came up with it. Randy. He chuffed. He wondered if the night clerk *was* randy. He had promised the guy a C-note—yeah, right! When was the last time he'd seen one of those?—if Randy would keep the maids out of his room. Randy said he'd alert the day shift. Well, Randy hadn't done such a good job this morning. Of course, it might not have been the guy's fault, what with the maid taking over for her sick colleague and all. But then, Brennan wouldn't have had such a scare if that jerk had remembered the Do Not Disturb sign. He'd give Randy a few choice words about that, then remind him of the hundred bucks.

A sigh stumbled over his lips. He felt as if gravity was pulling his organs out through his throat and leaving his body a shell.

His life had come to this.

He thought about all the energy that he'd expended over the past five years to conjure up temporary solutions for his dirty addiction. He had lied, cheated, stolen, betrayed, and destroyed. He thought of Lynda. Her soft eyes and shy smile were etched into his brain.

He knew he was a pile of shit.

Suddenly his blanket womb felt claustrophobic. He threw the covers off and stared at the ceiling, lamenting his lost dreams.

He had always wanted to be a mathematician, but that damnable wheelchair had thwarted his dreams. Instead of exploring Euclid's "beauty bare", he'd been a drudge, moving mind-numbed through each day as he cared for his crippled mother while his dad worked two jobs.

He'd left home a week after high school graduation, the week his mother died. He'd lost his twenties in a futile search for his childhood. And then, just before he turned thirty, he'd met Lynda Johansson. She had brought the light back into his life. He had gotten his accounting degree and had felt that his life was back on track.

It was, that is, until he'd made the decision to go the racetrack. He should have known he had an addictive personality. His gambling had become an obsession and had eventually consumed his paycheck and most of his time.

When he'd thought his life couldn't get much worse, he'd think about the fact that he still had Lynda. In spite of his addiction, she'd stuck by him.

Then came that terrible accident, and he'd been driving!

In the past two years since he'd lost her, when he wasn't *trying* to work at his profession, he was gambling with money embezzled from his employer or money borrowed from Benny or, most recently, Quinn Stevens, and trying to solve his problems at the bottom of a beer mug at the Pigpen. Now, both Benny and Quinn were after him.

Right now, in this motel room, most of him wanted to die. But that delicate thread that attached his soul to his body wasn't quite ready to break. He looked up at the motel ceiling.

Richard Brennan prayed for divine intervention.

He lay almost lifeless, staring at the ceiling for what seemed like hours.

Then, as if an invisible hand formed the script, he saw a name unfold on the ceiling. In that one moment of epiphany, he knew what he had to do. He'd call late tonight. When he was sure of reaching his party.

CHAPTER 3

❁

SATURDAY 3:12 P.M.

"What's the matter, mom?" Sam asked as she slid behind the steering wheel of her plum-colored Honda. "You seem distracted. Didn't you enjoy Dan Brown's talk?"

"Yes, dear," Elizabeth said, lacking her normal exuberance.

Sam glanced through the windshield at the mounted display of a newspaper clipping in the bookstore window. "Imagine. His new book was written up in the New York Times."

"Mmm. Interesting."

There was that word again. Sam looked at her mother as she engaged the ignition. "You know the old Chinese curse," she said as she backed out onto Water Street in Exeter and headed west, toward home.

"What's that, dear?"

Sam squinted, lowered her visor against the glare of the westering sun, and said, "May you live in interesting times."

"That's nice." Elizabeth sat motionless, staring straight ahead.

Sam reached over and lowered the passenger visor.

Elizabeth's voice was a monotone. The conversation wasn't registering. Something was on her mind.

A young woman in shorts, her hands curled around the handle of a baby stroller, waited by the crosswalk in front of Ocean Bank. Sam stopped to let the woman cross the street while she recounted how, many names ago, Ocean Bank was the Exeter Co-operative Bank, and on the opposite the side of the street, there used to be a Woolworth's. She had loved going in the old store with its narrow wooden floor boards, the soda fountain where you could get a sandwich and a drink, and the many aisles where you could buy one item instead of a package of twelve.

So many changes; it saddened Sam in some ways. Well, she told herself, the only constant is change.

The woman waved a thank you as she crossed in front of the Honda.

Sam smiled back. *Kneel. A child is born.* Spring had definitely sprung. She pressed on the gas pedal.

Lowering her window, she rested her elbow on the frame. As the breeze tickled her neck, she gave her mother a look. "Is this too much air on you, Mom?"

Elizabeth stirred, then patted her starched white hair. "No, dear. It's fine."

An F5 tornado couldn't disturb that lacquered twist, Sam thought, chuckling to herself.

She glanced at her mother once again. "Are you worried about leaving the Inn on a busy weekend?" Elizabeth owned and operated A Loosened Spirit, the bed-and-breakfast next door to Samantha's home.

"Oh, no, dear. Caroline and Sadie are very competent. You did a good job raising those two girls." Elizabeth worked at an imaginary wrinkle in her rose-colored skirt.

"With your help. Okay, mom. Give. What's bothering you?"

Her mother's hands fell silent as she looked out her side window. "I'm fine, dear."

"Come on, mom," Sam persisted. "I know you too well. Shall I turn the tables, and get out that ubiquitous cup of tea you always manage to have at hand when I'm having a problem?" A steaming cup of Earl Gray tea, Elizabeth Blackwell's secret weapon, was the equivalent of the Rorschach inkblot test.

Elizabeth looked down at her hands, now folded tightly in her lap, and sighed. "It's Mary Frazetta. I'm worried about her."

"Isn't she one of your Thursday Bridge club members?"

"Yes. She's also a good friend."

"Why are you worried?"

Elizabeth twisted the plain gold band on her hand, the ring placed there by her beloved husband, now twenty years dead. Finally, she said, "Last month Mary's husband, Claudio, died. Well, actually," she spoke so softly that Sam barely heard her "…he took his own life."

The story came back to Sam. "That's right. I remember now." She paused. "I take it Mrs. Frazetta's not doing too well?"

"She's not doing well at all."

"I did hear that her hardware business is in trouble."

Elizabeth nodded. "Mary's afraid she may have to declare bankruptcy. She had no idea they were in trouble until the bill collectors started calling her business, then her home. Of course, she's concerned about her children. They work in the business with her."

Sam slowed to allow a red Vandalay Construction truck to pass before bearing left onto Middle Road. She added the numbers on the license plate. A four. This vehicle was dependable, rarely broke down, and was a real workhorse. It rumbled past. Sam then wondered how the Vandalay murder trial was progressing. She, Nick, and Charlie, Georgetown's chief of police and her childhood friend, had spent a fateful weekend last year at the dead man's mansion.

As she accelerated, she asked her mother, "How many children are there?"

"There are two boys," Elizabeth answered. "The oldest, Frank, is from a previous marriage. The second boy is Claudio, Jr. The youngest is their daughter, Rita. She was adopted about…" her brow wrinkled in thought as she smoothed her skirt again…"I think it was about ten years after Claudio, Jr. was born. Mary had realized at that point that she couldn't have any more children, and she wanted a girl so badly."

"So," Sam said, "the kids may be out of a job, too?"

"Yes. It's a family run business." Elizabeth shook her head. "It's such a tragedy."

Sam clucked. Elizabeth would be devastated if her Inn failed, and her granddaughters had to look for other jobs. "I recall something about an accountant."

"Yes. Their accountant had been embezzling money from the business for some time, and successfully covering it up. Until recently, that is. Mary discovered that Richard Brennan—that's his name—this Mr. Brennan has a nasty gambling addiction. Mary said she hasn't seen him in weeks." Elizabeth shook her head.

They rode in silence until the houses thinned and the land opened. Sam let her eyes drift off the road and over the pastures. Cows grazed by Dudley Brook. The sky was that clear blue that only spring seemed able to birth. The afternoon sun hung in the west, beckoning them home. Sam thought about her family, about her haiku, about living in New Hampshire, and felt blessed.

She also thought about the tomatoes, red peppers, butternut squash, and cucumbers she would plant after Memorial Day, the date when New Englanders determined that the danger of frost was past. And on that weekend, as reliable as the first robin's return, the women of the Good Neighbors and Friends Committee would envelop old William Hornblower Coldbath's statue in the center of the Georgetown common in a blaze of petunias, marigolds, and geraniums. Never disturbed, of course, were the cowberry garlands strung from every lamppost and festooned over every doorway in town. They hung as tribute to the world-renowned Coldbath Cowberry Chutney. That recipe, passed down by William's wife, Hannah, through generations of Coldbaths, now lay irretrievably locked in the mind and Spice Cupboard of the last heir, the elderly maiden Agatha Beatrice Coldbath.

Sam figured the statue in the center of the town green should have been dedicated to Hannah Coldbath.

Pulled from these thoughts by concern for her mother, Sam commented, "The Frazetta family must be pretty torn up."

Elizabeth nodded. "They are." She began to describe the emotional toll that Claudio's death was taking on the Frazetta family. "That's the part of the story that is never reported in the newspapers. And it's such a shame. Mary is becoming…well, the best way to describe her is hard. I don't know how else to put it. She is very angry at her husband for…" her voice drifted. "But, it's more than that. I've made it a point to visit her twice a week. She lives outside of Manchester, you know. Anyway, I could almost feel the angry spikes in her…aura. Isn't that what you call it, dear?" Elizabeth cast watery blue eyes at her daughter.

Sam nodded as her thoughts segued to the story told by the famous psychic, Edgar Cayce, the man known as the Sleeping Prophet. Cayce could never remember a time when he didn't see colors emanating from the heads of human beings. One day, after examining sweaters in a department store, he was about to step into an elevator when he hesitated. The interior of the cab seemed dark. Surprised, he stepped back. Moments later, the elevator cable broke and the car fell to the basement. Everyone inside was killed. He later explained that the darkness in the cab was attributed to the fact that none of the occupants had an aura. Their energy colors had vanished just prior to their deaths.

"…so that's what worries me," Elizabeth said, her eyes fixed on nothing visible.

"I'm sorry, mom," Sam said. "Say that again."

"I was saying that Mary seems to have gone through a personality change. It's so unlike her but…I'm afraid she's bent on revenge."

CHAPTER 4

❀

SATURDAY 11:30 P.M.

They were after him again, taunting, "Hannibal knows about noses. His is nothing to sneeze at." Billy Bob Meaney and Johnny Benson laughed. "Honk, Hannibal. Honk! Honk!"

Billy Bob stopped to pick up a huge rock and throw it. It tumbled in slow motion and hit Hannibal on the right arm.

Hannibal grabbed his arm, struggled to run, but felt as if he was moving through deep water. They were right behind him. "Honk, honk, Hannibal, honk!"

Hannibal ran and ran until his heart felt about to burst out of his chest. He saw his own blood coursing down his body and filling the landscape around him. But he couldn't stop running. He had to keep on. Billy Bob was gaining.

He looked back. Billy Bob metamorphosed into Hannibal's father and he had the buggy whip!

Hannibal was terrified.

He struggled through a sea of waist-deep blood. He looked back once again. His father's face had melted into that she-devil. Her green eyes snapped, her mouth curled in a snarl. She swiveled her hips, mocking him with the whimpering baby she held just out of his reach. The baby reached for him, mewling like a newborn kitten. On the little girl's shoulder, he saw the pulsating heart-shaped birthmark.

He reached out for the baby but she was beyond his grasp.

His pulse pounded in his head. His eardrums were about to shatter. He clutched at his ears to stop the incessant beat of the drum.

Suddenly, the earth cracked open, the ocean of blood drained into an abyss and Hannibal tumbled into a blue haze of silence. He couldn't hear his own screams. He could only hear the terrible slicing silence...

...and that ringing in the distance...

Reverend Hannibal Loveless fought his way upright through the twisted sheets, his body bathed in sweat. He grabbed his head, trying to get his bearings and calm the banging muscle in his chest.

Slowly, relief washed over him as he realized that he'd been dreaming. It was the nightmares again. And the ringing that had awakened him was the telephone in the hallway. He smirked, ashamed of his fears. He was safe in Georgetown, New Hampshire, in the Victorian parsonage next to the Second Puritan Church on the town green, his unholy past behind him.

And it was spring, the season of resurrection and new life. He wondered if this season of hope and rejoicing would finally resurrect him from the kaleidoscopic nightmares that tormented his sleep.

Hannibal swung his long legs over the edge of the bed carefully, so as not to disturb his wife. Emmaline mumbled and changed position, but his thrashing hadn't wakened her.

A rectangle of light from a streetlamp on Black Skillet Lane filtered through the window, bathing her upper body in a surreal glow. Hannibal's eyes caressed her exquisite profile, her alabaster skin, and the way her long chestnut hair lay in tangles over the pillow. The scent of *Ocean* that she dabbed on each night graced their bed and offered absolution for his unholy past. If only he could immerse himself in that absolution and let go of the memories.

His gentle Emmaline, how he loved her! And how ashamed he felt because of his dreams. Hannibal didn't know how Emmaline could love such an ugly man as he, but he thanked God every day that she did. Her love had changed his life.

As if she had heard his thoughts, Emmaline stirred once again, then burrowed deeper into her pillow.

Hannibal turned toward the bedroom door and let his feet rest on the floor for several seconds. Then he slipped into the hallway and flicked on the small lamp beside the telephone.

His watch read 11:35.

He prayed for a wrong number. In his business, late night phone calls usually brought messages of pain and tragedy.

"Yes. Who is it?" he whispered.

"Is this Hannibal Loveless?" The voice was unsteady, but familiar. Hannibal wiped a knobby-fingered hand over his forehead.

A trace of *Ocean* lingered on his skin. He closed his eyes and inhaled the light scent, soaking up the memory of Emmaline's soft body against his. He swallowed. "Yes, it is."

"This is Richard Brennan. Do you remember me?"

Hannibal froze, then yanked the phone away from his ear as if he'd been stung. He stared at the mouthpiece as his heart went into overdrive.

He could still hear the voice pleading, "Please, Hannibal. I'm down to my last twenty dollars. I need your help."

CHAPTER 5

❀

SUNDAY 12:05 A.M.

A few minutes after midnight, Rita Frazetta pulled open the door of the CircleTo Motel in Portsmouth. She painted on a dazzling smile.

The night clerk was alone. He was reading a pornographic novel behind the oak counter when he looked up into the empty lobby and saw her stepping through the front entrance. At first glance, Randy Sturgis resented the interruption. He liked the night. He liked being alone.

With the motel only one-quarter full, he had expected to spend a quiet evening finishing his book, *Thrusting Passion*. Then he planned to poke through the guests' mail slots, check the change return pockets on the telephones and drink dispensers, and stroll through the function room on the lookout for forgotten items. He would add whatever he found to the store in his tiny third floor apartment on the other side of town. Unless, of course, the items were really worthless.

His plans changed when he got a good look at the svelte redhead who had sauntered into the lobby. Suddenly he was very interested in having company.

Rita Frazetta turned heads. She had a mass of flaming red hair that cascaded over her shoulders and a chest that made grown men weep. Even though her nose was a bit too long, and there were the prerequisite freckles that came with being a redhead, she had good skin, full lips, and wide-set eyes. She had learned to apply makeup to accentuate the positive.

Most men never looked at her face.

Randy Sturgis slipped the battered novel, which he had bought secondhand at Salty Peter's Videos and Books, under the counter. He rose, his pitted face displaying what might be construed as a smile, and straightened the thin black tie at his neck.

"Yes. Can I help you?" *Get undressed?*

Down boy, he told himself.

He coughed, a short bark, the result of smoking two packs of Camels a day for twelve years, since he was ten.

The woman opened ruby lips. "Why, yes. You can."

She unbuttoned her white coat and let it slip off one shoulder. As she grasped the coat at her waist, it slid off her other shoulder. She moved closer to the counter and leaned toward him. "And what is your name?"

Mounds of pink flesh rose majestically out of the low-cut emerald green sweater.

Randy stared. His mouth went dry. All he could think of was a smoke. Yeah. He could really use a smoke right now.

Rita's smile widened. "Surely you must know your name," she said, running a moist tongue over her lips.

At the sound of her voice, Randy looked up into her face. His own words seemed to squeak from his throat. "Ah…Randy Sturgis, ma'am."

"Randy Sturgis." The name rolled off her tongue. "That has a nice ring to it. But please. Don't call me ma'am, Randy. It makes me feel so old. I'm only twenty-five and my name is Rita."

Randy swallowed hard. "Yes, ma'am. I mean, Rita." His trembling fingers were inches from the flesh that lay on his counter. Testosterone he never knew he had roiled up from his groin.

Rita laid a warm hand over his thin cold one. In dulcet tones, she said, "Randy. I'm so upset. And I don't know what to do. But, I know you can help me."

Randy frowned. A strange feeling began to burgeon in his chest. "What's wrong?" Randy desperately wanted to help this woman. He fantasized about how grateful she could be.

Rita pulled her hand away. She buried it in one side of her thick red hair. "It's my husband. He's unfaithful. I can't count the number of times I've suspected he's been with other women. And now, I think he's doing it again. Here. In your motel."

Randy couldn't imagine a man wanting anyone other than Rita.

"So, you see my problem." She looked down, let her fingers brush the back of Randy's hand. Her helpless eyes, fringed with black lashes, lifted to his. He forced himself to look full into her face. Her eyes were pale green, with a splash of yellow in the center. He hadn't noticed her eyes before.

"Ah, no. Not really," he said.

"Randy." Rita took a deep breath. "I know he's with another woman here in your motel. I'm going to file divorce papers and I need his room number so I can tell him face to face. Randy, I need a man who's going to love just me. Someone who'll take care of me. You know what I mean?"

Randy certainly did. But he wasn't sure about giving out a guest's room number.

"And another thing," Rita went on, "he probably didn't register under his own name. He never does. Perhaps you might remember him if I describe him?" She lifted carefully plucked brows at him and gave him a thumbnail description of the man.

It was the guy in Room 15, Randy thought. *Roberts.*

Roberts had just left for the Quickie Stop, but not before he'd let Randy know he wasn't pleased about him forgetting the DO NOT DISTURB sign. And then Roberts had reminded Randy about the promise of a C-note.

Randy thought about the hundred bucks. Then he gazed at Rita. For once in his life, his decision took about five seconds. He bobbed his head.

"Yeah. I know *exactly* who you're talking about. He's been acting kind of funny."

"Yes," Rita sighed. "I imagine he would, chasing every skirt in sight." She pulled a tissue from the delicious crease between her breasts and dabbed at the corner of one eye.

Randy wanted to bury his face in those mounds. Instead, he flushed and got angry. How could that jerk husband of hers be screwing around when he had a woman like this waiting at home? Randy knew if she were his woman, they'd never leave the bedroom. That feeling in his chest began to inflate like an inner tube.

"I hate to tell you this, Rita,"—he wasn't sure he hated telling her at all. And he liked using her name. Made him feel warm and tingly—"but your husband asked that everyone stay out of his room. No maid service, nothing. Who are we to argue? Saves on cleaning expenses, right? In fact," Randy glanced around the empty lobby. He leaned toward Rita and shielded his mouth with his hand. "He promised me a hundred bucks if I made sure no one went in his room."

He could smell cherries. *Oh, God! Cherries!* He knew the smell because he loved Cherry Cokes.

Some of the pits in Randy's cheeks disappeared into the folds of a leer. Mustering up the strength of Samson, he pulled back a few inches. Scenarios from the book stuffed under the counter titillated the nooks and crannies of his brain.

Rita's hand fluttered to her chest, faint creases wrinkled her brow. "Oh. I knew it! I just knew it." She paused and put the back of her hand to her forehead. "Would you get me a glass of water, Randy? I feel faint."

"Sure, sure," Randy said, stumbling over a wastebasket at his feet. "You just sit down over there, and I'll be right back." He disappeared into a room behind the reception desk.

When he returned, Rita was sitting on one of the couches in the lobby, her thighs barely covered by a black leather skirt. She was fanning her face with a magazine. Her coat and bag lay on an adjacent chair.

Rita placed the magazine on an end table and reached for the glass of water. "Oh, thank you so much, Randy," she said, as her fingers grazed the back of his hand. She took a sip and set the glass down. "There. I feel so much better now." She sighed and patted the nubbly cushion next to her. Her nails were long, painted ruby like her lips. "Please, Randy. Sit beside me for a moment. I need company."

Randy dropped onto the seat. Fighting off the giddy smell of cherries, he made a Herculean effort not to come into contact with any part of her body.

"Randy," Rita said, touching his knee. "You could save me a lot of trouble by giving me his room number."

Still flush from reading passages in *Thrusting Passion*, it took all Randy's restraint to control the stallion rearing inside him. She was so close to him. All he had to do was grab her, bury his hands in that flaming mane, devour her mouth in his, press…But, of course, he wouldn't. He couldn't. He could barely breathe.

Rita was still talking. "I promise I won't cause any trouble. I need to tell him in person that it's over. This is the first time I've ever stood up to him. I just have to face him. You understand that, don't you? Randy?"

Randy gazed into her green eyes as his fantasy faded from his mind. Her words began to register.

She wanted to stand up to her husband.

Yes! His head bobbed in agreement.

Randy did understand. He knew how hard it was to face up to authority. All his life he had tried to stand up to his father, the man who had supplied him with Camels and who had taunted him about being a man when, as a young boy, he had coughed and sputtered during those first few weeks of smoking. He had learned. But he would never have the chance to stand up to the old man now. His father had died of lung cancer five years ago.

He admired Rita's courage. He sat up and adjusted the frayed black tie at his throat. He was on the verge of making another rare decision.

"Actually, he's not in now. He left about…"—his eyes flicked to his wrist— "oh, fifteen minutes ago. Unless he came back when I was in the bathroom. I think he went to the Quickie-Stop. He asked me where he could pick up a six pack of beer."

Rita cooed. "Why don't I just slip on over to his room and see if he's back."

Randy thought about that. And the more he thought, the more he liked the idea. The bum deserved to lose Rita. And maybe…she seemed to like him. That strange feeling inside him burst loose. He felt like beating his chest. *Tarzan. Strongman of the jungle. Protect Jane.*

He made the decision.

"Rita," he said, looking straight at her, his heart in knots, his concave chest pumped with blood, "I'm not supposed to do this, but, for you, I'll break the rules." He swallowed hard and took the leap. "Your husband's in Room 15." Then his voice tightened. "But please, don't tell anyone I told you. I could lose my job."

Rita's eyes narrowed. She leaned forward and kissed Randy's pitted cheek. "Relax, honey. You're secret's safe with me."

The hall was empty and quiet. With her ear to the door of Room 15, Rita listened for several minutes. Then she pulled a steel tool from her handbag. Seconds later, she was inside.

The air smelled stale with an underlying dampness. There was no sound. Rita knew she was alone. Empty rooms cried out their loneliness in dead silences, a sound like no other.

A slash of light from under the curtained window on the far wall cut the darkness like a knife. When her eyes had adjusted to the shadows, she could make out inanimate forms. She figured it was safe to use her miniature flashlight.

She surveyed the room. To her left, the notched wall provided space for an open closet. Further down were a bureau, a television, and a folding suitcase rack. Beyond the bathroom to her right, the room opened onto a queen-sized bed flanked by nightstands and lamps. There was a large nondescript print hanging over the bed. A table and two tubular chairs sat before the casement window. Everything was standard motel issue.

The bed covers were rumpled.

Rita stuffed the flashlight into her bag, and set the bag on the carpet. She used the sleeve of her sweater to flick on the bathroom light. Randy Sturgis had kept his word. No chambermaid had been in here.

The toilet seats were up—a sure sign a man was in residence. There were dirty towels on the floor and the sink was spattered with toothpaste. The miniature bar of motel soap was open, and lay on the white-flecked counter in a puddle of water.

Stepping around the crumpled bath mat, Rita examined the tub area. The walls were damp from a shower. An empty bottle of motel issue shampoo lay on its side on the tub floor.

There were no personal items. He had either left for good or he wasn't leaving any evidence of his identity.

Guided by the light from the open bathroom door, Rita used a clean face cloth to open drawers in the bureau and the nightstand. Nothing. She checked under the bed.

Then she noticed the notepad lying next to the phone. With the face cloth, she took it into the bathroom. The stark fluorescent lights revealed impressions on the top sheet. With a pencil from her bag, she ran the tip back and forth over the indentations.

The handwriting was slanted to the right. Although the words seemed hastily written, they were neat. *An accountant's hand*, she thought. The words on the pad were unmistakable:

Monday 3 AM Pottles Pond Rte 125

Rita smiled. She crumpled the paper and tossed it into the wastebasket. Returning the pad to the nightstand, she took pains to lay it as she had found it. She replaced the face cloth in the bathroom, and once again used her sweater sleeve to turn off the bathroom light. She left the room the way she had found it.

The hallway was empty.

Randy looked up from reading *Thrusting Passion* as the redhead sailed through the lobby of the CircleTo Motel. She blew him a kiss and slipped out the front. The door made a soft sucking sound as it shut.

CHAPTER 6

❁

SUNDAY 3:15 AM

Quinn Stevens lay in his metal bed staring at the stamped tin ceiling. Another restless night, ruffling through the pages of his memory.

Fingering the quilt that covered him, his eyes tracing the zigzag cracks in the ceiling as he had since he was a young boy, he recalled how the sharp angles helped him ponder the mechanical puzzles his father had given him every Sunday night.

As he shifted under the weight of memory, the old bed creaked with that familiar crickety sound he'd been listening to for thirty years.

Quinn left home right after high school graduation and took an apartment of his own. The need for independent living ran strong in his blood. But a year later, when his father left his mother for a younger woman, Quinn moved back in. Annie Stevens never asked her son for help, but he knew it was the right thing to do.

He smoothed a loose thread back into the faded pine tree quilt as his mind drifted to the Red Dragon, the name Gramp Stevens had called the old '47 Chevy that he drove to work every weekday. Quinn's dad had told him stories about how Gramp Stevens would pile his family and a wicker picnic basket into the maroon jalopy for trips to the White Mountains or the seaside. Quinn's dad had loved Gramp's car and had claimed he would never let it go. But he did. The Red Dragon sat in the backyard, barely visible now, having been just about consumed by the rampant grapevine that choked the side wall of the garage. Quinn still couldn't believe that his father had abandoned his wife and only child, and the Red Dragon.

He stroked his black beard and closed his eyes. His father had been a good dad. What had gone wrong? Why had the man left his faithful wife and adoring son for another woman? Quinn felt the abandonment as deeply, albeit in a different way, as his mother did. Middle age crisis is what they called it, and his father had fallen its victim. Quinn thought of the pain his mother had suffered, and his eyes narrowed.

He could not imagine leaving the woman you loved.

The woman you loved...

Quinn felt drained as that familiar pain carved a deeper trench in his gut. He knew the exact date down to the minute. October 3rd, 1:36 P.M., two years and seven months ago, BRB. Before Richard Brennan.

His memories of that day would never leave him.

He didn't usually attend the annual Georgetown Cowberry Festival, but he knew *she* would be there. On an apple-snapping fall day with the sun dappling the street and town green, Quinn parked his Harley at the south end of Black Skillet Lane, across the street from the Coldbath mansion. The maples lining the green showed off their plumage in brilliant oranges and cardinal reds. Clumps of white, amber, and orchid colored mums circled the bandstand where, amongst the cowberry garlands, the statue of old William Hornblower Coldbath stood stony watch. Children raced and tumbled; teenage boys in droopy jeans and shaved heads shuffled past gaggles of girls; couples with backpacks pushed baby strollers; and seniors examined the handmade quilts and jams, and Coldbath Cowberry chutneys and homemade pies.

Booths and tents were set up along the three sides of the green while at the north end, across the street from the Second Puritan Church, games and activities took place: face painting by the high school art class, fortunes read for the benefit of the New Hampshire SPCA, hit-the-target-and-dunk-the-coach games to benefit the school's soccer team, a three-legged race, and the pie-eating and pumpkin-carving contests.

Quinn ambled through the crowd, through the aroma of apple and mince pies fresh from the ovens, and the smell of cotton candy and foot-long hot dogs and sizzling burgers. He passed the Coldbath Cowberry Chutney booth. Stacked shoulder high were the famous squat jars in dozens of flavors that had evolved over the years and that attracted tourists year round.

His eyes cut left and right in search of the Friends and Neighbors Committee booth. Lynda's mother was a member, and Lynda would be there helping to sell the jams and jellies and crocheted, knitted, and quilted items that the good women of Georgetown had made throughout the year for this one weekend, to raise money for their club's treasury.

Quinn had done his research, his plan was well thought out. He should have been calm, confident, in charge. He'd been over this a hundred times in his mind. It was time to approach her. His uncooperative heart thundered in his chest. He felt like he was walking on stilts. Drops of sweat broke out on his forehead.

He swallowed what moisture he had in his mouth. What was he afraid of? She was a fragile slip of a girl. He could pick her up with one hand. How could she be a threat? The muscles bunched at his jaw line as he frowned. He wouldn't quiver when she lifted the bluest eyes he had ever seen to look at him. He wouldn't lose his voice and puddle at her feet when her full lips curled around his name.

He could do this.

He had left the bandana and vest at home, and was wearing a clean white tee shirt, jeans and jean jacket. His hair was freshly washed and his beard trimmed. He checked his fingernails again for traces of grease and grime. They were red from the scrubbing the night before and this morning. His breath was fresh, and with a splash of Aqua Velva behind both ears, he could do no more. This was the best he could be. It was now or never.

Quinn kept on through the crowds, passing the table where Chief Charlie Burrows and his Deputy, Lenny, were handing out reflector tape for the Halloween trick-or-treaters. Burrows threw Quinn a quick mind-your-P's-and-Q's look, but Quinn just looked away. He didn't want any trouble today. And besides, Burrows wasn't a bad sort. At least he gave a guy a chance to explain himself, which had saved Quinn's ass a few times.

He ambled by the Blackwell woman who wrote those odd books and who had had her picture plastered across the papers recently. She and two girls were talking with a man by the Lincoln Landscaping and Nursery booth. Quinn remembered something about a guy named Lincoln who was involved in the Cowberry Necklace murders a few years back.

His chest heaved. He had to focus. He pulled his thoughts back to the mission at hand. A group of teenagers stepped deferentially around Quinn as he approached the Friends and Neighbors Committee booth.

And then he saw her.

Lynda Johannsen was slender, barely five foot three. She was dressed in tight jeans and a white turtleneck sweater, a red ribbon tied her hair in a ponytail. The angels in heaven were not as beautiful. Quinn couldn't catch his breath.

As if she sensed his presence, she turned and lifted her eyes at him. A smile graced the corner of her lip as she tipped her head in the way only she could.

"Hi, Quinn," she said. Her voice was soft and bashful.

Quinn stood on his toes and nodded his head repeatedly. His lips were clenched. He couldn't seem to get his mouth open to speak.

Lynda watched him for a moment, then lowered her eyes and began to turn away as if she were embarrassed.

It's now or never, Quinn told himself. He swallowed hard and blurted out, "Would you like to go to the movies tonight?"

Lynda's head swung back, her ponytail whipping around the corner of her cheek. "What?"

He was dead. He knew it. Why did he ever think this beautiful girl would want to go out with *him*? He hung in a mental limbo. His body was one pounding pulse. He couldn't ask her again. If, at that moment, the earth beneath his feet had opened and swallowed him whole, he would have welcomed it.

Then, as if Quinn's words had finally penetrated her brain, Lynda's smile reappeared. She gazed up at him. "Why, yes, Quinn. I'd like that."

He blinked. His mind shut down. He couldn't think what he was supposed to do next. He stood transfixed, lost in Lynda's blue eyes.

"Are you all right?" she asked.

Quinn blinked, gave a short dry cough. "Yeah. Okay. Thanks." He turned away to leave.

"Oh, Quinn."

He turned back. "What?"

Her eyes sparkled as if she were privy to a secret. "What time do you want to pick me up?"

"Oh, yeah." *Stupid*, he thought. He almost raised his hand to slap his forehead. "Around 7:00."

"Great. I'll be waiting." Lynda turned back to make change for an old woman who had just purchased a handmade quilt. "Thank you so much, Ms. Coldbath. That is a lovely quilt. I'm sure you will enjoy it for many years."

Quinn never remembered getting on his motorcycle and riding home. It was the happiest moment of his life.

Now, in the light from the full moon streaming through his bedroom window, Quinn Stevens looked down as his hand caressed the small tattoo on the left side of his chest, right over his heart. LYNDA. His eyes filmed over with wetness. He turned on his side in the squeaky metal bed and stared at the movie stubs he had mounted in a small gold frame and placed on his bureau, and he thought his heart would break.

At that moment, an image of Richard Brennan's face rose in his mind. Even after more than two years, Quinn felt the searing heat of hatred in his soul.

He fell back on the old mattress and stared at the tin ceiling. He had to prepare himself for the mission.

CHAPTER 7

❁

SUNDAY 8:30 A.M.

The sun struggled to break through the bank of gray clouds that clung to the underbelly of the sky. Outside the Frazetta home, sun poked through the old maples, limning the leaves with a halo of light.

The two-story New Englander sat in a quiet, tree-lined residential neighborhood on the outskirts of Manchester. The sounds of Sunday morning stirred—doors opened and shut as people left for church, kids laughed and shouted as they played street hockey, a lawn mower chugged then spurted into action, and old lady McDonough called her dog, Fritz, who routinely escaped his back yard enclosure. The comforting sounds signaling the continuity of life.

But the sounds were not a comfort for Mary Frazetta this Sunday morning. She sat stoically at the glass-topped table in her white kitchen while her two sons continued the argument over the hardware store's financial future. She was tired of the bickering. It had been going on for the past month, ever since Claudio took the coward's way out.

Claudio.

She breathed in deeply as she toyed with her scrambled eggs. The kitchen smelled of bacon and burnt toast and French vanilla coffee.

Mary was sorry she felt that way about her husband but he *was* a coward. He had left her with a business on the brink of bankruptcy, and a bleak future without the man she had loved since she was twenty-three years old. Not that their marriage had been perfect. There had been infidelities, especially his dalliance with that over-sexed teenage cashier. But that was years ago and she and Claudio had endured.

She moved the eggs around on her plate and took a bite. They were cold, but she didn't care. She didn't have much of an appetite anyway.

Her eyes turned flinty as her thoughts shifted to Richard Brennan, their accountant. Or should she say their ex-accountant, the man they had trusted with their financial life. Brennan had become part of their family, attending birthday parties and cookouts. She'd often sent him off from his visits to their home with fried chicken, leftover meat loaf for sandwiches, and oatmeal cookies. She even hand-delivered chicken soup when he was ill.

Mary's fist tightened around her fork as she thought about the hours the family had spent helping him through that horrific accident.

But Brennan had a terrible secret, one that even the Frazetta family—his closest friends, they thought—knew nothing about...until recently, that is. Richard Brennan was a gambler. And his addiction had brought ruin upon the Frazetta family.

Mary could feel the hate simmering inside her. She stuck her left hand into her bleached hair and winced as her ring caught some strands. After carefully disentangling her hand, she stared at the diamond in her ring. .68 carats. The ring Claudio had given her, down on Ceres Street by the tugs in Portsmouth, the night he'd asked her to marry him. As their business had prospered, he'd offered to buy her a bigger diamond but she wouldn't part with this one. They had been happy.

And now what?

Mary prayed she could pull herself and her children out of this downward spiral. They all depended upon the hardware store for their incomes. But her mind was too splintered to come up with a rational plan. All she could think about was Brennan. She was consumed by the desire to make the bastard pay. One way or another!

"Listen, Frank," CJ said, thrusting a finger up toward his brother's square face. "I don't care how many times you add it up, it still comes out to zero. The money's gone. Brennan bled us dry."

Frank grabbed his brother's wrist. "Don't point your finger at me, CJ!"

CJ leaped up from his chair, wrenching his wrist from his brother's iron grip.

"Stop it, you two!" Mary yelled, slapping her open hand on the table. The fork bounced off her plate. "We don't need this sibling rivalry shit, especially now."

The brothers glared at each other and slowly backed off.

CJ slumped back into the wrought-iron chair opposite his mother and ran both hands through his straight dark hair. His bangs fell back down over his forehead and brushed his eyebrows. Picking up a butter knife, CJ scraped at the burnt edges of his toast, laid it down on his plate and stared at it for a moment. Then he pulled a length of nylon rope from his pants pocket and began making a hangman's noose.

Frank looked down at his mother and spoke in his measured cadence. "If you'd just listen, ma. I'm telling you, we can do it. We'll go down to the bank and work something out."

When Mary came into her second marriage with a child, her new husband, Claudio, had taken little Frank into his heart. He had loved the boy as much as his own son, Claudio, Jr.—who was called CJ—who was born eighteen months later. Then, when Mary had the hysterectomy and couldn't have any more children, Claudio was delighted when his wife wanted to adopt a baby girl.

Mary gazed at the photographs of her grandsons on the refrigerator door, but she didn't see them. She was still thinking about her husband. He'd had one major flaw. He was too proud. It was his pride and his inability to face the public shame of his presumed failure that had driven him to hitch a hose to the car's tailpipe in the garage. The cruel joke was that if he had waited another few weeks, he would have discovered it wasn't his fault after all. So here she was, left to face the struggle alone.

Just then the phone rang. The all turned toward the wall phone hanging by the refrigerator.

After a second, Frank started for it.

"Don't answer it," Mary commanded. "The answering machine in the living room will pick it up." She pulled another hair strand from her ring. "It's probably that man again and there's nothing more we can tell him."

"I'm worried about you, ma," Frank said, scratching circles on his left elbow. "This Benny guy's been calling you ever since Brennan took off. He's probably a bookie or a loan shark."

Mary got up and dropped the hair pulled from her ring into the wastebasket beside the refrigerator. "I told him I'd let him know as soon as I heard from Brennan." She wished Frank didn't irritate her so.

"But, ma. He could be dangerous."

CJ scowled at his brother. "Back off, Frank. The guy's just hot air. He knows Ma had nothing to do with Brennan's gambling."

CJ looked down at his handy work, a slip noose with nine turns around the rope. He'd been making the hangman's knot since he was eleven years old, when he'd first watched Clint Eastwood in *Hang 'Em High*.

"What *I'm* concerned about," he said, "is my next paycheck. I've got kids to feed and clothe. How am I going to support them? Debbie will be all over me again, not that she needs an excuse." Under the table, his knee worked up and down.

Frank poured himself a cup of coffee from the Mr. Coffee on the counter. The sun had finally given up and grayness curtained the backyard.

Turning to face his brother, Frank closed his eyes over the rim of the mug and inhaled the aroma. He took a sip, winced, and set the mug on the counter behind him. "Getting back to business. We need to talk to the bank. We've done business with them for years. They know us. They know we're good for it."

"Yeah?" CJ snarled. "Well, that visit and a dollar will get you a cup of coffee." He examined the hangman's noose. He thought about slipping it around his brother's thick, hairy neck and hoisting him up over a tree limb, and watching his legs kick out and his body twitch. He stuffed the noose back into his pocket and rubbed his forehead.

"Do you have a better idea, you lazy bum?" Frank countered.

CJ's slender fingers played a staccato rhythm on the tabletop as his right knee jigged under the table. Through slitted eyes, he viewed his stepbrother. "I work as hard as you do," he said.

"In a pig's ass," Frank muttered, glancing at his mother who had dropped back into her chair and was shredding the paper napkin beside her plate.

Even as CJ's fingers fell silent on the table, his knee picked up speed. "Don't give me any crap, Frank." The menace was clear in his voice.

"You don't do diddly squat and Ma knows it." Frank clutched the counter behind him, the muscles at his jaw line rippling.

"Leave him alone, Frank!" Mary snapped. "Can't you see your brother's upset?" A small pile of paper scraps was accumulating on top of her eggs.

Mary glared at Frank who, once again, scratched lazy circles on his left elbow. Frank reminded her of Anthony, her no-account first husband who had run off and left her with a baby and no money. Big, square, bull-headed. She wondered where *her* genes were in her first son.

When she swung her attention back to CJ, her eyes softened. Her second son was high-strung, sensitive. It hurt her to see him so upset. Regardless, she loved her two boys, her daughter, her grandsons, and she would do anything to ensure their financial futures.

With Claudio gone now, she was solely in charge.

Claudio.

Again, the bitterness against her dead husband rose like hot lava in her chest, threatening to erupt and send her into a boiling frenzy. She wanted to storm through the kitchen, pull every dish out of the cupboards and smash them into tiny shards on the kitchen floor, and scream until her throat was raw. Her family was hovering on the brink of ruin. Thoughts from which her priest would recoil dug their way deeper into her mind. Unstoppable, the words rolled across her mental screen: *Revenge is mine, sayeth Mary Frazetta.*

She stared into space, unconsciously shredding the last remnants of her napkin.

"Ma, please" Frank had his big hands spread in supplication. "Let's talk to the bank."

At that moment, a breathless Rita Frazetta rushed into the kitchen. "I found him, Mom! And I know where he's going to be at three tomorrow morning."

CHAPTER 8

✿

SUNDAY 7:30 P.M.

"You two have got to stop bickering," Rita said as she paced across the floor in Frank's apartment over the garage. "We have to work together to figure a way out of this dilemma. There's got to be an answer."

Frank stood with his hands clasped behind his back, staring out the open window at the back of his mother's house twenty feet away. The sun had finally rent the gray curtain of day and now, sinking behind the trees, cut long sharp shadows across the yard behind Mary Frazetta's two-story home. In the shade of a spindly lilac bush, ground phlox struggled over the stone wall he had installed as a gift last Mother's Day.

The lilac needs lime, he thought, *and I should trim the branches of the maple to let a little more sun into the backyard.*

He could smell the newly spaded earth where yesterday, from this window, he had watched his mother gouge the ground in preparation for the flats of multicolored pansies she had just bought. She then set the pansies in the earth as tenderly as if she were lowering a newborn baby into a basinet. Her mood swings frightened him.

Frank turned towards his siblings. "As I said this morning, we should talk to the bank. Maybe they'll help us work something out."

CJ laughed. He undid the hangman's noose he'd just made and stuffed the length of rope into his pants pocket. "You and your bank. You think those bloodsuckers care about us." He sprawled out on the black leather sofa and sighed. "You got any beer?"

Frank paced the few steps to the galley kitchen. "Want one, Rita?"

"Yeah, thanks."

Frank handed out the beer cans, and settled into the matching leather recliner. He popped the tab on his Budweiser and took a mouthful.

"I think Frank's right, CJ," Rita said, nudging her brother's feet aside. She put her Bud on the coffee table, pushed her hair back over her shoulders with both hands, picked up the beer can, and settled back with a sigh. "We do need to talk to the bank. At least they'll know we care and we want to work something out. That's got to count for something." She took a sip and cradled the can against her chest.

"You always think Frank's right. Frank, the best quarterback in our high school's history, still thinks he's carrying the ball."

"Stuff it, CJ," Frank grumbled. He set down his beer and began scratching circles on his elbow.

"That's not fair," Rita said. "I don't always think Frank's right. But he does happen to be, this time. Come on, CJ. Let's have a little cooperation here. We've got to do something. I'm also worried about Mom. I've never seen her so angry."

Frank nodded.

After a moment, he chuckled and looked over at his brother. "Remember when we were little and got the paint can out of the garage and painted the kitchen floor black?"

CJ nodded, and half smiled. "Yeah. Ma came home with an arm full of groceries and walked across the wet floor. And we said we didn't know who did it."

Rita laughed. "The fact that your hands were covered with black paint was a dead giveaway."

"Boy, was she mad," Frank added.

"And when she gets mad, it's scary," CJ said, suddenly sober. "More scary because she doesn't say anything. It's the look in her eyes."

"As I recall," Rita said, "you two not only had to remove the paint, but you spent two weeks in your bedroom. You were only allowed out to go the bathroom. I know because I delivered your meals three times a day."

"Yeah. And it was summer, and hot as hell," CJ said.

"And we missed the Fourth of July cookout and the family baseball game," Frank said, taking another mouthful of Bud. His eyes cut over to CJ. "Ma let you out of the room four days before she let me out."

"That's because you're older. You led me on."

"Yeah, right."

"Those were good times," Rita said, anxious to dampen the smoldering animosity between CJ and Frank. "I wish you two could get along like you used to." She sipped her beer, thinking about how easily her brothers slipped into the combative mode these days. She couldn't recall exactly when it started. The anger between them had just seeped into their lives like a leaking sewer pipe, unnoticeable at first, then slowly polluting what had once been a clear stream running through their childhood.

"A lot has happened since then," CJ said, staring at the half-empty can of Budweiser resting on his chest. He pushed himself upright and finished it off. "Got another one?"

"Get it yourself," Frank said.

CJ got up and went to the small white refrigerator, favoring his right ankle as he walked. "Rita?"

"No, thanks. How is Debbie making out with the kids?"

"Fine. Her folks are helping financially, but it's really not enough. I'm thinking about selling my Ram and buying an old pickup." He looked off at nothing in particular, a wistful expression on his face. "I've got to do something so I can give her a few bucks."

Frank tilted his head and lifted one eyebrow at his brother. "Yeah. I'm *sure* it will be a *few* dollars."

CJ's head swung back. "What's that supposed to mean?" His eyes narrowed.

"Admit it, CJ. You're tighter than a drum."

"Not when it comes to my kids!" Clutching his beer can, he approached Frank threateningly.

"Calm down, you two," Rita said. "Come on now. We've got a major problem here to solve here."

But Frank wouldn't let it go. "You should sell that gas guzzler. That's why you obsess about keeping the tank full. You're always afraid you'll run out of gas and have to pay a tow truck to haul you back. I never saw anyone so paranoid about his gas gauge."

"You looking for trouble, Frank?" CJ said in a low voice, the bones of his knuckles showing white.

"Friday was five cents off at the Quick Fill Up. I suppose you were the first one in line as usual," Frank sneered.

CJ bolted toward Frank, losing his beer in the process. The can bounced on the floor, and rolled a few feet, leaving a foamy trail behind it.

Rita sprung between her brothers, landing in Frank's lap from the force of CJ's thrust.

CJ pulled up short and backed away, his face twisted with anger. He bit at his top lip as he plunked back down on the leather sofa. Rita pulled herself out of Frank's lap with a little push from him.

"Will you guys ever get over this animosity?" she said, running a hand over her hair. "What is it with you two? Why do you argue all the time? We're supposed to be a family." Both men looked away from her and toward each other, silent, unmoved by her entreaty. "Our business is on the brink of bankruptcy and you two act like little bullies on a playground."

She let that sink in for a moment. She didn't even know why she tried.

She shook her head as she moved to the kitchen. She pulled a length of paper toweling from the wooden roller on the counter, and returned to pick up CJ's beer can and wipe the floor. After dropping the can and wet toweling in the wastebasket, she rinsed her hands in the sink, pulled another beer from the refrigerator, returned to the sofa, and handed the can to CJ. Her beer miraculously still sat on the coffee table where she had put it before leaping between her brothers.

Settling back against the cushions, she said, "Something's got to break. We can't go on this way."

"It's all because of that bastard, Brennan," CJ blurted. "He's the one responsible for this mess. He stole our money!"

"I'd like to wring his scrawny neck," Frank said, his eyes focused on CJ. "After all we did for him."

"You mean what Ma did for him," CJ retorted. "She treated him like a member of the family. And then he does this to us?" A muscle bulged behind his jaw line as his eyes narrowed. "He'll get his."

"He should," Rita added, as she thought about the devastating loss of her father, and the sadness plaguing her mother, and the turmoil now surrounding the family.

The room fell silent as the three of them stared into their beer cans.

CJ couldn't get his mind off his dad. He was so angry with his father, the father he had loved and admired, his hero since he was able to understand the meaning of the term. He paced his bedroom.

Claudio was a quiet man, unassuming, thoughtful. He didn't say much, but he always had a look that said he understood exactly what was going on but wasn't going to get involved unless things got out of hand. And then, you knew he could handle the problem. There were depths to the man that others would never know. His dad reminded him of Clint Eastwood, an enigma in a quiet package, seemingly loose and easygoing but, beneath the placid surface, a tightly coiled presence. CJ could find nothing wrong with the man. Not until he had stuck a hose in his mouth and left them all in the lurch.

But it wasn't his fault!

CJ pounded his fist on the wall of his bedroom again and again until he left a small crater in the wallboard. Cradling his hand against his chest, he felt the pain as a hate for Brennan that flooded through his veins like a raging river tearing at the embankments that held him on course. He dropped on the edge of his bed, fighting the loss of control. He had to calm down. He had to make plans.

It was Brennan's fault…the bastard took away his father as if he had physically pushed the hose into his dad's mouth and left him there to die…

CJ's wet eyes shut tight against the memory.

Pulling his thoughts back, he flexed his hand slowly and stared down at the side of his palm. No damage. His eyes cut to the wall beside the bedroom door. He'd have to repair that before his mother saw it.

He pushed the dark hair from his eyes. He had to find a way out of his dilemma. He wanted to avenge his father's death. He wanted to turn the business around. He turned his damaged ankle in slow circles. And he wanted his big hero brother out of the picture forever. There had to be a way to achieve all three.

CHAPTER 9

❀

MONDAY 3:00 A.M.

Nick and Sam were asleep in their rented motor home at Pottle's Pond in Georgetown, New Hampshire when the shot rang out. Sam bolted upright. The luminous dial on the travel alarm clock read exactly 3:00.

She stared at the green numbers while straining to hear any other sounds. Inside the mummy sleeping bag, her fingers crawled to her left side to rub the fleshy scar, the result of a shooting incident from her past. Then she thought about their gun. It was at home, locked in a closet.

"Nick," she whispered.

Rumblings rolled from the shelf over the front seats.

Sam fumbled for the zipper, found it, and released herself from the bag. The motor home was chilly. She shivered as she grabbed the edge of Nick's mattress with one hand and poked at her husband with the other.

"Nick."

"Mmm…"

"Did you hear that noise?"

"Whatever you say, honey," he mumbled, then turned away and stuffed his face into the pillow.

"Nick!" she cried. She poked again. "Wake up!"

He rolled back toward her. Sam's naked silhouette was backlit by the dim glow of the motor home's nightlight. His eyes popped open. He grinned. "What? You want sex again?"

"Nick!" Her voice was strained. "I heard a gun shot. Outside. Close by."

For a moment Nick stared at her. Then he kicked out of his sleeping bag and swung his legs over the edge. "Get something on," he said, blinking his eyes. He sat for a moment, clutching the edge of the mattress.

Sam grabbed her plaid bathrobe off the seat beside her and pulled it on. Nick slipped down into the narrow aisle of the twenty-two-foot Coachman and stuffed his legs into the jeans he'd left draped over the driver's seat. His eyes darted around the camper. "Where's the gun?"

"We didn't bring it," Sam said, annoyed with herself. She was sitting on the edge of the sofa bed, with the sleeping bag bunched against her chest. Trembling.

Nick scowled.

Sam dropped her head. Having a gun nearby had become a habit since the Cowberry Necklace Murders in their town two years ago.

"I should have thought to bring it," he said, squeezing her hand.

Sam looked up at him. "You'd think we could come to the Pond for a few days without worrying about carrying a gun."

He hesitated. "Well, I'm sure we don't need it. What you heard was probably a car backfiring. Or some kids with firecrackers." He scooped up their flashlight and headed for the back door.

"Be careful," Sam whispered after him.

Nick had rented the Coachman with an eye to buying it—if things worked out. He was still dreaming of taking Sam across country if he could pry her away from her entrenched lifestyle. Sam had agreed to a few nights camping by Pottle's Pond, close to home. Just in case she forgot something. Or the girls or her mother needed her. Or the cat got sick. Or a client called.

They hooked up the unit around five o'clock the previous evening and, joined by the couple parked next to them, they'd had supper over a community grill. Nick and Sam excused themselves around 8:30, and after a romantic walk around the pond, fell into bed around 9:30 to read.

Nick had been hopeful. He would love nothing better than to have Sam accompany him on winter camping trips, snowshoeing through the White Mountains, and on canoe rides down the Dead River. (She did query him about how the river got its name.) But Nick would settle for a trip across country in the camper. Sam, on the other hand, preferred the fireplace, hot chocolate, and a good book. The motor home was a compromise with which they could both live—for now.

At the thought of Nick leaving the camper by himself, the adrenaline took hold. Sam called, "Hold on. You're not going out there without me."

Donning a manly air, Nick said, "Calm down, babe. I'm sure it's nothing." He didn't look so sure. He knew that Sam was familiar with the sound of gunfire. "Stay put. I'll be right back."

"Halt!" Sam jumped up. She threw the sleeping bag aside, and pulled a black skillet from under the sink. "If we go down, we go down together." She slipped into her old Reeboks by the bathroom door, spooned her body behind Nick, and said, "Okay. Let's go."

Nick rolled his eyes, but he didn't argue. Sam flinched when the door lock made a metallic click.

Nick inched the door open, then stepped down, Sam on his heels. The damp air and fecund smell of earth closed around them. The ground was wet from a brief evening shower. Clouds had moved in during the night, blotting out the waning moon. The campground was dark and eerily silent. In the misty distance, a light flickered over the entrance to the office/grocery store. Beyond the office, a string of smudged lights lined Route 125.

Nick swung the flashlight in an arc. The beam barely penetrated the carbon veil of night. "I don't see anything," he said over his shoulder.

"I think the sound came from the other side of the motor home," Sam whispered in Nick's ear. "The side where I was sleeping." She could feel the dampness creep up her bare legs as Nick's shoulders rose and fell.

As one, they moved toward the back of the Coachman. Their feet made little noise on the damp dirt. With the flashlight as point, Nick poked his head around the rear of the coach, and then pulled back. He darted a second look.

"What do you see?" Sam asked.

"Shhh. Wait."

They inched forward. Sam, one hand at Nick's waist and the other weighing the frying pan, kept looking back over her shoulder.

Once again, Nick stuck his head out and pointed the flashlight toward the next motor home, twenty feet away. Sam felt his body stiffen as he gasped. "My God!"

She froze. "What is it, Nick?" She felt a shiver run through his body.

Nick's arm curved back to hold Sam in place. Then he turned and put his arms around her.

"Don't look, Sam. There's a man on the ground beside the next camper. And he isn't moving."

The interior of the Silver Stream motor home parked next to theirs was dark. In the cone of the light by the unit's rear door lay the body of a man. He wore sneakers, slacks, and a windbreaker. A puddle of dark liquid had pooled under his neck.

He wasn't moving.

By the time Sam convinced Nick to approach their neighbor's camper, Earle Bankes had already called 911 on his cell phone.

"Is he dead?" Nick asked.

The big man snuffed. "Well, I can tell you he won't be whistling Dixie any time soon. I felt his wrist for a pulse. There isn't one. Didn't touch his neck. Might have destroyed evidence." He cleared his throat.

Sam thought his reluctance had more to do with the sight of all that blood, but she had to agree. It was a ghastly enough scene without sticking your fingers in the poor man's fluids.

Bankes added, "I heard a tapping message right after the shot."

Standing in the open door of their luxurious coach, Lulu Bankes quivered in her pink satin robe. "I told you it wasn't a message!" Exasperated, she looked toward Nick and Sam for support. "He thinks the tapping sound was a message from the dead man." Lulu had a head full of pink rollers and an arm full of white poodle. Sweetums was minus her pink ribbons from suppertime.

"I know what I heard!" Bankes huffed at his wife.

"It was just tapping," Lulu persisted in a tremulous voice as she crouched against the steps. She kept kissing the top of Sweetums tufted head.

"It wasn't just tapping!" Bankes roared. "I'm a card player. I know signals when I hear them."

Sam was afraid there was about to be another homicide, if that's what this was. And it looked like it was.

"Whoever did this could still be out there," Sam whispered, her eyes sweeping the darkness around them. She flinched and grabbed Nick's arm with one hand and pointed toward the street. "Look!"

A pinpoint of light seemed to be moving closer.

Maybe it's the police, Sam thought. *The shooter wouldn't march up to us like that, would he? The generic he,* she added, and then wondered how her mind could consider the proper use of pronouns in this horrendous situation.

The light grew radially, bobbing like the bouncing ball over the old sing-a-longs on the movie screens. A man emerged from the gloom.

"What's the problem, folks?" Kenny Pottle politely leveled his flashlight's beam at their chests. Then he saw the body. "What the…" He directed the shaft of light at the prone figure.

Sam winced as a circle of light pooled on the dead man's head.

"Jesus in a jumpsuit!" Kenny said. His bloodshot eyes were now wide open. He stared as his head began to swing back and forth. "I knew that sound I heard wasn't a car backfiring. Is he dead?"

"Yes," Earle offered, scowling down at the unmoving figure. "I called 911. The police should be here any minute."

"Who is he?"

Bankes flung his hands wide. "I don't know. I heard a shot, then some tapping. When I came out here and found this guy, I called the police."

"Does anyone know this man?" Nick asked.

There was a unanimous shaking of heads.

"The police said not to trample the scene," Bankes said.

The group stared at their feet as if expecting to find a weapon or footprints or maybe a gaping hole that would swallow them all.

Once again, Sam was aware of the cold seeping under her bathrobe and up her bare legs. She hugged her chest, bunching the robe tighter at her neck. Her breathing was shallow as a tremor ran through her.

"Strangest thing," Bankes said again, shaking his head. "This guy was tapping some kind of code on the side on my motor home."

Lulu rolled her eyes. "It wasn't a code."

"Did you hear it, woman!" Bankes roared.

In spite of the tension coiling inside her body, Sam drew a mind-picture of Earle Bankes, huffing and puffing and blowing his motor home down and dispatching Lulu and Sweetums in a maelstrom of hard pink plastic rollers.

"You were sound asleep! Gurgling, by the way," Bankes roared again. "You couldn't have heard Mighty Joe Young beating his chest and bellowing his mating call. I heard it, and I'm telling you, he was sending a message. Look at the guy! You think he could yell with that bloody throat?" Lulu shuddered. "He was reaching out the only way he could."

Lulu scurried up their steps and turned at the top. "If you need us," she said, with her nose in the air, "Sweetums and I will be inside where it's warm." The door shut with a bang and the interior light went on.

Sam turned toward Route 125 where she heard a car slue to a stop. Several moments later, Charlie Burrows's form parted the soupy night. "Someone called about an incident."

Sam thought she saw her old friend flinch when he spotted the body on the ground. "Everyone step back, please." His voice was gruff, detached, professional. But Sam knew him. He would never get used to violence. He had witnessed too much of it as a child.

Charlie went down on one knee and shone his flashlight on the victim while he felt for a pulse. Then he patted the pockets of the windbreaker. From the man's right pants pocket he extracted a folding leather wallet. Holding it by the edges with two fingers, he flipped it open, then placed it by the victim's side. He pulled a notebook from his breast pocket and made notes then grunted as he pushed himself up.

"This man is dead." His eyes flicked at Sam and Nick, but there was no break in his cadence. "Stay exactly where you are. Please don't move until I get your statements."

The area was cordoned off with yellow plastic police tape. After statements were taken and the medical examiner and crime lab people were done, the body was carted off. An officer was posted at the entrance to the campground to prevent any unauthorized vehicles from entering or leaving.

"Not that I have much business at 4:30 in the morning," Kenny grumbled.

"I hope we're not suspects," Bankes said, when they were free to return to their motor homes.

"How could we be? We don't even know the guy," Lulu said, poking her head around the door of the coach. She looked to the chief. "Are the police going to stay here tonight?" Her voice broke with fear. "I don't want to stay here unless the police are guarding us."

"Don't worry, ma'am," Charlie Burrows assured her. "Someone will be posted here all night." With a glance at Sam, he turned and left.

"Thank goodness," Lulu said, pressing a hand to her chest. "Are you coming to bed, Earle?"

Sam sidled up to the big man. "What were you saying earlier about the tapping you heard?"

A cavernous smile spread across Earle's face. When he turned to respond to his wife, Nick poked at her and whispered sternly, "Sam. It's not our affair."

"Well," Sam said under her breath, "you never know. What if Charlie wants my help?"

"What if, Sam?" Nick muttered. "Your 'what ifs' get us into more trouble than a one-armed paper hanger."

Sam elbowed him.

"…and, Lulu," Bankes commanded, "pull down the blinds. We're not living in Macy's department store window, you know."

Lulu nodded and closed the coach door. The blinds went down.

Earle turned to Sam. "Well, I'm glad someone believes me."

"I do," Sam assured him, looking up wide-eyed into his face. "A man with your experience would know the difference between a simple knocking and a tapped message."

"You'd better believe it, little lady." His chest puffed up.

"Exactly what did you hear?"

"Well," he drawled, as he looped large thumbs into his jean pockets, "I distinctly heard a rapping sound that went…tap…tap…tap-tap…tap-tap-tap. And the guy did it a second time before he died."

"So," Sam said, "it was one tap, one tap, two taps, then three taps?"

"Exactly!"

"Sam," Nick interrupted. "It's late." He edged away, his hand firmly around her arm above the elbow.

Sam locked his hand against her side, ignored him. She gazed into Earle's face. "Do you suppose it's some kind of Morse code?"

"I don't rightly know, little lady," Bankes said, rocking back on his size thir-teens. "Never learned Morse code. All I know is, the man was trying to tell me something. That tapping was his dying cry for help."

CHAPTER 10

✿

MONDAY 9:30 A.M.

CJ came late to work on Monday morning, his hair rumpled, his eyes hollow. He was in a foul mood.

"What the hell is this?" he cried, waving an invoice at his stepbrother. "I thought these guys had been paid way back. What are they trying to pull? Double bill us or something?"

In the clutter of the windowless office, Frank looked up from his chair behind the metal desk and snorted. "What's the matter, CJ? Can't handle a wild night in front of my TV?"

"I never turn down an offer of free beer."

"Yeah. Well, you drank enough of my beer last night."

"Don't start, Frank! You drank more than I did." CJ tossed the bill at him and began pacing in his odd gait in front of the desk, rubbing his temples. "I've got a headache."

The bill fluttered to the floor.

Frank rolled his chair back and picked up the invoice stamped with bold red letters—OVERDUE—and placed it in the metal tray to his left. "Yeah, I drank as much as you did, but I don't have a hangover." He wasn't feeling so hot either, but he wouldn't let his brother know that. "By the way, when are you going to stop sponging off Ma and move out of her house and get your own place?"

CJ swung toward him. "What about you?"

Frank's eyes narrowed as he said, "I pay for my apartment over Ma's garage. And I buy my own food. So don't use that for an excuse."

CJ's voice dropped. "I'm looking," he said.

"You've been saying that for months. You keep saying that because you think Debbie's going to take you back, but she's not, so you'd better get used to the idea and move on."

CJ waved a dismissive hand at him. "Where's Ma?"

"She's getting her hair done. Rita went with her. You and I are on today."

CJ slumped into the Morris chair opposite the wall of filing cabinets. His head was pounding. He stared at the letters carved into the nameplate on the desk. FRANK BONACCI. His stepbrother. Frank wasn't even a Frazetta, for God's sake. And the jerk barreled around like he was in charge of the whole stinking business.

CJ didn't like Frank much. Maybe he even hated him. He wasn't sure. He knew he hated Frank for his muscular body and his legendary prowess on the football field. Some of CJ's classmates, and even a few of the parents, still came into the store and talked about the great quarterback Frank Bonacci and how he should have gone on to the National Football League. Frank had that take-charge attitude in the hardware store. The big hairy bum was still trying to be the high school quarterback, calling the plays, running with the ball, and with the women. Nothing had changed. The broads still hung all over him like balls on a Christmas tree.

CJ loved Rita as a sister, but Frank would never be his brother. He saw the irony in this, but it didn't change things.

"What's the use?" he went on. "We're going to lose this goddamn place anyway." He leaned forward, his elbows on his thighs, his head in his hands. "And all because of that bastard Brennan."

Neither of them spoke for several minutes. The only sound in the room was the hum of the overhead fluorescent light. CJ looked up to see Frank lean back in his chair and glance at the ceiling. A few dead bug carcasses lay scattered inside the glowing tube.

Finally Frank got up. "I'm going to the john. And as for Brennan, he'll get what he deserves."

"You can be sure of that," CJ mumbled into his hands.

"Where are you going?" Frank demanded. "It's not even lunchtime yet."

CJ flinched at the sound, then squinted at his brother through a veil of pain. Inside his head, the pounding had not abated. "We've got customers to attend to, you know."

CJ looked around the nearly empty store. "Yeah. I can see them all lined up at the cash register. Now, get out of my way, Frank, before I deck you."

"Don't push your luck, little brother."

Frank's eyes narrowed. He began tracing circles on his elbow.

CJ knew he had to try and control his temper. He was smaller than Frank, but he was a scrapper. He and Frank had their fistfights through grade school and into high school, and they both had stitches from those encounters. More than one bully who thought CJ was a weakling because of his size carried battle scars to this day. CJ's slight limp was the result of a scuffle in the hallway outside Miss Cranston's third grade classroom when Frank landed hard on his ankle. CJ sustained a fracture that kept him in a cast for a month.

CJ glowered at his brother, then stepped around him and headed out. He could see Frank's reflection in the closing glass door. He grumbled all the way out to his truck. He had matters to attend to, and he wasn't going to let his big oaf of a stepbrother get in the way. The guy needed a head adjustment. CJ didn't know why he put up with Frank. Maybe it was time to find a way to get rid of the prick for good. The family was rid of Brennan. Maybe it was time for Frank to disappear, too. Hang 'Em High, he thought.

"I can't believe I slept so late," Mary Frazetta said to her daughter as they left the beauty salon and headed for the supermarket.

"Did you take more Valium last night, mom?" Rita asked, with a note of disapproval in her voice. This morning, her mother seemed to be running on high octane. Rita was concerned that Mary was mixing her medication with caffeine and who knew what else.

"No. But some nights I do," Mary admitted, "when I can't sleep."

She narrowed her eyes against the glare from the sun glinting off cars in the mall parking lot. "But I was out like a light last night. And then, this morning, I was so tired it was almost as if I had taken sleeping pills. I had to have three cups of coffee to get started. But, as far as the Valium goes, I can handle it."

Rita wasn't so sure. Her mother had seemed distant since her husband died. Sometimes Mary seemed to be in a drug-induced haze; other times, she was wired for sound.

Rita thought about her dad. God! She missed him too. The family had been through so much the past month. She wanted the pain to end. With gut-wrenching bitterness, she thought about Brennan once again. He was as guilty of her father's death as if he had done the dirty deed himself. She hoped Brennan would rot in hell.

"Did you notice that Lisa was awfully quiet today?" Mary asked.

Rita blinked. "Uh…yeah. I did actually. Lisa's usually so bubbly. Maybe she's worried about her business." Rita bit her lip. She wished she hadn't said that. She added quickly, "Most likely she was just tired from the stress of having two of her hairdressers out with the flu."

Mary and Rita stepped aside to let a harried woman pass. She was pushing a loaded grocery cart and dragging a weeping child by the hand.

That's when Rita saw it.

In the metal news dispenser chained to the supermarket wall, the headline screamed:

SUICIDE'S ACCOUNTANT MURDERED

Rita looked at her mother who was frowning. Neither one spoke.

CHAPTER 11

❀

MONDAY 12:10 P.M.

Moments earlier, Sam had turned off the noon news. The lead story had been the homicide at Pottle's Pond on Route 125 in Georgetown, New Hampshire. Richard Brennan, accountant to recent suicide victim Claudio Frazetta, murdered by an unknown assailant at three o'clock that morning.

Sam wondered when Charlie Burrows was going to call.

She sat at her desk with her chin in her hands, staring at page 341 in volume 8 of the *Encyclopaedia Britannica*. She couldn't help it. She had to know if Earle Bankes was right about the tapping. Not that she was going to get involved. She was just curious.

Nick was fond of reminding her that curiosity killed the cat. To which she would respond, "Yeah. And satisfaction brought it back."

Besides, Sam thought, *a cat has nine lives, and I've just begun to meow.*

Picking up her Saga pen, she grabbed a sheet of scrap paper by her printer and started.

Bankes had said that Brennan had rapped on his motor home in sequence. Two times. Certainly the repetition of the first series of taps couldn't be a coincidence.

She wrote:

1	1	2	3
X	X	XX	XXX

Her eyes fell back on page 341.

The encyclopedia stated that Samuel Morse invented the first system of dots and dashes that comprise Morse code in the 1830s. A modified and simpler version was devised in 1851 at a special meeting of European nations. This newer code was called the International Morse Code, or the Continental Code.

Operators in the United States used the original version until the late 1920s. Because Brennan was middle-aged, Sam reasoned, most likely he would have used the International Morse Code version. Based upon that premise, she began.

Sam peered at the table in the encyclopedia.

There was no way of knowing the cadence of the tappings, so Sam noted the corresponding letters of both dots and dashes.

The single taps were either an "E" or a "T"; the two taps, the letters "I" or "M"; and three taps, an "S" or an "O".

She wrote the letters under the original two lines.

1	1	2	3
E	E	I	S
T	T	M	O

If the tapping from the dead man was Morse code, the letters before her could contain the answer to who his murderer was. She rubbed the side of her face and stared at her neatly penned and aligned script.

It was as clear as the calculus course she had taken her freshman year at the University of New Hampshire. And that was a disaster. She just passed with a 2.5. It was a case of misplaced number fascination, she told her mother years later, after she'd fallen in love with the metaphysics of numbers.

Sam leaned into her hand as she scowled at the sheet before her. The code could be all dots, all dashes, or a combination of the two. Surely the letters were in the proper order to form a word. That's if Bankes was right about what he'd heard.

She doodled.

EEIS

TTMO

TEMS…the river Thames?

ETMO

TTIS

Could the letters stand for an organization? She wondered if there was an alphabetical list of acronyms somewhere. She twiddled her pen as she pondered the possibilities.

ETIO

ETIS

Something in Latin maybe?

Sum, es, est, summus, estis, sunt.

She found herself conjugating the verb "is" from her high school Latin class. She wondered why pieces of seemingly useless information take up space in a person's brain.

Latin? Right! A Latin scholar who speaks dead languages murders an embezzling, gambling-addicted accountant and escapes down the river Thames. She was getting nowhere fast.

She diddled with the original Morse Code, but that made no sense either.

Sam crumpled the scrap of paper and tossed it into her overflowing wastebasket. After all, she wasn't involved. It was not her business. The police would handle it—and very efficiently. They didn't need her help.

She slid the encyclopedia back into the bookcase under the sun porch windows and took the wastebasket into the garage. She had to shake it a few times to loosen the contents. Her mind was working overtime as she watched the catalogues, ripped envelopes, advertisements, Ring Ding wrappers, and odd pieces of paper fall into the pail.

She replaced the lid, turned to go back into the house, and stopped. She stood in the cool of the garage rubbing her top teeth over her bottom lip.

Setting the wastebasket on the steps leading into the breezeway, she removed the lid once again and gingerly fished through the debris, taking pains to avoid the fuzzy leftover beans she dumped earlier that morning. She found the scrap paper she had written on—free of growing things she didn't want to think about—laid it on the top step, smoothed out the wrinkles, and folded it into a neat square. She stuck the paper in her sweatpants pocket, just in case.

By cat reckoning, she figured she was only on her second life.

CHAPTER 12

❀

MONDAY 12:15 P.M.

Randy Sturgis sat in his apartment, coughing and staring at the television screen. He couldn't believe his eyes.

It was the same guy who was staying at the CircleTo Motel, the one the gorgeous redhead was looking for. Only the guy didn't check in under the name Richard Brennan. He said he was John something. John Roberts, that was it. And now he was dead? Murdered?

The newscaster's expression modulated from serious concern to bright optimism. "So, Mike, what does the weather have in store for us?"

Randy shuddered as he thumbed the remote button and the set crackled into silence. He dropped the remote on top of *Thrusting Passion*, the book that lay on the rickety table beside him. He flopped back against his chair and plucked at the stuffing fanning out from its arm.

He thought about the note he fished out of the wastebasket in the dead guy's room at the motel. Someone had rubbed a pencil over the note pad. Randy had to hold the note directly under the lamp to see the writing. The letters showed as white wisps, ghost-like, against the gray smudge.

Monday 3 AM Pottles Pond Rte 125

Randy wondered why Brennan would make a rubbing of his own note? Then, in a moment of unfamiliar clarity, he reasoned that Rita the Redhead might have done it. He'd given her the guy's room number! Maybe she was so mad at her husband for screwing around that she'd gotten into his room somehow, found the note, then followed him to the campground and shot him.

A crime of passion!

Randy leaned forward and rubbed his forehead hard.

Should he call the cops and let them know about Rita and the note? He shook his head. No. If he did that, he'd be implicated.

He grabbed his Camels off the table, shook one out, and lit it. Taking a deep drag, he held the smoke in his lungs for a moment, then let it out slowly as he leaned back into the chair. He coughed again.

I've gotta think this thing through. If I tell the cops about this broad, and she tells them I gave out the guy's room number, I could lose my job. It ain't much, but it's all I got.

Then a more terrifying thought struck him. What if the cops searched his apartment? They'd find all the stuff he'd lifted from the motel. He flicked an ash onto the pile of butts in the ashtray next to his elbow and chewed at his bottom lip.

The final scene in this play of what-ifs caught him with a quick jab to the gut. The cops might say he helped her, that he was an accessory to the murder! He'd go to prison. Bad things happened to guys in prison showers.

For the first time in Randy Sturgis's life, he knew the true meaning of some-one's blood running cold. He began to shiver. He mashed the butt in the ashtray, pushed himself out of the chair, and began to pace.

See what making a decision did for you, you stupid jerk! You couldn't mind your own business, could you? You let yourself get sucked in by a pair of tits.

Terrified beyond speech, Randy knew he had to make another decision. He had two options. One, go to the cops and spill his guts and maybe go to prison, or two, stay the hell out of it and maybe, just maybe, no one would know he talked to this broad.

His body broke out in a cold sweat.

Suddenly, he began to cough. And cough. He ran to the bathroom, gagged, and spit up a mouthful of phlegm into the toilet. Back in the living room, his tripped on the loose threads in the carpet and caught himself before he sprawled headlong into the television set.

Great! That's all I need. Bruises and bandages. Then it'd look like I fought with the guy who was murdered.

He almost choked when he tried to swallow. His throat felt raw. He clenched his teeth so hard that his jaw muscles began to ache.

He didn't want to get involved. He had to think!

He paced.

Even if the cops checked the local motels, he reasoned, the CircleTo register would only show that some guy named John Roberts had checked in. The dork wasn't killed at his motel. Besides, there was nothing to place Brennan in the motel room because the guy had left nothing behind, except the note in the wastebasket, and Randy had that. It was as if the Roberts/Brennan guy had never been there. If, for some strange reason, the police did find a way to trace Brennan to the CircleTo and if the news was right and the guy had been shot around three in the morning...well okay, Randy had been on duty that night. The eleven to seven shift. He couldn't be in two places at once. That was something in his favor.

Randy stopped pacing. He nodded vigorously. *I was working that night. I never met that broad before. I'm in the clear.*

Randy chose the latter of his two options. He'd keep his mouth locked tighter than a virgin's legs on a hot date.

A shiver registered down the back of his neck. If he was so goddamn sure he'd made the right decision, why was he still in a cold sweat? He leaned a clammy hand against the wall.

Through the sole window in his apartment, he stared down into the narrow alley separating his building from the three-story apartment building next door. A mangy dog was nosing through a split in a plastic garbage bag. Nearby, a rusted tricycle lay on its side, its front wheel missing. A scrap of paper, caught by a sudden burst of wind, jerked and twisted crazily down the alley, caught in the spokes of the bike's wheel, and then, on another gust of wind, pinwheeled into the shadows beyond.

Life's castoffs, Randy thought, feeling like a member of that sorry group. *Used, abused, and dumped.*

Randy found himself picking at pieces of the putrid green wallpaper under his hand. Once again, he felt like he was going to barf. He pulled the window open, stuck his head out and took in deep breaths of the cool air.

In the alleyway, the mangy dog stopped foraging, lifted its head as if listening, then looked up at Randy in the window. Its lips curled back over sharp teeth.

"Get out of there!" Randy yelled, waving his arm at the dog. He grabbed the edge of the windowsill as a coughing jag bent him over.

The dog stared up at Randy with yellow eyes.

That's when Randy's subconscious kicked in. Unknown to him, a third option began to formulate in the smoke-filled regions of his mind.

CHAPTER 13

✿

MONDAY 7:40 P.M.

"Your name's in the paper again, mom," Sadie said. The accusatory tone came through the portable phone loud and clear.

Nick and Samantha had just laughed themselves silly over a Seinfeld rerun—a much-needed release after the episode at Pottle's Pond early that morning—and had settled in for the evening.

Nick sat in the rose brocade chair by the fireplace with his feet on a matching footstool. He was reading the hardcover, autographed copy of *Not Without Peril* that Sam had given him for Christmas.

Across from him, Sam lay sprawled on the couch with a book on her chest, trying to pretend she didn't smell the aroma of chocolate from the freshly baked cookies on the kitchen counter. Attitude changers, she called them. She'd already eaten nine—six, that Nick knew nothing about, while she was baking them, and three after supper, for dessert. And her attitude had definitely improved.

The 6:00 evening news featured sketchy details that the reporter had wheedled out of someone. Sam was relieved that she and Nick weren't mentioned in the news clip, but she did wonder if the reporter had spoken to Earle and Lulu Bankes or Kenny Pottles. Sam figured Kenny would have clammed up. He was probably already tabulating the lost dollars as a result of the murder. After the police left the scene of the homicide, Kenny railed about how the negative publicity would affect his business, stating that he could see the headline in the next edition of Publick Occurrences. "Person Popped at Pottles" were his exact words.

Somewhat bemused at Kenny's alliteration, Sam smiled. Then she sobered. Murder was a heinous crime. But she knew that Kenny was a wily businessman and that he might eventually take full advantage of the incident. His campground was not quite up there with Lizzie Borden's guesthouse yet, but who knew how he might capitalize on the incident. When the investigation was over, Kenny might well be embellishing his campground's fliers. He might even post a sign marking the spot, and sell little pistol souvenirs with his logo stamped on the side.

Ashamed, Sam told herself to be kind, to give Kenny the benefit of a doubt. She also wondered where her thoughts came from, and was a bit afraid of knowing. She contemplated the possibility of putting her suspicious mind to work writing a mystery.

"Mom? Are you there?"

"Yes, honey," Sam said tiredly, sticking a marker in her book and laying it on the coffee table. "We saw the papers, too. Believe me. Dad and I just happened to be there when it happened. We're not involved." She reached down to feel the note still stuffed in her sweatpants pocket.

Sadie snuffled. "Is this the 'I did not have sex with that young woman' defense?"

Sadie told her sister, "Mom says they aren't involved."

In the background, Caroline responded, "Ask her if she's sure."

"We're not involved!" Sam said, too emphatically. She switched the portable to the other ear, and with three raised fingers, motioned Nick toward the cookies on the kitchen counter. She always ate cookies in threes. Things happened in threes and she enjoyed the challenge of happenings.

Nick raised one eyebrow at her, challenging her decision.

She raised two eyebrows in return. Nick put his book down and got up.

Sam decided she needed a really *big* attitude change after talking with Earle Bankes in the wee hours of that morning. Three more cookies would make an even dozen that she had consumed this day. She patted the bulge rising above her waist.

*I start dieting tomorrow and I'm not going to get involved in the murder at Pottles' Pond. No matter how curious I am about that tapping. ETIS…EEMO… TTIS…*Her mind began to wander.

"What happened, mom? The paper says that…

Sam blinked. She could hear rustling sounds.

"…here it is. 'Richard Howard Brennan was the accountant for Claudio Frazetta, who recently committed suicide. An unknown assailant shot Brennan at Pottles' Pond Campground early this morning.' And then it mentions you and dad and another couple."

"All I know is what I read in the papers," Sam said.

"Come on, mom!"

Nick placed a china plate with three cookies and a paper napkin on the coffee table. He winked at Sam, who smiled up at him, took his chair and began reading once again.

"And Gramma said," Sadie continued, "that this Brennan guy worked for her friend, Mrs. Frazetta, and that the Frazettas might be in financial trouble because of him."

"Tell mom that's no reason for her to get involved in this." Caroline must be hovering over Sadie's shoulder, Sam thought, because her voice came through loud and clear.

"Caroline says…"

"I heard her," Sam said, her eyes locked on the three cookies.

An admonition from the eternally young exercise guru, Jack LaLane, popped into her mind. "*It's on your taste buds for a minute, but on your front porch forever.*" She re-crossed her ankles and tapped her right forefinger on the valley between the sand dunes of her stomach and her chest.

It's mind over matter.

Her finger picked up speed.

I don't need any more cookies.

As she inhaled the smell of warm chocolate, her salivary glands got down on their knees and begged.

All right already!

She'd have three cookies, no more, and she'd start exercising tomorrow and get rid of the extra thirty pounds she'd been carrying around for too long.

"Please, honey," Sam said to Sadie. "I don't want you two to worry. Dad and I are enjoying a quiet evening reading. What could possibly happen?"

"Isn't that a line from the old television series, '*Crazy Like A Fox*'?" Sadie asked. "And didn't the lead character say that at the beginning of every episode, just before he got into trouble?"

"Sadie, the historian." Sam grabbed the biggest cookie off the plate and examined it. "I'm not involved. Believe me."

Sadie transmitted to Caroline, "Mom said she's not involved. Believe her."

After a very loud pause, Sam said sweetly, "Can I go now, *mother*?"

"Well," Sadie's voice was stern, "sometimes you do need a keeper. Okay, Mom. You can go. I love you."

"Me, too," Caroline added.

"And I love you both."

Sam smiled as she set the phone on the coffee table. She took a generous bite of the cookie and tapped the crumbs into her mouth before placing the remaining half back on the plate. She nestled back into the sofa pillows, and once again opened the book that had come in the mail that day: *The Theoretic*

Arithmetic of the Pythagoreans. She hoped she'd be able to understand some of it.

She had plowed through eleven pages of the introduction by Manly P. Hall, and was frowning over a table of Greek and Hebrew glyphs when the phone rang once again. Sam glanced at Nick. He stirred, frowned, and lowered his head into his book.

Sam reached for the phone.

"Hello."

"Samantha?"

Sam hesitated, and then sat up, cradling the book against her chest. "Hannibal?"

"Yes. I hope I'm not bothering you."

"No. Of course not."

Nick looked over his book with a question in his eyes. Sam shrugged, her brows arched.

The Reverend Hannibal Loveless calling numerologist Samantha Blackwell? In all the years that Hannibal had been in Georgetown, he had never once telephoned her.

The minister cleared his throat. "This is very difficult for me, Samantha. One might say, role reversal." An intake of breath. "Might I make an appointment to speak with you soon? It's extremely important."

There was just the briefest pause.

"Why, yes. Of course, Hannibal. And you don't need an appointment. Would you like to come over now?"

Come over right now! was what she really wanted to say.

"Thank you, Samantha. I appreciate your kindness, but I wouldn't impose on your evening. Would eleven tomorrow morning be convenient for you?"

"Eleven o'clock is fine." It really wasn't fine, but she was an adult. She could wait.

There was a pause before Hannibal said, in a voice betraying his uncertainty, "I must ask you to exercise the utmost discretion in this matter, Samantha. Please don't mention our appointment to anyone, not even to my wife."

Sam was really curious now. Hannibal worshipped Emmaline. "As you wish. Good-night, Hannibal."

"What was that all about?" Nick asked as he laid his book in his lap.

"I don't know," Sam mumbled, nibbling on the remaining half-cookie. A gooey chocolate bit fell on her sweatshirt. She didn't notice.

Hannibal didn't know if he had done the right thing in calling Samantha Blackwell. The woman was a partaker of forbidden fruit. But her intentions were good, and he was sure the Lord would forgive her for dabbling in dangerous subject matters. Just as he knew the Lord forgave Emmaline her harmless hobby. He shook his head, truly bewildered. Numerology. Palmistry. How could these intelligent women fall under the lure of the Occult?

Hannibal ladled two scoops of steaming clam chowder into a crockery bowl, and headed for the living room with yesterday's Sunday edition of Publick Occurrences under one arm. He knew he was not the one to sit in judgement. Heaven knew he had broken many commandments in his youth. And yes, he had to admit, even well into his thirties. Until the day he met Emmaline. His precious wife. God had given him a great gift on the day they met. He looked down at the soup bowl in his hands. Emmaline had made the chowder for him just that morning. The warmth from the bowl seeped into his hands and—it seemed—up his arms and into his heart.

Hannibal knew that Emmaline liked and trusted Samantha, and even though his wife was involved in the study of palmistry, a subject of which he disapproved, he trusted her judgment. That fact made him feel more confident about putting his trust in the Blackwell woman.

Hannibal noticed that his hands were shaking as he set the newspaper and the chowder on the table beside his easy chair. His wife had gone to visit her mother for the day and, as much as he adored his wife, part of him was glad to have this time alone. He sank into his faded blue chair, picked up the television remote and pressed the power button.

Niagra Falls thundered over him!

He jumped as his heart gave his chest a good thump. He jabbed at the remote.

Bullets ricocheted off the walls!

Hannibal almost dove for cover before he realized it was the television, a gun battle on the dark streets of L.A., and not bullets shattering his living room windows.

He sighed. Instead of pressing the volume down button, he had hit the scan button and changed the channels. The memory of Richard Brennan's death by gunfire was haunting him.

Hannibal shut off the television and slumped back against his chair. He wasn't aware that the remote slid from his hand and into the crack between the cushion and the upholstered arm.

So many secrets!

He felt his stomach roil. He was ashamed about keeping his shady past from his wife, afraid of what she would say, what she would think of him, and ultimately, what she would do because of it. He couldn't bear losing her. Those fears compounded the terror he felt at what had happened at the Pond early this morning. He looked over at the creamy chowder made by his wife's loving hands, at the crockery bowl they purchased at last year's Cowberry Fall Festival, and his stomach lurched violently. He bent forward, grabbed his head in both hands, and began to rock.

Could he ever forgive himself?

Would God forgive him?

Hunched over his knees, he continued to rock. It was as if the world was flat, and he was standing on its edge. He could feel the universe waiting for him to leap into its void. But even that thought was not as terrifying as the answer to the primary question. The only answer that really mattered.

Would Emmaline forgive him?

CHAPTER 14

❁

TUESDAY 8:30 A.M.

Sam sucked on the finger she had just nicked.

Then, brandishing a paring knife, she said, "If you're looking for trouble, young lady, you're going to get it. How do you expect me to make an apple pie with you rubbing your tail under my nose? Now, get down off my counter before I hug you to death."

The tabby that Sam had picked up at the SPCA a few years back and who had subsequently decided to move in to her mother's Victorian Bed & Breakfast next door, landed on the floor with a flomp, then waddled under the dining room table. Sam leaned over the counter and looked into Selket's lime eyes. She chuckled. "What's the matter? Didn't my mother fill your bowl twice this morning?" The cat ventured forth to wind around Sam's legs.

Holding the knife off to one side, Sam tugged the cat under her free arm and kissed her orange face. "I would think, with all the guests at the Inn, you'd get enough attention." She elbowed the handle on the storm door, held it open with her foot, and lowered the cat onto the stoop. Selket stuck her whiskers in the air and crossed the yard with queenly grace. Sam watched her climb the side steps of her mother's Inn and disappear through the kitty door.

"I see Selket's on his high horse again," Charlie Burrows commented as he approached the breezeway door. "You busy?"

"*Her* high horse, Charlie. And I'm never too busy to talk with you. Come on in. I was wondering when you were going to show up here. I'm making Nick an apple pie, and I don't have a client until 11:00."

The door clicked shut behind them.

As Sam waved Charlie toward the kitchen, he said, "Be careful with that knife, Sam. I'm too tired to wrestle even a woman to the ground right now..." Sam eyeballed him "...though you might be a handful even on one of my good days." He grinned, a sharp contrast to the dark circles under his eyes.

"You do look like something the cat dragged in, Charlie. Take a seat. Don't tell me Brun decided to trade you in for a newer model."

"She's too smart for that," he chuckled. "Nope. I got a call early this morning and had to go out to the Cooder place again. Old Leroy was three sheets to the wind and waving a butcher knife as big as a machete." He eyed Sam's paring knife, his demeanor suddenly more sober.

Sam paused to look at her childhood friend. She had to wonder if Charlie's early morning tussle with Leroy Cooder had dredged up that old memory. No one knew exactly how ten-year old Charlie Burrows got the slash down the left side of his face. The official story was that he had tripped over the wood stove hearth and fallen on his father's hunting knife, which he supposedly had in his hand at the time. But Sam would never forget the look in Charlie's eyes when he'd come to school the next day, his face sheathed in bandages. He'd said it was nothing. He'd just fallen. The following year, Charlie's father had had that fatal shooting accident in the woods. To this day, Charlie had never again spoken of either incident.

The sun pouring through the bow window laid squares against Charlie's back and over the table. On his shadowed face, the spaghetti scar running from his forehead past his left eye and onto his cheek looked white against his leathery skin. He looked tired.

Charlie let out a man-sized sigh and unzipped his Red Sox jacket. "Took both Lenny and me to calm old Leroy down. 'Course the bucket of cold water took some of the fire out of him. He'd never hurt Maggie or the kids, but he sure scares the stuffin' out of them every time. What's wrong with him anyway, waving a knife like that at his family."

Sam knew it wasn't a question to be answered, so she asked, "Where's Leroy now?"

"Sleeping it off at the police station. Lenny's wife is making Leroy breakfast 'cuz Maggie's mad as a wet hen. Says he can cook his own meals from now on. That'll last about two minutes," he chuffed. "Them apple muffins?" He hitched his head toward the tin on the breadboard next to the stove.

"Sure are. Would you like one?"

"Two, if you don't mind." He ran a hand through hair the color of acorns, what there was of it. "A couple of eggs and a few sausages wouldn't be refused either." He grinned at Sam. "That's if you don't mind. I don't want to interrupt progress on Nick's pie."

"No problem, Charlie. I was just peeling the apples. Where's Brun?"

He smiled at the thought of his big blond wife. "She was going out the door as I was getting home this morning, to some breakfast meeting. Ladies

Historical Society of Georgetown, this time. I think." He shook his head and leaned back against the captain's chair. "Never can keep her schedule straight."

Sam placed the paring knife in the sink out of sight, wiped the counter where Selket had settled, and then washed her hands before popping two muffins in the toaster oven. "Fried, with the yokes runny. Right, Charlie?"

"You got it." He inhaled. "Those apple muffins sure smell good. So, how are you doing? Recovered from your camping trip to Pottle's Pond?" He looked hard at her face.

"I'm fine, Charlie. Still a little shook up though. Where did the Bankes go, do you know?"

"They've gone home. I guess the experience spoiled their appetites for vacationing. Anyway, we've got their vital information. They come from Massachusetts and have good standing in their community. We know where to find them if we need them. I doubt if they had anything to do with this."

He paused.

"Them muffins ready yet? I'm starved."

"Just about. Butter?"

"Don't mind if I do."

Sam reached up into the cupboard and pulled down a jar of honey.

"I don't want honey, Sam."

"I know, Charlie. It's for my cut." She held up the offended forefinger.

"Honey on a cut? Where'd you get that idea?" He didn't appear surprised.

"If it's good enough for Imhotep, it's good enough for me."

Charlie snickered. "I feel a story coming on."

"It's true, Charlie. According to a Discovery special I watched recently, Imhotep was an Egyptian physician and wise man who lived about 2700 B.C. He practiced medicine that would astound doctors today."

"So, what's honey got to do with it?"

"Because bacteria can't live in honey, Imhotep used it on wounds to combat infections. He also used moldy bread—you know, like penicillin. The man was so revered that he was one of the few non-royals to be deified by the Egyptians. The Discovery special said that perhaps doctors, instead of taking the Hippocratic oath, should swear to the Imhotepic oath."

Charlie tipped his head and looked at her. "I'd rather use iodine."

"To each her own, Charlie," Sam said, lathering her finger with honey. "I'll be right back." She returned with a Band-Aid wrapped around her finger.

Moments later, the toaster oven clicked off. With a fork, Sam toppled the muffins onto a small plate, gathered up silverware, a napkin, and the butter dish, and set them on the table. Charlie hunched forward and proceeded to slather on the butter.

"Umm, good," he mumbled around a mouthful.

"Glad you like them." Sam wasn't about to spoil his appetite by telling him the muffins were made with organic wheat flour, and the butter and sausages were soy. She felt good about slipping in healthy food when the occasion arose. She pushed thoughts of her Ring Dings into the recesses of her mind.

While the sausages sizzled, Sam leaned against the counter and pulled a pointed fork from the utensil jar. "Do you have any leads on the Brennan homicide?"

Ignoring the napkin, Charlie wiped a corner of his mouth with the back of his hand and then swiped his hand along the side of his green work pants. "We're looking into a few possibilities." He sat straighter in the chair and arched his neck, straining to view the frying pan.

"I'm sure Mary Frazetta and her children are suspects," Sam said, eyeballing Charlie. "They all had a good reason to want Brennan dead because of Claudio Frazetta's suicide. The bankruptcy only added fuel to the fire."

"Eggs, Sam?" Charlie said.

"They're coming. And then, of course," she said with a gleam in her eye, "there's Quinn Stevens." She studied the frying pan. "I heard he and Brennan had words of sorts at the Pigpen a few days before Brennan was shot."

"Jesus, woman! Where did you hear that?"

Sam thought of Clarence at Clean As A Hound's Tooth Cleaners across the green. The scribe of Georgetown, recording the town's history as he received more than dirty shirts and soiled suits from his customers. But all Sam said was, "I have my sources."

Charlie just shook his head.

Samantha folded one arm across her waist, and drew triangles in the air with the fork as she looked at him. "Isn't Quinn part of some motorcycle club? Seems I remember seeing his name a few times in the Police Log in Publick Occurrences."

"Yup. His name's been there. Nothin' real serious, but he can be a trouble-maker, no question about that, especially after the accident with Brennan and that Johanssen girl."

"Wasn't that awful. I heard she and Quinn had gone out a few times."

"How's them eggs and sausages comin', Sam?"

"Patience is a virtue, Charlie."

Sam knew that Charlie's chuckle was at her expense. She stabbed at the sausage. "So, what's this visit really about, Charlie?"

A buttery corner of the chief's mouth curled. "You mean beyond getting a great breakfast?"

"Give, Charlie."

Charlie finally wiped his mouth with the paper napkin instead of his hand. He sat back. "It's the homicide at Pottle's."

"Ah." Sam rolled the sausages to the side of the skillet and dropped in two eggs. She pulled the Save the Whales dishtowel off the refrigerator door handle, flipped it over her shoulder, and reached for a dinner plate.

"Ah? Is that all you're going to say?"

"What do you want to hear?"

"Come on, Sam. I heard you talking with that Bankes guy, something about the code he swears the victim tapped out as the guy was dying. And if I know you, you're already working on it."

"Who? Me?" Sam said as she delivered the eggs and sausages. "Do you want some orange juice? Coffee's gone, but I can make more."

"OJ's fine, thanks. Okay. Let's hear it, Sam."

Behind Charlie's laid-back country boy façade resided a keen intelligence and honed gut instinct that Sam recognized and respected. She set the orange juice on the table and sat.

As she toyed with the grapes in the fruit bowl in the center of the table, she watched Charlie shake too much salt on his eggs. "It's just like I told you the other night, Charlie. I heard a shot about 3:00 that morning. Nick and I went out to investigate and found Earle Bankes standing over this guy—Richard Brennan—and Lulu Bankes hovering on the steps of their camper with that little dog. Brennan was on the ground, already dead, shot through the neck. None of us saw anything."

Charlie's fork paused halfway between the table and his mouth. Long yellow strings of egg yolk dripped to his plate. "The code, Sam."

"Oh, that."

Charlie shook his head, and began scarfing up the fried eggs again, punctuated this time by sausage segments, but his eyes never left Sam's face.

She wondered how he did that without sticking his cheek with the fork. "Earle Bankes swears that Brennan was tapping out a message on the side of his motor home."

Charlie nodded, and after he finished chewing, he said, "What do you think?"

Sam regarded Charlie for several moments. "I believe him," she said.

"Hmm. That's what we thought."

Sam's eyebrows lifted in unison. "We?"

"Yeah." He paused to swallow. "We want you to see what you can come up with on that code. Unofficially, of course."

A Cheshire cat smile spread across Sam's face. She now had official, if not public, permission.

CHAPTER 15

❀

TUESDAY 10:15 AM

"CJ. Can I borrow your truck for a few minutes? I can't get my car started. It must be the battery again."

"Take ma's," CJ said as he backed out of his truck parked in front of the hardware store where he'd been taping FOR SALE signs on the windows.

"Ma went out." Rita held out her hand.

Reluctantly, CJ reached in his pocket and pulled out his keys. "You're not going far, I hope. I just took the truck through the car wash."

"Nope. Just going to the post office. We're out of stamps."

"Okay. And there isn't much gas."

"How come? You usually fill it up on Mondays."

"I'm selling it. Why waste the money? Besides, I need all the cash I can scrounge up for Debbie and the kids."

Rita climbed into the Ram. "Be back in a few minutes."

Rita's body felt like lead as she pulled out to the street. She buried a hand in her hair, glanced in the rearview mirror and grimaced. She hadn't put on any makeup this morning and her freckles stood out like spots on a giraffe. There were dark smudges under her eyes and her lips were nearly invisible without color.

She grabbed the steering wheel with both hands and stared straight ahead. Her looks were the least of her troubles.

She had made a really stupid mistake stopping at that gas station Sunday night. Actually, 3:00 Monday morning, she corrected herself. What had she been thinking? But her throat had been so dry at the thought of what she had been about to do that she'd needed a drink of water before she had gone into coughing convulsions.

Traffic was heavy and the light at the corner turned red before Rita could gun her way through. Her hands dropped to her lap as her eyes moved over the commercial buildings and the people milling up and down the sidewalks and cutting across the street with purpose in their gaits. A scene she saw every day, but at this moment the geography was as surreal as if seen through a drug induced haze and the only sharply defined acreage was in her mind. Where the pain was.

She missed her dad.

She buried her face in her hands, felt the tears coming.

The driver behind her leaned on his horn.

Rita flinched. Her head went up. She sat unmoving for another few seconds as the guy in her rear view mirror stood on his horn. At that moment, Rita understood road rage. It took all her willpower not to grab the gun from her purse and pump four bullets into the guy's fat face.

Instead, she raised a significant finger out the cab's window and inched forward, the driver behind her a hairbreadth from her tail. Shaking his head, he turned at the next corner.

Rita wiped the corners of her eyes with the back of her hand. Rage was grabbing hold of her too often these days. Eating her up. And yet there she was admonishing her two brothers for fighting. What a hypocrite she was.

Her mind drifted back to that night.

No one had seen her well enough to recognize her, she was sure of that. Her distinctive red hair, braided, had been tucked inside a black hat that had been pulled down over her eyebrows. An oversized dark coat gave no indication of the body hidden beneath.

Rita had identified the cameras in the station and had kept her head down and her chin buried in her black turtleneck. She didn't think the attendant had even looked at her. He had seemed more interested in what two kids were doing in front of the beer cooler than in who she was. She had paid for her bottle of water and left. She now wondered if the sunglasses had looked too suspicious at 3:00 in the morning. She shook her head. This wasn't the time for second-guessing. The clerk had not noticed her.

Rita looked down at her bag lying on the seat beside her. It was so easy to get a gun today, legal or otherwise. She knew she had to get rid of it.

I'm carrying a concealed weapon without a permit, she thought, and laughed at the insanity of that crime after what she had done. No gun permit was the least of her troubles.

CHAPTER 16

❁

TUESDAY 11:00 A.M.

I have permission, Sam told herself.

Unofficially, of course. Now she could tell Nick that the police had asked for her help. How could she say no?

Charlie had just left and Sam was cleaning up the kitchen, wondering exactly how the Frazettas fit into the puzzle. Could her mother's friend and bridge partner be a murderess, a woman so devastated by her husband's suicide and the possible loss of the family business which supported her and her children that she took revenge on the man who drove her husband to the deadly act?

What about the family? The modern nuclear family: two half-brothers and an adopted daughter. Did one of the children kill Richard Brennan to avenge the father, or kill him because he ruined their business? Sam needed to find out more about the dynamics of the Frazetta clan.

Then there was big Quinn Stevens who hated Richard Brennan because of Lynda Johanssen. What might Quinn have done to avenge that loss? The burly biker certainly looked the part of a crazed killer with those intense eyes and that bushy black beard. He'd strike the fear of God into the bravest of souls. She shuddered at the thought of meeting him in a lonely alley in the middle of the night. Actually, even on a well-lit populated street under the noonday sun, he'd part the crowd like Moses parted the Red Sea. And Quinn had had scrapes with the law. Charlie said they were nothing serious, but who knew what Quinn might have done that he'd gotten away with. When issues of the heart were involved, people committed unspeakable acts in moments of passion.

And that tapping, what was that all about? Sam wondered if she were really way off base assuming that the dying man had really meant to leave a message. Was her fertile imagination galloping away with her again? Should she reign in the wild thoughts that plagued her about this homicide? But Earle Bankes swore he distinctly heard tap…tap…tap-tap…tap-tap-tap…

That stirring in her gut told her she was right. She used to get that same feeling when she was a child solving puzzles in the magazines her parents had bought her every week. With a dash of melancholy, she thought about the nights she had spent under the red quilt with a flashlight and her puzzle books long after her parents had gone to bed. She recalled the pleasure that had suffused through her as she worked with her pen filling in the squares and working out the letter sequences. She didn't realize then that her skills would be put to work solving homicides. Or at least helping, she thought.

How she wished that this homicide were merely an intellectual exercise.

Hannibal was punctual.

It was precisely 11:00 when the doorbell chimed. Sam met him at the door, in her sweats and stocking feet.

Moments later, Hannibal Loveless stood awkwardly on the sun porch, waiting for direction. Sam thought that the minister, with his jet black hair, sallow complexion, stern demeanor, and somber black suit, could easily slip back in time and merge with that staunch group of Puritan settlers who endured those first few harsh winters in the New World. His dark specter stood out in stark contrast to the sun that streamed through the sun porch windows behind him. The joyful day seemed to beg him to smile and be happy.

Sam gazed past Hannibal's lank frame and into the back yard. It was one of those gorgeous May days that wiped away memories of the dreary tail end of winter. Lush mounds of pot-of-gold hugged the base of the aboveground pool. The white magnolia bush had already dropped most of its blossoms, which lay scattered at its feet, and, beside it, the flowering quince's dark salmon-colored arms draped over the mulch that Nick had lain so neatly around the plantings. A chickadee splashed in the birdbath. Sam could hear its sweet chirping through the open windows.

She smiled then turned her attention toward Hannibal. "Please, sit down. May I get you a drink? Coffee, tea?"

"No, no. Thank you," Hannibal said, as he lowered himself into the red rocker. He arched his neck like a great black crow. His ebony eyes took in the room in a restless search for somewhere comfortable to perch.

Sam unhooked the desk phone and turned down the volume on the answering machine. The band-aid on her finger was loose so she pulled it off, folded it and dropped it in the wastebasket. A quick rub of the nick with her thumb caused no pain. *Thanks, Imhotep*, she said to herself.

Settling into the sofa, she tucked her feet up under her and said with a smile, "Hannibal. We've got to stop meeting like this."

The Reverend's brows crinkled. "I beg your pardon?"

Sam laughed. "It's supposed to be a funny line, Hannibal. I'm sorry. I know you have something serious on your mind."

She massaged her foot. She wanted to toss her ragg socks—that seam was rubbing the toes on her right foot again—but she didn't know if the act of undressing her feet would put Hannibal at ease or ruffle his feathers even more. Maybe she'd just take the socks off and turn them inside out. She looked at the black clad minister. Well, maybe not.

Hannibal examined his knotted fingers as if it were the first time he had ever seen them.

Gathering his courage, she thought.

Sam had never seen him this uneasy. Nervous, perhaps, but not so agitated. She wondered about his past. No one knew much about this strange Ichabod Crane look-alike. What they did know was that the Second Puritan Church had hired him from his last ministry in Trumbullton Corners, New Hampshire. Seems he had found a body in the basement of his church. Although the killer had been apprehended and Hannibal had never been a suspect, still people had talked and Hannibal had felt it was better to move on. Perhaps his proximity to those homicides was why the deacons of the Second Puritan Church of Georgetown had hired him after all. A little scandal does wonders for attendance.

"This is most difficult, Samantha," Hannibal finally said, his voice breaking at the start. "I don't know where to begin."

"The old cliche," Sam said gently, "is to start at the beginning."

He bobbed his head but remained silent.

Finally he said, "I was wrong in coming here, Samantha. You don't need to get involved in this." He started to rise.

"Sit, Hannibal!"

No way was Hannibal leaving her sun porch. You don't hold a Ring Ding in front of Samantha Blackwell and then snatch it away.

Startled and half out of the chair, Hannibal halted.

Startled herself, especially at her intensity with the conservative minister, Sam said more evenly, "Please, Hannibal, sit down. Not only have you stimulated my curiosity, but I also care about you and Emmaline. If you have a problem, then I want to help if I can. So, what do you say? Shall we talk?" She gave him her biggest smile.

Hannibal hovered in the air a moment longer, then folded his body down into the chair like one of those big cardboard Halloween scarecrows that Sam's daughters used to hang on the breezeway door every October, the kind with the little metal rings that bend at the joints.

The minister crossed his legs and cleared his throat. He proceeded to pick imaginary lint off his pants leg. His shiny black suit lay in ripples over his body, except at the points where his elbows and knees jutted out.

Finally, adjusting his half-glasses, he said, "This is most private."

"My lips are hermetically sealed," Sam assured him. "Please, Hannibal. Just start at the beginning."

"The beginning. Ah, yes." He looked at Sam, but his eyes were lost in a vision of the past.

Sam found herself focusing on the center of Hannibal's face, on the large wart that nestled at the base of his right nostril. It moved slightly when he talked. It was such a distraction she wondered why he didn't have it removed, but he would probably consider it vain and just plain wrong to alter the appearance that God had given him. If God saw fit to give him a huge wart for all the world to see, then he would wear it proudly. She had to admire the gumption of the man, although *she* was vain enough that she would have disposed of it long ago.

"Although I'm a minister," Hannibal said, grasping the arms of the rocker, "my life has not always been what you might call exemplary."

"Few of us are without sin, Hannibal," Sam said, falling easily into the Biblical reference. She could see a slight tremor in the minister's knobby fingers. "Let me get you a glass of water."

"Thank you, Samantha. I could use one after all."

Sam returned with a glass filled with ice water. Her socks were now turned inside out. She sat in the rocker adjacent to Hannibal, and hoped he wouldn't notice.

The ice cubes clinked as Hannibal took a sip of water.

"About twenty-five years ago," he said slowly, "I left an abusive home. I was 16, right off the farm and totally unprepared for city life. I had managed to save enough money for bus fare to New York. I didn't know what I was going to do when I got there, but anything was better than the way I was living."

He set the glass on the table between them and shifted in his seat. A pained expression rumpled his face as he plunged on.

"I arrived in the city in July. It was hotter than I had ever experienced on the farm in Kansas. All those tall buildings seemed almost smothering. At any rate, I fell in with the wrong crowd. There are those who wait at bus stops for the young, the naive, and the frightened. And I was a ready victim. I am not excusing my behavior, you understand, just explaining it."

Hannibal took another sip of water, set the glass down again, and looked down at Sam's socks.

Sam ruffled her toes. She wondered if he noticed that the thick seam of her ragg socks was now on the outside.

But Hannibal was in another place, beyond wondering about sock seams. "A world of alcohol and drugs followed," he said. "I won't go into the sordid story. Suffice it to say that I never stole to support my habits, like some of my…friends. I managed to keep a job at a restaurant, washing dishes. My father's preaching must have sunk in."

He laughed bitterly.

"Then," he hesitated, "there was the baby. She was so tiny and she had a heart-shaped birthmark on her shoulder." His hand went to his shoulder as if to demonstrate the placement. Then his eyes cut to the floor. He didn't speak for so long that Sam thought he had forgotten where he was. Finally, he blinked a few times and shook his head, as if warding off an evil thought. His breathing seemed more labored.

"Hannibal, are you alright?" Sam asked, reaching out to touch the back of the hand that had now fallen to his lap.

It took a few moments for him to come back. Then he said, "Yes, I'm fine, Samantha. Thank you. I just need a moment. I have never told anyone about this until today." He pushed his half-glasses up on his nose and drank the full glass of water.

Sam got up to get him another.

"You mentioned a baby," Sam urged after returning from the kitchen.

Hannibal took a few more gulps of water and set the glass back on the table. His head bent to his chest. He seemed spent with the effort of the telling; the only visible motion now, his bony fingers twisting in his lap like spiders embraced in a death dance.

Sam gave Hannibal the time he needed. There was nothing she could say at this point, and she had learned over the years, with clients, when to remain silent and just listen. But she wanted to scream, *What about the baby! Talk to me!*

The clock on the wall ticked away the seconds. Sam glanced out the window. Two chickadees sat on the birdbath as if contemplating their images in the water.

Two, Sam thought, *the number of companionship and inner work toward peace and harmony.*

As she wondered if the chickadees were also waiting for Hannibal to speak, one of them cocked its little head toward the sun porch. *Bird telepathy,* she thought, smiling inwardly in spite of her frustration.

She heard the click of the answering machine as it took its message.

Hannibal clutched at his water glass once again, as if stilling the motion of his hands could overcome the turmoil in his heart. He stared down into the clear liquid. Finally, he took another drink and spoke into the glass, almost as if he was embarrassed to look Sam in the eye, "Why am I telling you this?"

"We all need a good ear once in a while," Sam said. "How many life stories have you listened to in your position, Hannibal? Surely you have the right to unburden yourself like the rest of us."

He leaned back in the rocker—the confessional, Sam called it—having lost count of the number of clients who had shifted, twisted, and ultimately relaxed on that simple red print fabric as their life's problems poured out. Just having someone impartial listen to their problems was often enough to shed light on the "dark night of the soul". Self-revelation was often cathartic.

Hannibal looked straight at Sam and laughed without humor. "I have no idea why I've told you what I have. It wasn't my intention. I came with another purpose in mind. You see…" He swallowed so hard that Sam thought his Adam's apple would slide down his gullet and disappear forever.

"You see…" he said again, his body was rocking forward in the chair, "the man with whom I did drugs decades ago on the streets of New York is the same man who called me late Saturday night and begged me to meet him at Pottles' Pond at three o'clock Monday morning. That man was Richard Brennan. And I was there when he was murdered."

CHAPTER 17

❀

TUESDAY 11:10 A.M.

The third option surfaced.

It had started subliminally Monday morning, just before his shift ended at 7:00 A.M. With Rita the Redhead still on his mind, Randy Sturgis noticed that John Roberts' car wasn't in the parking lot behind the motel. So he snuck into the guy's motel room before the maids arrived to clean. Practiced at this sort of thing, he routinely rummaged though the rooms of early checkouts for any forgotten items of interest. He would add these to the stash in his apartment to be kept for his personal use or sold at some later date.

In Room 15 where John Roberts had stayed, Randy found the crumpled sheet of CircleTo notepaper in the bathroom wastebasket. He decided to keep it in the remote chance it might be a connection to the stacked redhead. And he was going to grab onto any possible thread that would give him an excuse to see her again. After all, she had expressed an interest in him.

A few hours later when he saw the noon news about the shooting, Randy knew that the man who had been shot in the middle of the night by an unknown assailant at Pottle's Pond was the same man who had registered at his motel as John Roberts. And Roberts was Richard Brennan, the accountant to that Frazetta guy who had offed himself in his garage with a hose. And somehow Rita was connected to Roberts or Brennan, or whatever the hell his name was.

Now, as Randy sat naked in the stuffing-challenged orange chair in his living room, his head was spinning. His shoulders slumped as his eyes fixed on the smudged piece of notepaper in his hands. He realized how his life had changed in the few days since he'd met that she-devil. He also realized that the idea that had flitted into his mind this morning when he first opened his eyes had been a good one.

His tiny cheek craters collapsed into the folds of a smile. He remembered Rita's hand on his knee. And those boobs! His shoulders lifted as he inhaled, and a warm and tingly feeling coursed through his blood. She liked him. He could see that now. He knew he had to see her again.

Randy cleared his throat as a tickle threatened to erupt into a cough. *Concentrate*, he told himself.

He leaned forward as his mind once again stumbled over the facts as he knew them, the cogs of his mental machinery grinding laboriously.

He reasoned that the Brennan guy wouldn't rub a pencil over his own notepad. After all the fuss Brennan had made about his privacy, as far as Randy knew, no one had gone into his room except Rita the Redhead.

The possibility then hit him! *Rita* had done the rubbing on the notepaper. And because of that, she had known that Brennan was going to be at the campground at 3:00 that morning.

Jesus Christ! he thought. *She went there and popped the guy.* A tremor ran through him. He fell back into the chair, surprised at his conclusion.

Even though he heard about shootings all the time on the news, murder had never hit this close to home. U*sually,* he thought, scratching under his armpit, *it was the guy who shot the broad.* Randy had to admit he was aroused by the picture: a flaming redhead, her long legs tented for balance, her extended hands gripping the cold steel of a magnum, her painted nails coiled around the trigger. She was right out of a goddamn Mickey Spillane novel. He shivered. And probably as dangerous.

Although Randy wouldn't have recognized it, his feelings struck some primal mating call deep within him, the merging universes of orgasm and death. He felt that same inexorable draw that some women feel towards dangerous men, women who go so far as to send offers of marriage to convicted murderers and rapists. For some people, living on the edge of death made life more delicious.

Rita filled his mind as he rubbed his thumb over the edge of the wrinkled notepaper. W*as she really married to this Roberts/Brennan guy like she said she was?*

Randy had caught a glimpse of Rita's car when she'd left the motel. It had one of those magnetic signs on the side that read: Frazetta's Hardware Store. Did she work for the Frazettas? Or, maybe she was the daughter, mentioned on the news as one of Claudio Frazetta's kids. The Frazetta daughter was named Rita. How many Ritas were there? It wasn't as if it were that common a name, like Mary.

Randy blinked his eyes as he felt a headache at the edge of his forehead. He rubbed at the spot. His brain cells were straining now. A line of sweat broke out on his forehead.

If she was a Frazetta, then she wasn't married to this Roberts/Brennan guy or her last name wouldn't be Frazetta. Unless she was one of those feminists types. But she was too beautiful and sexy to be one of those. Those types could never get a man. Randy was convinced that Rita was a Frazetta. But even if she wasn't, he figured he could find her at the hardware store. Otherwise, why would she be driving a car with a Frazetta Hardware sign on the door?

He leaned back in the chair and scratched at his groin, his brain now so overworked it was slogging.

Plucking mindlessly at the stuffing that splayed out of the split in the arm of the chair, he thought about wandering into the hardware store one day and taking a look. See if she was there. Maybe let her see *him*, and see what her reaction would be. Now that he had this note, he had another good reason to see her.

Randy's head dropped back against the chair. His eyes closed, and soon he fell into a light doze.

Minutes later he awoke with a start. He felt energized. Maybe he'd just had a dream, he couldn't remember. But whatever it was, he had that funny feeling in his chest again, like the one he'd had when he talked with Rita at the motel. That unfamiliar feeling. Like he could be in charge. Like he had some power. Like he was somebody! And he liked the feeling.

Maybe Rita would be grateful to have this note back. Maybe she'd be *really* grateful. He had a vision of her red hair spread over his pillow, her full pink breasts pointed up at him, her murderous green eyes staring into his. His loins tingled. He felt himself rising like the Pillsbury Dough Boy.

"Down boy!" he chortled, and sucked in a deep breath. He coughed, three hard barks, then settled his shoulders.

Before he saw Rita, he would make a copy of this note and put the original in a safe place along with his own account of what had happened. Just in case she got some ideas about getting rid of him. He's seen enough cop shows to know that was the thing to do. He wasn't a dummy.

He laid the note down on the end table and rubbed his hands together. This was just too good to be true. He had to share it with someone. Someone who would appreciate his talents.

Randy Sturgis reached for the phone beside him.

"Hey, Vinnie. How's it hanging?"

"Bigger and better than ever, man. What's going on?"

"Are you still working the night shift at the gas station?"

"Yeah. And it's boring as hell, I got to tell you. Not too many people tank up in the middle of the night. 'Course there's always the bums coming in for a six pack and smokes. Little excitement the other night down at the campground, though."

"You mean the murder at Pottle's Pond?" Randy was *really* interested in what Vinnie might have to say about that. Maybe Vinnie would provide another nail in Rita's coffin. Murder? Coffin? He realized what he had just said and smiled at his cleverness.

"Yeah," Vinnie said. "It happened just down the road apiece."

"I thought you might have heard something about it. So, you're off today?"

"Yeah."

"Want to meet me for lunch? You can tell me what happened that night, and I've got a whopper of a story to tell you."

Vinnie belched. "Sure. And speaking of whoppers. How about you meet me at Burger King up the road from you, say…about noon?"

Randy glanced at the white digital readout on the VCR. 11:13. "You got it, man. I'll be there."

CHAPTER 18

❀

TUESDAY 11:15 A.M.

Sam gasped audibly, her eyes widened in disbelief. "You were there when Richard Brennan was killed?"

A shudder rippled the length of Hannibal's body and his voice quivered as he spoke. "Yes. I was there." Hannibal rocked back and forth in his chair, his eyes staring into empty space.

Sam lowered her lids and pinched the bridge of her nose between her thumb and forefinger as the enormity of the situation sunk in. A lump settled midway down her throat as she opened her eyes to look at Hannibal. She didn't speak for several minutes.

Finally, under her gaze, Hannibal wet his lips and shrunk back into the rocker. His body seemed to cave in on itself, leaving the impression of a black suit laid out over a pile of sticks.

He cleared his throat. "Well, I wasn't at the exact spot where he was... umm...where he was..." His voice trailed off. He ground his middle finger into the spot between his eyes as if to release the pressure of a great weight.

A thousand questions battled for position in Sam's mind, but the one that gained purchase at the front line was "Exactly where were you when Richard Brennan was murdered?"

Hannibal's Adam's apple bobbed numerous times before he answered. He looked straight at Sam, his eyes pleading for her support. "I'm not sure of the exact time he was killed. I was approximately a mile from Pottle's Pond. It was 2:56 A.M. by my car clock. I had a flat tire within sight of a gas station. I asked the attendant to change the tire for me. I'd say the entire incident took about a half hour. As I approached the entrance to the pond, I saw the police cars. I knew something terrible had happened. I was so terrified that I drove past. Later that day I heard what had happened." He lowered his head, and shook it back and forth. "I'm so ashamed of myself. I should have stopped and inquired about the incident. I should have told the police about Richard's call and our plan to meet."

"Do you know why Richard Brennan wanted to meet you?"

"No. All he said on the telephone was that he had twenty dollars left and he needed my help. He never said why he needed that help."

"How do you know him?"

"He was one of my friends in New York so many years ago. I haven't seen or spoken to him since then."

"So, this phone call came as a complete surprise?"

"Yes." Hannibal was breathing heavily and rubbing his lips together.

"Brennan called you Saturday night, and you agreed to meet him Monday at 3:00 in the morning. Why Monday and why 3:00?"

"He wanted to meet right away, but I told him I had church duties Sunday morning and a meeting in the afternoon with the church deacons. I also had an appointment with Agatha Coldbath for late afternoon tea. She is a dear lady and a staunch supporter of the church and it wouldn't do to disturb her schedule."

Sam would have managed a smile at that comment if the situation weren't so serious. The diminutive Ms. Agatha Beatrice Coldbath was one crusty octogenarian to whom you didn't make excuses—unless you'd broken both legs and been airlifted to Boston Medical or you had been kidnapped. Even then, you'd have some explaining to do.

As the last heir to the Coldbath Cowberry Chutney fortune, the elderly maiden guarded the secret chutney recipe, locked in the Spice Cupboard within her sparkling clean plant, like Cerberus guarding the gates of Hell. And since that business supported the town's economy, no one refused her invitations. For some wildly weird reason, Agatha had chosen Sam as the next keeper of the world famous recipe.

Hannibal continued, "Richard Brennan didn't want to be seen in the daylight. He was obviously frightened. He felt that at 3:00 in the morning, there would be fewer people around."

Rightly so, Sam thought, as she recalled a line from F. Scott Fitzgerald: *In a real dark night of the soul it is always three o'clock in the morning.*

Hannibal's chest rose and fell rapidly. His breathing became even more labored.

Sam rubbed her lips with the flat of her fingers, then said, "So, you think if the police find out you once knew Richard Brennan, and that on Saturday he telephoned you for a meeting, they would think you are somehow involved in the man's murder."

Hannibal nodded.

"And the police would want to know, since you agreed to meet him and were in the vicinity of Pottle's Pond at 3:00 in the morning, why you didn't stop if you are innocent."

"Yes." The minister's response was barely discernible.

"And, of course, they'd want to know what the meeting was about," Sam said to herself.

Hannibal's eyes dropped to his fists, buried in the dark folds of his lap. He let out a breath that seemed to further deflate his concave chest.

Sam rubbed the back of her neck. "And you said you don't have an answer to that question?"

After a moment, the minister looked straight into Sam's icy blue eyes. "That's right. I have no idea why he wanted to see me."

"Why did you agree to meet with him?"

A puzzled look settled on Hannibal's face, as if he were trying to figure that one out for himself.

His shoulders dropped. "The man sounded desperate. He needed my help. I'm a man of the cloth. How could I refuse him? And now, if I report this aborted meeting to the police, I could be implicated. Then my past could become public knowledge. It's bad enough that I left my last position under a cloud but this…"

His face contorted into a mass of wrinkles.

"Emmaline knows a little about my past," he said, "but I've never told her the whole truth." He paused. "For a man of God, it seems I'm a little short on the truth lately. But what I've told you today *is* the truth." His eyes locked on his fists. "I don't know how Emmaline would take the full story." A tiny sob caught in the knob of his throat. He closed his eyes as if, in the act of shutting his lids, he could erase the events of the outside world and retreat to an inner place of peace.

Sam knew his unspoken words. Hannibal was afraid that, if he told Emmaline about his past, he would lose her. He was less afraid of being arrested for suspicion of murder than of losing the woman he loved. His torment was almost more than Samantha could bear.

Hannibal leaned toward her, his face a study in desperation. "What am I going to do, Samantha?"

Sam caught the faint scent of perfume. From a morning embrace, she thought. He and Emmaline were such an unlikely couple. The pious black-clad Ichabod Crane minister, with that wart nestled at the base of his hawk nose, and his beautiful, gentle, palm-reading wife. Certainly Hannibal didn't approve of his wife's involvement with palmistry. Sam wondered what he would do if he knew Emmaline advertised anonymously in the local newspapers for palm readings, by mail, to be sent to M. Lines, care of a post office box in the next town. It seems that both husband *and* wife had secrets from each other.

What had drawn them together was less of a question in her mind now than what she could do to help him.

Sam chewed at her bottom lip and looked past Hannibal out into her back yard and up over the treetops. The sky was clean, the palest of blues, like a wash on a canvas waiting for the artist's touch. Sam waited for an inspiration, the merest brush stroke of an idea that would lend some composition to the palette of events of the last few days. She believed that Hannibal wasn't involved in the murder, and she believed that he'd had a flat tire and had arrived too late for his appointment.

Her eyes drifted.

Two yellow-breasted gold finch sat at the slender bird feeder hanging from a limb of the maple tree by the back porch. They pecked at the openings in the feeder, sending seeds spinning out around their heads. A red-winged blackbird flew onto an upper branch.

A low grumbling rolled inside her. She pushed the thought of a salad with low fat dressing, followed by a package of Ring Dings, out of her mind as she put a hand to her stomach and looked back at Hannibal and said, "Do you think the gas station attendant would remember you?"

Hannibal sighed. "I don't know. Probably. I can't imagine he has that many requests to repair flat tires in the middle of the night."

Sam nodded and slowly massaged her stomach. Because it was close by, the police might stop at the gas station to find out if the attendant had seen anything suspicious. If they did, it wouldn't take them long to find Hannibal. He was a distinctive looking man. But if they didn't…

Sam wondered what good it would do for Hannibal to tell the authorities about his aborted meeting. He said he hadn't seen Richard Brennan for years. Brennan called him out of the blue. And Sam believed Hannibal. So why should he get involved in a homicide? Especially when he was terrified of telling Emmaline about his past indiscretions.

If he went to the police and told them his story, he could be in trouble. Those two homicides in Trumbullton Corners at his last post wouldn't help his case. One of the bodies had been found in his church. The killer had been arrested and confessed, and Hannibal had not been involved. But still—that wouldn't look good for him. She could imagine what the tabloids could do with this story. The Reverend Hannibal Loveless flaps into town on ebony wings, cloaked in black, his past shrouded by bodies in the church basement at his last assignment. The paper would not come right out and say he was a murderer, but the innuendo would be devastating.

On the other hand, what if he didn't say anything and the police somehow learned he was near Pottle's Pond, close to the time Richard Brennan was murdered? They would want to know what he was doing there and why he hadn't come forward and, Hannibal, being a minister and all, couldn't lie. Then he'd be up the proverbial creek without the paddle.

Hannibal had a right to be scared. His situation was tenuous at best.

"I believe you're innocent, Hannibal," Sam said, leaning toward him, her fingers stacked over her belly. "I can't advise you on what to do about going to the police. But I will do everything I can to help you."

Sam now had another good reason to get involved in the investigation. As if she needed another one.

CHAPTER 19

❀

TUESDAY 12:10 PM

"Hey, what's up-chuck?" Vinnie LaRoche said, laughing and dropping into the Burger King's hard plastic seat. He let out a loud belch.

"My world's shaking and moving, man," Randy said with anticipation in his close-set eyes and a smug curl around his lips. He leaned back, his arm draped over the back of the seat. He nodded at his friend as if to punctuate the importance of that observation.

Vinnie yawned.

A bit deflated but not deterred, Randy persisted. "You won't believe what I've got to tell you." His voice was low as he leaned forward, his eyes cutting over the crowded room, taking in the yellow walls and the sweeping gray and blue seating, like something out of *Space Odyssesy 2001*. The noise level was rising as more customers pushed their way through the swinging glass doors to make grabs for food on their lunch hours.

"Yeah?" Vinnie's pug nose wrinkled as he inhaled the smells of frying meat and sizzling fries. His eyes calculated the number of people queuing up at the counter. "Well, first, I've gotta eat, man. I'm starving." He got up quickly.

Randy sighed and sat back to wait. "All right. Get me a Whopper with fries and a large Pepsi, would ya?"

"You got money?"

"Yeah. Don't worry about it."

Vinnie hurried off to stand in line.

In order to emulate the cool guys from the fifties' movies, Vinnie LaRoche kept a pack of Luckies rolled up in the left sleeve of his dingy white tee shirt. Built like a gnome, he routinely shortened the legs of his jeans to accommodate his short legs. White threads hung from the cuff's raw edges.

Vinnie hitched his jeans over his stocky hips as he moved into line behind two teenage girls in shorts and tight tee shirts.

Randy's eyes ran up and down the girls' legs. He wondered how big their boobs were. The tall leggy blond, with straight hair that cascaded halfway down her back, turned to say something to her friend. Randy's eyes bulged. She had a pair of knockers that put Pamela Anderson to shame. Splashed across the blonde's chest, were the printed words: *So many men, so little time.*

Eyelevel with this sentiment, Vinnie turned and rolled his eyes at Randy.

Randy just shook his head as he conjured up fantasies about the blond and Rita the Redhead. Then he felt it. Quickly, he hunched over the table.

He needed a smoke. He looked through the plate glass window.

An old guy with a cigarette in his mouth was climbing out of a pick-up truck. Randy watched as the guy took one last drag, dropped the butt on the hot top, and mashed it with the toe of his boot while he blew a stream of smoke from his mouth. Wisps curled from his nostrils.

A golden retriever stuck its head through the open window, it's muzzle white with age. The dog's tongue lolled to one side of its mouth as its mournful eyes looked up at its master, waiting for the signal to get out of the truck. The old guy kissed the dog's head and ruffled its ears while he spoke a few words. The dog watched the man disappear through the entrance to Burger King, then turned and lay down on the seat.

Randy tapped his forefinger on the table for what seemed interminable minutes. He was about to get up and go outside for a smoke when his friend returned with a food-filled tray. He grabbed his Pepsi as Vinnie set the tray on the table and plopped down on the seat.

Vinnie hitched his head at the register slip and said, "You owe me $4.29." He peeled back the wrapper on his Whopper, and took a hunk out of the burger. "Let me tell you what happened the other night," he mumbled through his food. Juice dribbled down his chin and on to his tee shirt. He chewed and swallowed hurriedly.

Randy unwrapped his burger and smoothed the paper. "Okay. You first." He grabbed a long steaming French fry from the paper bag in front of him, juggled it in his hands, and finally dropped it on the grease-slicked wrapper under his Whopper. "Christ! These are hot." He licked at the tips of his fingers.

In the adjacent booth, a woman with two small children frowned at Randy. She lowered her head and busied herself with her little ones' meals.

They probably hear a lot worse than that in school, lady, Randy thought.

"Usually fries *are* hot when they just come out of boiling fat," Vinnie said laughing. He got serious, cleared his throat, and said, "About the other night."

"Yeah?" Randy blew on his French fry.

Vinnie looked around the room as if he expected all ears to be bent in his direction. He leaned over the table toward Randy. "That murder down by Pottle's Pond."

Randy cocked an eyebrow. "What about it?"

"Well, I was workin' that night, you know. It was a little after three in the morning when all hell broke loose. Police cars came screamin' down the road, blue lights flashing. Seems some guy was shot at Pottle's Campground."

"Yeah. I heard about it on the news."

Randy scowled at his friend while he picked up the fry with his fingertips and nibbled at it. He was getting impatient. If Vinnie didn't have anything more to add to the story than a bunch of cops speeding by the station, Randy wasn't interested. He wanted to tell his story.

"That ain't all," Vinnie said. "The cops came in to question me about any unusual stuff that happened that night between two and three. Usually it's quiet, you know. But that night, seems like people was coming out of the woodwork. Some guy looking to borrow the gas can. He ran out of gas. Another guy dressed in black like some undertaker asked me to fix a flat tire for him. He was just down the road apiece. I could see his car from the station, so I did it. Charged him good, too, I want to tell you. Then, a broad stopped to buy something. Bottle of water, I think."

At the mention of the word "broad," Randy's jaws stopped in mid-chew. Noticing the pause, Vinnie sat back with a satisfied look on his face. He had Randy's attention.

So as not to lose the spotlight, he hurried on. "And then some guy who was three sheets to the wind stopped for gas. At first, when the cops went screamin' by, I thought it was this drunk who got in an accident. Anyway, the cops questioned me and I explained it all real careful like to them. Always smart to keep on their good side, you know what I mean?"

Randy didn't care what side of the cops Vinnie was on. He was thinking. "What did the broad look like?"

"I didn't notice her all that much."

"Why not?"

Vinnie shrugged. "Don't know. She was wearing a big coat and one of those hats that looks like a bucket pulled down over her head. I couldn't see her face. Wasn't really lookin' at her when she came in. Had my eye on a couple of kids in front of the beer cooler. You know how them underage kids try to steal beer." He laughed. "Remember when we used to do that."

Randy didn't laugh. He was wondering if the woman with the bucket on her head was Rita. Maybe she covered up that gorgeous red hair deliberately. Maybe she was on her way to Pottle's Pond to kill her husband—if that

Brennan guy really was her husband. Her red hair would have been a dead giveaway." He thought about the note in his pocket.

Vinnie took a few mouthfuls of Pepsi and belched again. "So. What's your shakin' news?"

Randy took a deep breath and leaned over his food. The steam from his fries had dissipated, but he could feel the warmth under his chin and smell the cholesterol clogging grease. His mouth watered as he said, "You're not gonna believe this, Vinnie." His eyes slid around the crowded room and then out the window as if he expected to see the local fuzz slue to a stop outside the building and dash into Burger King to arrest him for withholding information on a homicide.

The noise level in the room was getting louder, a chattering sound like monkeys in a zoo at feeding time.

Randy lowered his voice, but still spoke loud enough to be heard above the teenagers hoots and snorts and bumping in the seats on one side of them, and the broad in the seat on the other side yelling at Adam to sit down or she would smack him. The same broad, Randy thought, who gave him the evil eye when he said *Christ*. The bitch needed a head transplant.

Randy brought his attention back to the matter at hand. "That same night you're talking about," he confided to his friend, "this stacked redhead came into the motel around midnight looking for her husband. At least she said it was her husband. She said she was going to divorce him." Randy sat straighter, puffed out his chest. A smile spread across the pitted moonscape of his face. "And she came on to me."

"No kidding?" Vinnie looked up from his burger, impressed.

"Yeah." Randy nodded a few times, examined his nails, and let the silence work its magic.

"Anyway," he said, "she described the guy she was looking for and it was this John Roberts guy who was registered at my motel. Well, the next day I saw on the news that this Brennan guy had been killed at Pottles Campground." He grabbed a few fries and stuffed them in his mouth and, in seconds, had chewed and swallowed.

"Yeah, so? What's one got to do with the other," Vinnie asked.

"I'm getting to it." Randy waited a moment to gather his thoughts. "The thing is, I think this Roberts guy who was at my motel, the guy who the redhead was looking for, is Brennan, the same guy who was killed at the campground."

Vinnie frowned. "Why do you think that?"

"Because. I went into Roberts' room before I quit work, and I found this piece of paper in his wastebasket." Randy pulled the note from his pocket and smoothed it out on the table in front of Vinnie who pushed his burger aside to lean over it, squinting.

"Look. It's a pencil rubbing. I think she got into this John Robert's room somehow—he had gone out for about a half hour when she was there—and she made this. Probably from the pad by the phone when the guy took a telephone message."

Vinnie read.

"*Monday 3 AM Pottles Pond Rte 125*"

Light registered behind Vinnie's eyes. "Holy shit! That's where that Brennan guy was killed. You think the redhead did it?"

"I don't know. I saw her car when she was leavin' the motel and it had a magnetic sign on the side that said Frazetta Hardware. And the TV said that Brennan was an accountant for the Frazettas. So maybe Brennan and Rita knew each other through the store. And maybe Brennan really was Rita's husband and maybe he really was fooling around with another broad." He chewed another fry as if it provided fuel for his thoughts. "But...what if..."

Vinnie rubbed the side of his face. He wasn't ready to process much more. He said, "What if what?"

"Well, what if Rita is a Frazetta. The papers said that old man Frazetta had a daughter. Maybe Rita's out to revenge her old man."

"Let me think," Vinnie said. "You think this Roberts guy is really Brennan, the dead guy? And you think Rita is Frazetta's kid and was mad because her old man piped himself?"

"Right." Randy ran his fingers over the note. "Maybe old man Frazetta committed suicide because his business went under. Brennan was his accountant and he might have stolen money from the business and that's why it went bankrupt. Then Rita shows up at my motel looking for her husband, so she says, and it turns out that this husband is none other than Richard Brennan who had written Pottle's Pond on the motel note pad, the very place he was murdered. Don't you think that's kind of strange?"

Randy's brain cells were cooking.

Vinnie sat with his mouth open, exposing bits of partially chewed burger behind his yellow teeth. He was struggling to keep up with the mental sharpness of his friend. "It's kind of confusing," he said.

Randy gave Vinnie the condensed version.

"Look. Old man Frazetta commits suicide because Brennan stole his money. His daughter, Rita, finds out where Brennan was gonna be Monday morning because she broke into his motel room and found the note pad and made this rubbing." He hitched his head at the note on the table between them. "Then she goes to the campground and pops him."

Vinnie's eyes crossed. "I guess."

Randy realized his friend had followed the beginning of the story but got lost along the way.

"I've thought about this a lot," Randy summarized, "and I think she's involved somehow. I don't know if she was really married to this Roberts/ Brennan guy or whatever the hell his name is, or how she's connected to the hardware store or if she was mad enough to kill Brennan because of her old man or because Brennan was messing around with other women, but," Randy felt that full feeling in his chest again, "I'll tell you this, old buddy. There's treasure in them thar hills and I'm going to find out who this redhead is and how she's connected to this whole mess."

And the treasure doesn't have to be money, Randy thought as he licked his lips. He felt like beating his chest and letting loose a Tarzan roar that would clear the jungle monkeys out of the Burger King.

CHAPTER 20

❀

WEDNESDAY 1:35 am

His hand was shaking. He wiped the perspiration from his face and blinked, but the image lingered. Those long legs and that cruel mouth, taunting him.

He knew he must fight the sinful lust that threatened to consume his every thought and rack his chest with every breath or it would ruin his career, his life, everything he held dear. As he rocked, he chanted. He would not covet this woman. He would not covet.

He stumbled to the bathroom and threw cold water on his face. As he gripped the edge of the sink and stared at the reflection in the mirror, a gaunt face stared back asking, "Who are you? What have you become?"

A wrenching fear washed over him. He locked eyes with the bloodshot orbs in the mirror, boring in deeper. He knew those orbs held the answer to his despair.

But no answer came.

He collapsed on the john, buried his face in his hands, and began to sob.

Snap!

It was the buggy whip. His father was behind him, lashing his back and screaming, "Discipline and self-denial, discipline and self-denial..."

How odd. He felt no pain.

He stared down at the tiny kitchen table at his feet, at the spare breakfast provided for him—a half grapefruit and a mug of black coffee. "That's all you get," his father yelled, "that's all you deserve."

Snap!

Snap!

He looked out the window and saw the sultry Kansas sun laying waste to the fields of wheat and corn. The baby lay between the stubbles of wheat, blistered and burnt, her wasted arms reaching out to him. But the vamp was there, her tangled red hair blowing in the hot wind, her mighty arm raised, her claw-like hand clutching a scythe. She laughed as she delivered a terrible swift blow to the sweet hollow of the baby's neck.

"The poor farm!" his father yelled, "We're going to the poor farm."

Reverend Hannibal Loveless bolted up, bathed in his own sweat, his heart beating like a jackhammer. It was the nightmares again!

Clutching the sheet against his chest, Hannibal looked over at his sleeping wife, his dear precious wife Emmaline, his heart heavy with despair and guilt.

CHAPTER 21

❁

WEDNESDAY 9:47 A.M.

Sam poked through greeting cards at the Paper Patch on Market Street in Portsmouth, and found the perfect card for her mother for Mother's Day.

As she stood in line at the cash register, waiting while the elderly woman in front of her rummaged through her large bag looking for her wallet, Sam's eyes wandered over the displays of magnets on the counter. One particular set caught her eye. There was a photograph of the fog-shrouded tugs off Ceres Street with the Interstate Bridge in the background, shots of Prescott Park in full glorious color, images from Strawbery Banke, New England's largest outdoor museum, and pictures of the Nubble Lighthouse off Cape Neddick Point across the river in Maine. Sam recalled that the Nubble became part of history in 1977 when its photograph, along with those of the Great Wall of China and the Grand Canyon, was sent past Jupiter and into outer space on NASA's Voyager.

At $2.50, the magnets were a bargain.

She chose five, for stocking stuffers. They'd be placed in her closet in a box marked: DO NOT OPEN. She'd hidden gifts in there from the day she and Nick were married. No one dared breach that security.

She paid for her purchases and headed for the door, looking into the bag to double check the items: the Mother's Day card and the five magnets. She reached for the doorknob thinking, *Five. The number of activity, change, communication.*

Books.

The RiverRun Bookshop.

She stepped out into the brilliant sunshine and glanced to her right down Commercial Alley. The narrow bricked alleyway sat in shadows because of the three-story buildings on either side, but it was home to several quaint and popular shops. Maybe she'd pick up a book. But then, the sudden growling in her stomach turned her thoughts to a delicate pastry at Café Brioche in Market Square, in the opposite direction. Sam placed an assuring hand against her stomach and wondered which should come first, food for the body or food for the soul.

She looked up at the wedge of crystal blue sky above the buildings. Hesitating, letting the sun warm her skin, she breathed in the smells of the historic city. Portsmouth, with its eclectic collection of shops, galleries, restaurants, and historical houses, was also home to the tugs that escorted the tankers and other commercial ships dockside, and the occasional sloop that sailed gracefully up the Piscataqua River.

This warm spring morning, New Hampshire's only port city was a mix of mid-morning sounds: an animated conversation between a double-parked delivery truck and the owner of a small shop, the laughter of teenagers pushing each other down the sidewalk while dodging elderly tourists and parents with strollers, the honk of a car as the driver leaned out the window and waved to a friend, and the North Church bell tolling the hour in Market Square.

Sam glanced up at the clock on the tall spire as she stepped off the stoop of the Paper Patch and onto the sidewalk. Ten bells. Maybe she'd pick up a book first and then get a pastry and a hot chocolate. She felt absolutely cosmopolitan when she sat in the sunshine at the round metal tables on the sidewalk in front of Café Brioche. But if she did that, she'd lose track of time and end up sitting there for hours reading the book.

She looked up at the sky once again…. *On the other hand.* She snickered. *Now I sound like Nick.*

That decision, however, was made for her. Movement in the alleyway caught her eye.

The question mark that Nick said God should have branded on her forehead when she was born planted itself between her eyes. In the shadows, she saw Quinn Stevens, carrying a plastic bag, coming out of the RiverRun Bookstore.

She tipped her head, watching the big man walk away.

Quinn Stevens with a bag of books? Quinn, a reader?

She reminded herself not to form opinions about people because of their lifestyles and the way they dress.

As she thought this, she caught a glimpse of herself in the store window— gray sweatpants and an old UNH tee shirt—and wondered how she would like it if people judged her by the way she dressed.

Her eyes moved once again to Quinn's retreating back. She still couldn't reconcile his interest in books with his biker image and troubled past. For a brief time, he had dated Lynda Johanssen, and that had seemed an odd match, like Beauty and the Beast. Hannibal Loveless and Emmaline came to mind. Another seemingly mismatched pair, yet Hannibal and Emmaline adored each other. Sam was thinking in clichés: you never know what goes on behind closed doors, and you can't judge a book by its cover.

By now, the question mark on Sam's forehead was quivering.

Quinn reached the far end of the alley and headed across the street, in the direction of the post office. Sam decided she'd buy a book first. She needed a break from the Pythagorean book she'd been reading, something lighter, a mystery perhaps.

The plan was in place by the time she reached RiverRun and opened the door.

Sam took two steps down into the tiny glassed-in foyer, and turned left through the door into the bookshop. She was greeted by the soft jazz sound of Nora Roberts. Oriental runners lay on the floor and muted lighting hung from the natural beams overhead. The place felt warm and inviting.

To make her visit official, she spent a few minutes poking through the local authors' section before approaching the counter.

"May I help you?" the clerk asked.

Sam smiled sweetly. "Yes, you can. A man I know just left here with a bag of books. His birthday's coming up, and I was wondering if you could give me a suggestion as to what genre he likes." She wasn't really lying. Quinn was a man she knew, and his birthday was coming up *sometime* in the future.

The man hesitated, and said, "Do you mean that big fellow with the beard and the tattoos?"

"Yes, he's the one."

The man cleared this throat. "Well, he asked me if a Sandra Brown book was good. I told him that Brown's books were usually on the New York Times best sellers list. Then he went back to the shelf and picked up two more. He didn't say who they were for. I wouldn't want to steer you wrong. Perhaps the books are for his wife?"

Sam knew that Quinn wasn't married.

Quinn Stevens reading Sandra Brown? She didn't think so. Brown's books were on the edge of romance. Were the books for his mother? Even Quinn must have a mother.

Sam chewed on her bottom lip.

"You know what? I think maybe I'd better check with him to see who the books are for. I'll be back," she called over her shoulder as she hurried out of the bookstore, the mystery she had planned on buying erased from her mind.

CHAPTER 22

❀

WEDNESDAY 11:15 A.M.

Quinn Stevens stood in the back hall and called to his mother. No answer. She was probably at the library. He hung the RiverRun bag of books on one of the hooks lining the wall.

The aroma of brownies welcomed him into the spotless kitchen. Everyone raved about his mother's brownies. The joke was that she used the Betty Crocker box mix—with three eggs because she liked them cake-like. What made *her* brownies different was a cup of chocolate bits.

Quinn cut a large square of brownie from the corner of the glass baking dish sitting on the kitchen counter. He liked the crusty edges on the corner pieces, and often left the brownie sheet in the shape of a cross. That was just fine with his mother. She liked the center pieces.

Placing the brownie on a napkin, he moved to the table, pulled out a chair, sat, and stretched out his legs.

He glanced at the collection of postcards on the big cork bulletin board by the back door, postcards from Annie's friends, from places she would probably never see. His eyes slid over the glass-fronted cupboards to the café curtain across the lower half of the window. There were ships on the curtain. Annie said they reminded her of adventures to distant lands.

Among his mother's eclectic library were books by Thor Heyerdahl, Asa and Martin Johnson, and the explorers Richard Burton and Shackelton. Quinn told his mother that her penchant for rearranging the furniture in the living room was indicative of a frustrated traveler. She would smile and ask him to grab the end of the sofa. She would steer.

Quinn held the brownie beneath his nose and inhaled before taking a bite. Setting the rest of the brownie on the table, he leaned back with his hands locked behind his head, savoring the moment, the silence, the familiarity of home and his mother, the woman who had loved him first.

The clock on the wall behind him ticked. A fly buzzed under the window curtain.

For a few moments, his mind drifted.

Then the taste of chocolate melting in his mouth steered his thoughts to the one defining moment of his pathetic life. It was as if it happened only yesterday.

Lynda.

The soft blonde curls, the big blue eyes, the curves under that pink sweater, the moist tongue licking chocolate from a dainty finger.

Quinn rubbed the spot on his chest as he thought about the few times they had dated and how much in love with her he was from the very beginning. Then Richard Brennan had stepped into the picture and stolen the angel from his arms.

In the pit of his stomach, Quinn felt the familiar ache, the longing, the terrible need to hold Lynda close, to feel her breath on his cheek, to inhale the scent of her. But his arms were empty, his body hollow. He would never feel her soft flesh pressed against his body. He would never taste her lips again. He would never know the joy of having her carry their child. He would grow old alone. He knew that, but he lived for his fantasies. What else did he have now?

Then his eyes narrowed and his jaws clenched as he thought of Brennan lying dead in a pool of his own blood. Justice had reared her head and seen fit to take the scumbag. He looked down to find himself cracking the knuckles on his left hand.

"Hi, darling."

Quinn flinched.

Annie Stevens brushed her son's cheek with a kiss and placed a bag of groceries on the counter. "I didn't mean to startle you." She glanced at the baking dish and laughed. "I see you found the brownies."

Quinn loved the sound of his mother's laughter, round and full of love. She was the bright spot in his otherwise dark existence. Even when his dad took off with a younger woman ten years ago, Annie persevered. She never complained, just stoically moved on with her life. Quinn had learned a lot from his mother.

"My, it's getting warm." Annie pulled off her black cardigan and draped it over one of the chairs.

"Were you at the library?" Quinn asked.

"Yes." She busied herself with unpacking the groceries. The flesh under her plump arms jiggled as she lifted boxes and cans out of the paper bag. "That little Suzy is so adorable, and her reading skills have improved tremendously in the last few months. I'm so proud of her."

"I'm sure you had something to do with that," Quinn said, forcing himself out of his black fugue.

Annie looked down at the floor and scratched behind her left ear, something she always did when deflecting compliments. She turned to look at Quinn, hesitating a moment as her eyes swept over her son before saying, "The child is quite smart. She just needed someone to tell her that. Her parents couldn't give a hoot about her. They fill their lives with meaningless trivialities. What could be more important than your child?"

What indeed, Quinn thought. He watched his butterball of a mother pull the aged footstool out from between the Kelvinator refrigerator and the counter, then open it.

He rose. "Here, mom. Let me do that." He took the box of Cheerios from her hand and looked down at her. "Why don't you let me lower that shelf for you so you don't have to pull out that foot stool every time you want something up here?"

"You have enough to do, darling, what with your long hours at the motorcycle shop. Besides, I like the cabinets just the way they are. Your grandfather built these."

She says that every time the subject of the cupboards comes up, Quinn thought. Family. Annie Stevens loved her family. And now there was just the two of them. Everyone else was gone. How Annie would have loved to have grandchildren. How Quinn would have loved to produce them for her.

He sat back at the table, his mind on *her* again. He rubbed at his curly beard and looked at the last bite of brownie, not sure he wanted it.

Annie cocked her head and lifted one eyebrow. "What is it, Quinn?"

She knew what was wrong, and Quinn knew that she knew.

He shook his head. "It's nothing, mom. I'm fine."

Anne Stevens looked hard at her only child. She'd heard the news about Richard Brennan, and she was scared out of her mind.

CHAPTER 23

❀

THURSDAY 8:45 A.M.

Nick rubbed his hand over his mouth. "I've got to get to work, Sam. The printing press waits for no man."

Nick owned and operated Georgetown Printers and employed five people. On big orders with tight schedules, as with Agatha's Annual Cowberry Chutney Catalog, Sadie and Caroline would work with their father late into the nights to be sure that every 'i' was dotted and 't' crossed. Sam would help too. Only once had there been a tiny error and, if it hadn't been for Sam saving Agatha's life that year, the crusty matriarch would never have let Nick live it down.

"Okay. You can go," Sam said, setting the dirty dishes from the table over the divider and on the kitchen counter. They had just finished breakfast, and Nick was hovering in the breezeway door.

Nick hesitated. "I know you're up to something."

She looked straight at him. "What could I possibly be up to?"

"Signals, Sam, signals. You hardly said two words at breakfast."

"So?" she said, wandering into the kitchen.

"Since when do you say only two words at breakfast?" He shook his head. "Usually, your mouth can hardly keep up with your mind."

Sam glared at him.

"Did I say that out loud?" he asked. The little smile that crept over his face cut a deeper dimple in his check.

To soften the blow, Nick walked over and took Sam in his arms. "Those beautiful blue eyes are turning icy," he said, as he kissed each lid. He held her at arms length. "I didn't mean that quite the way it sounded. It's just that you had that obsessed look on your face all through breakfast. You can run, my dear, but you can't hide from me. I know those expressions. We've been married for twenty-five years."

101

"Almost twenty-six," she said, and then tried to smile. "I was thinking about codes, that's all."

"You know, Sam. Instead of thinking about codes and homicides, why don't you spend time like most women do, thinking about hair and clothes and exercise?"

Sam thought about challenging him on the words 'most women,' but decided instead to focus on the word 'exercise'. She scowled at him. "You're skating on thin ice there, big boy."

"What do you mean?" Nick feigned ignorance.

Sam's lips tightened. "I'm going for a walk this afternoon."

"Good for you. That's what I like to hear."

"I can think better when I'm walking."

Nick lifted one eyebrow. "Wouldn't it be better to just take a walk and enjoy the outdoors, let your mind rest?" He chuckled. "Like that's possible. I know what you're going to be thinking about, Sam. The homicide, and that guy in the camper."

"Earle Bankes."

"I suppose you still believe what he said at the campground about the tapping he supposedly heard. I thought you weren't going to get involved."

"I'm not involved. I'm just curious."

Nick started to open his mouth.

"I know, I know," she interjected. "Curiosity killed the cat."

"Right again. And I don't want to find any dead felines around here when I get home. I'll see you tonight." He grinned, pecked her on the check, and as he made a strategic withdrawal through the breezeway and into the garage, he called back to her, "Don't forget to take that walk. And think about nothing. Zen stuff, right?"

Sam stood in the middle of the kitchen with a dirty plate in one hand, listening to the sound of the garage door rolling up.

She drew a soft breath as her forefinger beat the rhythm on the counter top: tap—tap—tap, tap—tap, tap, tap.

One, one, two, three. Why does that sound so familiar?

She closed her eyes. Behind her lids, she saw the bed of plantings at the base of the aboveground pool in the backyard. Frowning, she wondered what those plants had to do with the dying message of a gambling-addicted accountant. The vision might simply mean she needed to tend to her garden. The weeds would soon be mushrooming into mutants and marching toward her house like Tolkien's forest of tree herders creeping inexorably toward Isengard.

Maybe the focus of her vision wasn't so much the plants as it was the swimming pool. She thought about the lime green bathing suit she had bought on sale last fall and had planned to wear this summer when she was thirty pounds thinner. She looked down at her belly. *Yeah. Like that's going to happen.*

She handed the thoughts off to her higher mind and finished stacking the dishes in the dishwasher. She was wiping down the counter when the breeze-way doorbell rang. Grabbing a dishtowel off the side of the refrigerator to dry her hands, she went to answer it.

"Emmaline! What a nice surprise," she said, pulling the door open. "Come in."

"I hope I'm not disturbing you," Emmaline said. The minister's wife look sad. Everything about her turned down; her eyes, the corners of her mouth, the slope of her shoulders. "I should have called first. Are you busy?"

"Don't be silly. You don't have to call. We're friends. You drop in anytime you want. When I have a client or I'm working, I hang a sign here." Sam pointed to a small gold hook protruding from the strip of wood between the glass panes. "Would you like coffee or tea?"

"No, thank you."

"Well, then. I'll meet you on the sun porch." Sam disappeared into the kitchen.

Moments later, she took up the rocker opposite her unexpected visitor. Emmaline gazed out the window. "You have a lovely back yard, Samantha. I like the white trellis against the pool. Is that a new addition?"

"Yes, this spring. I planted butternut squash at the base of it. I got that idea from a book on square foot gardening. Instead of having the plants trailing over the ground and taking up a lot of space, they grow up over the trellis. The vines look quite pretty with their bright yellow blossoms."

Sam heard the distinctive call of a red cardinal. She reminded herself to hose out the birdbath after Emmaline left.

"That's a nice fragrance, Emmaline. What is it?"

Emmaline's eyes grew soft. "Hannibal bought it for me. It's called Ocean, by Calvin Kline."

Sam nodded.

She was uneasy. She sensed the reason for Emmaline's visit and, in her mind, was lining up subjects to discuss in order to avoid the inevitable. Her conversation with Hannibal, as it was with all her clients, was sacrosanct. She couldn't tell Emmaline that Hannibal had left the scene of a murder. She couldn't tell Emmaline that Hannibal knew the dead man. And she certainly couldn't tell Emmaline that there was a baby somewhere in her husband's past. Whose baby it was or what it had to do with Hannibal, she didn't know.

Emmaline leaned forward in the rocker, her chestnut hair sliding gracefully over one shoulder. Her gray slacks and light blue tailored silk blouse were a stark contrast to Sam's black sweatpants. "Samantha. I need some advice. It's about Hannibal."

"Oh." Sam nodded her head like one of those odd bird figurines that bobs its head into a container of water. She felt a flush creep up her chest and onto her cheeks. She tucked a loose strand of dark blond hair into the flowered scrunchie at the nape of her neck and heard herself saying, "Would you like a Ring Ding?"

"Excuse me?" Emmaline said, a slight furrow on her forehead. One of her eyebrows was slightly crooked, an imperfection that only emphasized her beauty.

Sam grinned as she got up. "Would you like a Ring Ding? I'm going to get one. Want to share a package?"

Please share. I don't want to eat both of them.

"All right," Emmaline said, smiling. "Chocolate is good anytime."

"You've got that right." Sam disappeared through the doorway.

After the women had finished their Ring Dings, Emmaline dabbed at the corners of her mouth and wiped chocolate from her fingertips before placing her napkin on the dessert plate. "Thank you, Samantha." She laughed. "That was surprisingly good." She picked up her glass and examined the liquid. "You have well water, don't you?"

"Yes, eighteen gallons a minute. We have it tested periodically."

"It's very good." Emmaline took a drink and set the glass down.

Thankful that she had shared the package of Ring Dings, Sam said, "You know, there's no such thing as bad chocolate. I have a client whose father was a Navy man. He'd been to the Antarctic on the icebreaker, the Atka, back in the fifties. The ship had spent some time down there examining the base camp called "Little America" that Admiral Byrd had set up in 1928. Her dad brought back chocolate that Byrd had left. It had been frozen for over thirty years, and it was still good. Imagine."

"How interesting," Emmaline said, and leaned forward.

There was that word 'interesting' again. It was her mother's response last Saturday on the way home from the book signing, just before Elizabeth let loose with her fears about her friend, Mary Frazetta. From Sam's experience with clients, she knew that the word 'interesting' hung in conversations when the listener was distracted by other thoughts, following pathways that often led to subject matter unrelated to the topic at hand. 'Interesting' preceded what the listener really wanted or needed to say. Nick's handsome face flashed through her mind. And then again, sometimes the listener was just bored out of his skull.

Sam plumbed the depths of her mind for a detour, but it was too late.

"Samantha. I need to talk with you about Hannibal."

Sam allowed herself a deep breath and settled back in her rocker.

"Something is wrong with my husband," Emmaline continued, "something very serious. It started Monday morning. I've never seen him this distant and distracted. Just yesterday he hung up on Agatha before she had finished talking. He had to call back to apologize."

That must have taken some undoing, Sam thought, visualizing the diminutive matriarch of the town. Agatha Beatrice Coldbath brooked no interference from mere mortals. Only God in His heaven had any power over Ms. Coldbath and her uncompromising opinions, and even then He'd have to make an appointment.

"I'm sorry to hear that, Emmaline," Sam said, reaching for her glass of water. She took a sip and set the glass back down. She found herself staring at the few crumbs of chocolate left on her Rose Chintz dessert plate and wondering if it would be impolite to moisten her fingertip and pick them up. She wanted out of this conversation.

Emmaline clasped her hands tightly in her lap. "Hannibal's always had nightmares, but they seem worse the last few nights. He hasn't slept through the night since Sunday. I pretend I'm asleep, but I hear him downstairs in the kitchen or in the living room watching television."

"Have you talked with him about this?"

"Yes, I've tried but it doesn't do any good. He assures me that everything is fine, and I'm not to worry. But I know something is wrong. You know how it is when you've been married for years. You know the mood of your partner."

Sam knew that was true.

"He talks in his sleep," Emmaline continued. "He's called out the name Trudy a number of times. Just last night, I woke to hear him mumbling, 'No, Trudy, please, no.'" Emmaline started to cry softly.

Sam reached over and touched Emmaline's knee. "I'm sure it's nothing. Maybe Trudy was a relative who died a long time ago. Or a parishioner who had a problem that Hannibal couldn't help her with. Maybe something happened to this Trudy and Hannibal blames himself. There could be a hundred reasons why Hannibal is having these nightmares." Although Sam suspected that Trudy had something to do with the story Hannibal had told her about his past. *And that baby.*

Emmaline's tears flowed freely now. Sam opened the door under the table between them and pulled out a box of tissues. She handed one to Emmaline.

"Thank you." Emmaline dabbed at her eyes. "I'm sorry for making a spectacle out of myself." A sob caught in her throat as she closed her eyes and leaned back into the chair. She looked drained. There were dark circles under her eyes, and her normally creamy skin looked almost ashen.

Sam said, "You know, Emmaline, there are few men so in love with their wives as Hannibal is with you."

"Thank you, Samantha. I know my husband loves me. It's just that sometimes my imagination blows things out of proportion. Hannibal is the first man in my life that I've been able to completely trust. The night we were married, I told him I'd given him my heart. He said that he would handle it with gentleness and abiding love. And he has done that ever since. I couldn't have asked for a better husband."

"Hannibal is a good man," Sam agreed.

Emmaline nodded in agreement. "Up until a few days ago, I thought we had no secrets." She hesitated. A corner of her lip lifted. "Except for my palm readings through the mail." Emmaline had told Sam about that some time ago during an especially stressful period. "But something has happened. I feel as if a huge wedge is being driven between us. And Hannibal won't talk to me."

Emmaline stared out the window behind Sam's head as she said slowly, "There's something else Hannibal says in his sleep." Her eyes filled with hurt. "He calls out in a pleading voice, 'Give me the baby. Please, give me the baby.'"

CHAPTER 24

❁

THURSDAY 9:15 A.M.

"Where's Frank?"

"I don't know. He's probably out back screwing around with the checkbook."

"Please, CJ," Mary Frazetta said glancing around the hardware store. "We have customers." She toyed nervously with her diamond ring.

CJ slumped against the wall behind the cash register, a half-made noose wrapped around his fingers, and said sarcastically, "Right! Have you seen the receipts for the past few days? We should be sitting out on the sidewalk wearing dark glasses and waving tin cups."

"That's no excuse for foul language. Where's Rita?"

"She's upstairs in her apartment."

"Call her and tell her to come down to the office. We've got to work something out here."

Mary examined her son. He looked tired. She worried about him now that Debbie had decided to file divorce papers. CJ needed money. Didn't they all? But CJ had two children to support. And the poor kid was so sensitive. The word volatile crept into her mind. As much as she hated to admit it, she knew that CJ took after her when it came to his temper.

He certainly wasn't like his father. Claudio had been a calm man, taking things in stride. The last thing Mary Frazetta expected was for her quiet, introspective husband to kill himself and leave his family behind. Well, the past was past. There was nothing she could do about Claudio. But she could protect her family. Then she thought about Richard Brennan lying on the cold ground with blood seeping from the hole in his throat. And she smiled.

"Ma?" CJ said.

Mary blinked. "What?"

"Are you okay?"

"Yes, I'm fine. I'll be in the office. Don't forget to call Rita." She headed for the door at the back of the store.

CJ finished making the noose, smiled at his work, and then tucked the nylon rope in his pocket. He was hanging up the phone when two men pushed through the swinging glass doors. CJ noticed one of the guys in particular. He looked like something out of the James Dean movie, *Rebel Without A Cause*. Hair slicked back in what used to be called the duck's ass style, pack of cigarettes rolled up in the sleeve of his tee shirt, black boots under his jeans. The guy had really short legs.

But it was a passing thought as CJ turned to ring up a young woman in a soiled shirt and dockers. "Been out gardening, Lucy?" he asked.

"How can you tell?" she laughed, setting a box of Rapid Gro and a bundle of long green stakes on the counter.

"Maybe it's those dirt smudges on your cheeks."

The back of Lucy's hand went up to wipe at her face. She laughed. "Yup. It's that time of year. Oh, and add a bale of peat moss to that, would you, CJ."

When Randy and his gnome-like friend walked into Frazetta's Hardware on the outskirts of Manchester, the place looked like a morgue. Except for the skinny guy behind the counter to their left, waiting on some broad, and an old guy shuffling along with his cane and examining little plastic boxes of nails lined up along the right wall's shelf, the store seemed deserted.

"Not many people in here," Vinnie said.

"That's good," Randy said. "The fewer people around the better. Now, let's hope Rita shows up."

Like a general planning battlefield strategy, Randy quickly assessed the layout of the store.

The tall shelving that ran parallel to the front of the building was intersected by a wide center aisle over which hung identifying signs. Spring items were everywhere: seed racks, trellises, potting soil, garden gloves, trowels, and lawn chairs, along with the traditional tools, batteries, sundry motor oils, light bulbs, and wood and metal ladders.

If we stand between those shelves, Randy thought, *we won't be seen. Unless someone walking down the center aisle happens to look left or right.* He smiled. *Perfect.*

Everything was set in motion. All they needed now was the final ingredient. Rita the Redhead. Randy's groin tingled as he visualized the fun he was going to have.

Vinnie snuffed, interrupting Randy's fantasy. "How do you know she'll come in?" he asked, small creases forming a fork between his eyes. "We could be standing around in here for days. We'd look suspicious if we came in every day and just hung out."

"I checked around," Randy said, that feeling in his chest now full blown. "She has an apartment up over the store here. And her car's out front, at least it's the same one she drove Sunday night. So, let's give it a few minutes. If we have to, we can wait across the street in that mini-mall and watch the place." Randy inclined his head toward the street. "Come on. Let's poke around." His pockmarked face spread into a leer. "Need any screws?"

"Just one big one." Vinnie laughed and rubbed his nose.

Together they sauntered down the main aisle.

Randy watched as Vinnie caught his reflection in a car mirror hanging on a rack to his right and stopped to smooth back the sides of his greased hair. He examined both sides of his head, and said, "Cool."

Randy shook his head and turned into the aisle marked "HAND TOOLS, TOOL BOXES" with Vinnie close behind.

Rita pulled on a pair of jeans and a blue work shirt. Tucking in her shirttails, she hurried down the stairway outside her apartment. She had wanted to sleep in this morning, but duty called. The family had to find a way out of this dilemma. And when Mary called a meeting—well, none of them dared to defy their mother. She ruled the family with the proverbial iron fist. And there was no velvet glove in Mary's bureau drawers, except when it came to CJ. It bothered Rita that her mother's soft spot for CJ was so obvious. It never affected her—she was the only girl. But poor Frank. He had tried so hard to please his mother all these years, and got little in return.

In the store, Rita waved to CJ and walked down the center aisle.

"Excuse me."

Rita turned toward the voice coming from her left. "Yes?"

"Could you help me here, please?"

Rita hesitated. Her mother was never one to wait patiently, but lately, since her husband's death, Mary was dynamite waiting for someone to light the fuse. Rita didn't want to be the one to ignite her. But, Rita had been brought up with the merchant's mantra: the customer comes first. As she approached the two men, she said, "How can I help you?"

"Rita, Rita," Randy said. "I'm hurt that you don't remember me."

About three feet from the two men, Rita stopped dead in her tracks.

"Don't you remember the kiss we shared Sunday night? Or was it Monday morning?"

Rita's mouth went dry. It was that pocked-marked night clerk at the CircleTo Motel in Portsmouth. *Jesus Christ! What now?*

Rita Frazetta drew in a long breath. She wished she could blink her eyes and tap her shoes and, like Dorothy, whisk herself away to another land. "I'm sorry," she said, her chin in the air. "I don't think we've met."

Randy's eyes narrowed. He stood straighter and said, "Oh, we've met, baby, we've met."

Vinnie snorted.

"This is my friend, Vinnie. I've told him about you."

Rita's lips flattened out as Vinnie's eyes swept up her legs and hips and settled at her full breasts.

Vinnie said, "And *I'd* like to know you better, Rita." He grinned, leaned back against the shelving, and drew the cigarette pack from his sleeve.

"There's no smoking in here," Rita said, her jaw set. She thought about pulling a hammer off the rack to her right and pounding the two little runts into the hardwood floor.

Vinnie look defiant as he shook out a butt, stuck it between his lips, lit it, took a drag, and slowly blew out a stream of smoke in her direction. "Really."

Rita clenched her fists. "What exactly do you two want?"

Randy scratched the side of his head. "What we want, *Rita*, is to tell you a little story. Well, actually it could turn into a big story. We're sure you'll find it very interesting."

Rita glanced back over her shoulder, then turned back toward the two men. "I'm quite busy, so unless you want help in purchasing an item, I've got to…"

Randy stuck his hands in his jean pockets. "What you've got to do, Rita, is listen. You see, once upon a time there was this beautiful redhead."

Vinnie blew out a perfectly formed smoke ring.

"And this redhead visited me one night at my motel. It seems she was looking for her husband. But it turns out later that maybe this guy wasn't her husband, maybe he was the…" he leaned toward Rita, "…maybe he was the accountant for her family's hardware business."

Rita stepped back and drew in a sharp breath.

Randy moved closer to her. "And maybe this accountant stole money from this redhead's family and caused her dear old dad to cut out big time."

Vinnie chuckled.

Rita's voice broke as she tried to speak. She finally managed to say, "That's ridiculous."

"Not so, my pretty," Randy said. "And, to continue my story, maybe this redhead found out that her *husband* was going to meet someone at Pottle's Pond Monday at 3:00 A.M."

Rita was horrified. "How did you…" Her mind raced. How did this little bastard know about the meeting? Then it hit her. The note. *Stupid! Stupid!*

Stupid! She wanted to slap her forehead. She had crumpled up the rubbing she had done of the message on the motel note pad, and dropped it in the wastebasket. The little weasel must have gone through the room looking for things.

"You can't prove that," Rita said, trying to regain her composure.

"Maybe not by myself," Randy said. "But my friend here happens to work at a gas station about a mile from the campground. And he said he remembers everyone who stopped that night. Everyone."

Vinnie dropped his cigarette on the floor, ground it out with the toe of his boot, and said, "Yeah. I remember *everyone* who stopped."

Rita stared at the cigarette butt on the floor, then looked back at Randy. Fear, hate, murderous intent seemed to ball in her chest. She clenched teeth. "What is the point of all this?"

"The point," Randy said and smiled, "is that we could go to the cops and tell them all this. I could tell them about your visit to the motel just before Brennan was offed, and Vinnie could tell them about the broad who stopped at the gas station the night of the murder. The cops would find our stories very helpful."

Vinnie moved closer to Rita. "You know, Rita. Even if you didn't kill that guy, the cops will think you did."

"Yeah," Randy added, "and the news will spread. You, this business…" his eyes swept in an arc over her head "…could all go down the tubes." His smile was sickening.

Rita rubbed the back of her neck. Her heart was beating so hard she could hear it in her ears. She swallowed hard, and then said, "What exactly do you want? I don't have any money."

"Money is not what we want," Randy said, reaching out to touch a curl that had fallen over her shoulder. "What we want is to get to know you better. We happen to be free this weekend." He lifted the curl to his nose. He inhaled and looked straight into her eyes.

Rita wanted to smash his face in.

"Tell you what, doll. You meet us at the Pigpen in Georgetown around eleven this Saturday night."

Frozen in place, Rita felt as if the blood had drained out of her body. She thought she was going to be sick.

"Be there or be square," Randy said, as he let her hair fall back into place.

Vinnie gave a short bark of a laugh as the two of them turned and walked away.

The little bastard actually thinks he's won, Rita thought. *He doesn't know who he's dealing with.*

As that emotion overtook her, she reached out to grab the edge of a shelf for support. She knew she was going to be sick.

Rita had no way of knowing that, in the next aisle, a lone figure had overhead the last half of her conversation with Randy Sturgis and Vinnie LaRoche.

CHAPTER 25

❀

THURSDAY 9:50 A.M.

Sam flushed out the birdbath and filled it with fresh water. Returning to the sun porch, she opened a few windows and then sprawled on the floral print couch. She should take that walk now. It would do her good to get out in the fresh air, get her muscles working, clear her head.

She sighed as she rubbed the mound that sat on her stomach like a thirty-pound gargoyle. Gurgling. She had to chuckle. Gargoyles were grotesquely carved figures perched on the gutters of buildings, their open mouths draining water from the rooftops. Thus the word gargoyle meant to gurgle.

Exercise long forgotten, Sam closed her eyes and drifted in the comforting silence of the sunny room.

Emmaline had just left, and the scent of *Ocean* lingered in the air. A light, graceful fragrance, with a lingering hint of the depths beneath its surface. *Like its wearer*, she thought.

She wished she could do something to help Emmaline and Hannibal. They were both in such torment, albeit for different reasons. But her hands were tied. What could she do?

Nothing, at the moment.

She could *try* to help the police solve the crime committed at Pottle's Pond by attempting to decipher the code that Earle Bankes swore he'd heard, but Hannibal had to deal with the secrets he had kept from his wife. The Reverend was a good man. Sam knew he would eventually do the right thing and tell Emmaline about his past.

But what was all that about a baby? What if the baby Hannibal mentioned was his? What if Hannibal had had an affair or had been married before? What if he was still married when he married Emmaline? Was that why he couldn't tell his wife about his past? Sam couldn't get her mind around that one. No. Hannibal wouldn't do that to Emmaline.

113

Sam also knew that Emmaline was the kind of woman who, as the song went, who would stand by her man. She loved Hannibal deeply, that was obvious. If only Hannibal could see that. Surely their love was strong enough to withstand a few pebbles in the road. Sam sniffed. Boulders were more like it, with an avalanche of rocks and a microburst thrown in.

She threw one leg up over the back cushions of the sofa, and traced triangles on her thigh as she stared out at the bright sky.

The leaves of the maples rustled at the urging of a gentle breeze. A brazen bird chirped loudly from a treetop. A honeybee repeatedly bumped against the row of sun porch screens, determined to find a way in. The birds and the bees, nature's little creatures, instinctually determined to carry on the life force.

An errant breeze wafted in through the screens. Sam inhaled the cool delicious smell of spring, and smiled.

Nick often told her that she was determined. Actually, he called her the universal solvent—tireless, unrelenting, dogged, and stubborn, although he put it more tactfully.

Nick was tactful.

Sam's smile spread as she thought about the time he'd cut out a scrumptious-looking peach pie recipe from a magazine and left it on her desk with a note reading: "Doesn't this look good?"

She had waited a day, then put it back on his bureau with a reply: "Yes, it does."

A few days later, Nick had asked her, nicely, of course, if she would make it for him.

To which she had replied, "Of course I will. You know, if you had come right out and asked me to make it, you would have had it by now."

She could play these games with Nick for an eternity (and actually enjoyed doing so), but deep down she knew you couldn't change a leopard's spots. Her spots hadn't budged one millimeter from the second she was born.

Her eyes softened as she thought about her husband. Nick had such a nice way about him. He was one of those employers you thanked for firing you from a job you loved. A true gentleman in a world that seemed to have lost that sort of graciousness, if one was to believe the evening news.

Sam yawned deeply and rubbed her eyes as her mind shifted focus. She knew she couldn't tell anyone about Hannibal's visit, not even Charlie Burrows. Sometimes she felt like a priest, bound by the confessional, carrying around her client's secrets and sorrows. Her gut told her that Hannibal was innocent. That same gut had twisted as she listened to Emmaline relate her fears about the growing distance between herself and her husband. Her friends were in trouble and she had to do something about it.

Her thoughts turned to Quinn Stevens, and that bag of books. What was the big burly biker—she hesitated as she rolled the alliteration around on her tongue—big burly biker—what was he doing at the RiverRun Bookstore? Again she told herself that she didn't like to stereotype people, but somehow she couldn't imagine Quinn Stevens settling down beside a warm fireplace with a steaming cup of Earl Gray tea and a stack of Sandra Brown novels.

But then—she traced squares on her chest—*there was the big burly football star, Rosie Greer, who used to do needlepoint to unwind. Still...*

She rolled over on her side, stuck one throw pillow under her head and hugged the matching one to her chest. She thought about the tapping code again.

One...one...two...three...

Her instincts told her there was something hidden in that code. And it was a code. She had no doubt about that.

So, what do we have? Her eyelids drooped. *We have an accountant who committed suicide. And his wife, two sons and the daughter, who all had a good reason to want the embezzling accountant dead. We have a biker who briefly dated Lynda Johanssen, who later became the accountant's girlfriend. And now the accountant's dead.*

A cast of five suspects, it would seem.

And seven tappings.

Five and seven equal twelve, the number of months in the year, although the solar calendar was originally a lunar calendar corresponding to the thirteen full moons in each year. Huh. Twelve apostles. Jesus made thirteen. Twelve witches in a coven. The High Priestess, the thirteenth.

Sam blew out a puff of air. She was wandering again.

There was another possible suspect in the Brennan homicide, that bookie. What did Clarence say his name was? She chewed on her bottom lip for a moment.

Benny! Yes. Benny the Bookie. She wondered if Benny was the type to put a bullet through the throat of his less cooperative clients. Loan sharks in the movies had done worse things than that. An old Bobby Darren song came to mind. Words that went something like...*Oh the sharks, dear, have such teeth, dear, and they show them pearly white.* And there was a mention of a pair of cement shoes.

She shuddered.

It was fine to lie here and think about possible suspects, but she had to find a plausible excuse to contact some of them...to ask questions, to observe body language and mannerisms, hand and eye movements, and to listen for subtle shifts in speech cadence.

She had read somewhere that when people lie, their eyes turn down and to the left. And the carotid artery in the neck pumps harder. A study at the Mayo Clinic detected faint blushing around the eyes of those who were lying, and a police procedural she'd recently read told of thermal imaging cameras that detected hot spots in the eyes when someone was lying.

We reveal ourselves in so many ways, she thought as she adjusted the throw pillow between her knees.

The first step was to find a way to talk to the Frazetta family. Her mother had mentioned that she intended to visit with Mary Frazetta. Maybe Sam would tag along. She might get lucky and find all four Frazettas at home with one swoop.

She wondered if Hannibal ought to accompany them as well. He had met Mary on a number of occasions when she was in Georgetown visiting with Elizabeth. In fact, she remembered Mary and the gangly minister engaged in a lively conversation, about the pros and cons of the Coldbath chutney's superiority over other well-known New England producers, at last year's Cowberry festival.

After a nap, she'd take a walk and then call her mother and Hannibal.

Once again, her mind shifted to Quinn Stevens. How was she going to find out what was going on in the biker's mind? She couldn't just walk up to the man and say, "Why are you reading Sandra Brown novels?" or "Did you hate Richard Brennan enough to kill him?" The man could crush her in one hand like an empty beer can. But maybe she could find out where he lived and, more importantly for now, where his mother lived. Quinn's mother might be more amenable to questioning. She certainly couldn't be as threatening as her son.

Unless…. A vision built in her imagination of a scowling biker mama with bushy gray hair and one glimmering tooth, dressed in leather and chains, and with a heart tattoo on her fleshy shoulder that read "Quinn".

She shuddered as she quickly erased the mental image. Quinn's mother was most likely a rosy-cheeked butterball in a flowered apron, wooden kitchen spoon in hand, with only good intentions in mind.

Sam reached down, pulled off her socks, and threw them on the floor. She wiggled her toes, then settled back down into the sofa. For some time she lay very still, watching the treetops sway gently in the slight breezes. Their graceful branches reached up to the sky as if in homage to the life giving elements of nature.

She was reminded of Joyce Kilmer's poem about trees. She began to recite the poem, but stopped when she got to the line—a tree who lifts her leafy arms to pray.

Her leafy arms…

She closed her eyes.

Since childhood, she'd had the ability to see things on the movie screen behind her eyes. Unlike real theaters, with scheduled times for viewing films, on her inner screen something was always playing. She had learned to trust her visions.

Now, behind her lids, she saw the branches of the trees stripped of their leaves. Their bare arms beckoned her. They were trying to draw her closer so they could reveal their message.

She grasped the throw pillow tighter. The message was hovering in front of her mind, but tantalizingly out of reach. It was so frustrating, like when someone's name is on the tip of your tongue and you open your mouth to speak it, but the name lingers back there with your tonsils and won't come out.

She tried an old trick of hers. She started with the letter A, and turned that over and around in her mind. When nothing came, she went on to the letter B.

By the time the letter P rolled onto her screen, she knew what she had to do. That the thought she had was dangerous was shoved into the back reaches of her brain.

For now, after a fifteen-minute nap, she'd definitely call her mother to set up a visit with the Frazettas. Then she'd try to find out where Quinn Stevens lived and if his mother was nearby. And finally, she'd buy a black wig.

She had forgotten all about exercising.

It didn't take long on the Internet.

After calling her mother to ask her to set up a visit with the Frazettas, Sam made a quick Internet trip to Yahoo, then the white pages. There were a lot of Stevens in Manchester, but only one Quinn.

She discovered that there was also an Anne Stevens whose address was the same as Quinn's. Quinn wasn't married, so Anne Stevens could be Quinn's mother. Of course, Anne could be an aunt or a sister, maybe even a sister-in-law. At any rate, Quinn and this woman both lived in the same home. Time would tell.

She was amazed at how easy it had been to find Anne Steven's address on the Internet. Long gone was the time when you had to call the operator with scant information that might not get you anywhere, or you made a trip to the library, to search through a local directory for the city in question, to find an address or telephone number.

Gad! Even *her* address was there. There wasn't much privacy in this new Age of Aquarius. Funny, she thought. The air sign Aquarius is said to rule global networking. Along comes the Internet and we have instant global connections through the airwaves.

Her mind was once again wandering off on a side road but she was enjoying the trip.

She thought about how humanity, in the last one hundred years, had gone from walking on the earth to walking on the moon, from sending messages via weeks-long pony express rides to instant messaging. In this new Age of Aquarius, of satellites and space travel, independent thinking nurtured the seeds of rebellion against strictly organized thought. The symbol of Aquarius, a human, and its opposite sign Leo, a lion, could become the signatures of the world's new consciousness and emerging religions, just as the fish defined the Age of Pisces, along with the symbols of its opposite sign Virgo, the virgin and the bread and wine.

Sam wondered if two recent books that suggested Christianity hid a truth that threatened to crack the foundation of its teachings, *The DaVinci Code* by Dan Brown and *Daughter of God* by Lewis Perdue, were part of the revelations that would introduce the new Age of Aquarius.

She sighed and rubbed her eyes. Time to get back on the main highway.

She didn't want to face Quinn Stevens at the door of his home. She had other plans on that front. So she mustered her gumption and called the motorcycle shop where Quinn worked—she had gotten that information from Charlie—to make sure he was on duty that day. He was, but he was busy, the gruff voice said on the other end of the line. Sam was relieved she didn't have to make an excuse about why she couldn't talk with the biker.

She hung up the phone hoping that, when she took the thirty-minute ride to Manchester, she'd find Anne Stevens home alone.

She leaned back and gave her shoulders a good stretch, yawned, then massaged her scalp. She had to get moving. And she needed an opening line when Anne Stevens came to her door. Of course, that wasn't a problem. She could be clever when it came to, well, not exactly manipulating circumstances—manipulating had such a negative connotation. She preferred to think of her mental gymnastics as using all the resources available at the moment to achieve her goals. Yeah. That sounded much better.

On the way to the Stevens home, she'd pick up a wig. Long, black and curly.

CHAPTER 26

❀

THURSDAY 2:35 PM

Before stepping out of her Honda, Sam checked the contents of the bag to make sure she hadn't inadvertently picked up the bag containing the black wig. She could tell by the weight that she hadn't, but it didn't hurt to double-check. Obsessive-compulsive, Nick called it.

"Mrs. Stevens?"

"Yes?" The cheerful looking woman wiped her hands on the red-checkered apron wrapped around her middle and smiled.

"My name is Samantha Blackwell."

Sam judged the woman was probably in her late sixties, maybe early seventies. She obviously wasn't Quinn's sister, so maybe she was his mother, or an aunt. Sam hoped she was some relation. She'd feel pretty stupid if she were at the wrong address.

"I know Quinn," she said.

Actually, she knew *of* Quinn, but what's a little white lie when you're investigating a murder? Her throat felt dry, but she managed to force an acceptable sound through her constricted air passage.

"Oh. You're a friend of Quinn's?" the woman said, the smile now touched with a trace of curiosity.

Sam plunged ahead, the words tumbling out over her lips. "Well, sort of. You see, yesterday I was at the RiverRun Bookstore in Portsmouth. I had been shopping for a Mother's Day card for my mom in my favorite store, the Paper Patch. Do you know Portsmouth? Well, the gift shop is on Market Street, right off Market Square," She knew she was babbling but she couldn't seem to stop the flood of words "…and when I came out of the Paper Patch, I just happened to see Quinn leaving the RiverRun. It's right around the corner from the Patch, you see. And since I had to pick up some books anyway, I went into the bookstore and noticed that Quinn had left his bag. I know the owner, and he mentioned that Quinn had forgotten his bag. And since the owner doesn't know Quinn, I told him I would drop the books off at Quinn's home."

Sam took a breath and held up the RiverRun bag.

"Oh, how thoughtful of you," the woman said, reaching for the bag. "I'll let my son know."

Her son. Okay.

Sam flushed with the heat of the battle—she was not menopausal! She smiled and said, "Why don't I give you my card in case these are not Quinn's books." She began to rummage through her purse. "Now, where did I put my business cards?" She hesitated, frowned, then said, "Darn! I just remembered. I ran out of cards. I've been meaning to order more." Her eyes rolled up to the woman's face. "Mrs. Stevens. I don't even seem to have a pen and paper."

The woman hesitated, a small furrow formed between her brows "Do I know you? You look so familiar."

A glimmer of hope flickered in Sam's eyes. "I've written a few books and I write a numerology column for the newspapers. Perhaps you've seen my photo there."

"Of course! I saw your photograph on the back of a book jacket at the library." Annie Stevens scratched behind her left ear, then patted at the gray curls at the base of her neck. "Why don't you come in for a cup of coffee? I just finished baking a coffee cake. It's still warm. And I have a few brownies left from yesterday."

Ah, success!

Now Sam didn't have to use the excuse that she didn't have a pen. When she had pulled up in front of the small neat home, she had removed the small pad of paper and the three Saga pens she kept in her bag in case an idea struck; *three* pens because the number three stimulated the creative muse.

In addition, having backup pens was a necessity. What if she had a great idea and she ran out of ink? Then the only fluid available would be her own blood and, although that might be an option if the idea were good enough, she didn't relish the thought.

"Why thank you, Mrs. Stevens," Sam said. "I don't drink coffee, but a glass of ice water and a piece of coffee cake would be wonderful." *Maybe even a brownie after the coffee cake.*

"Please. Call me Annie. The only people who call me Mrs. Stevens are the IRS and the children I tutor at the library." She stepped back to let Sam in, then led the way down the narrow hallway.

Sam marveled at the apparent discrepancy between Annie Stevens and her troublesome biker son. But then, perhaps Quinn was more than he appeared to be. Perhaps beneath that rough exterior lurked the proverbial heart of gold. Appearances could be deceiving. She looked down at her sweats and chuckled.

Stepping into Annie's kitchen was like being folded into the bosom of a doting grandmother. The room smelled of cinnamon and freshly baked bread. Tendrils of steam wavered over the coffee cake on the linoleum-covered counter. On the windowsill above the porcelain sink, sat a chipped, blue pottery vase filled with the bright faces of pansies.

Guilt pressed down on Sam. She knew she was going to hell.

Annie Stevens placed the book bag on the kitchen table. "Please. Have a seat."

"Is Quinn a big reader?" Sam asked, forcing thoughts of damnation from her mind. As she sat down, she glanced around the kitchen, wondering if there were traces of Quinn in the room.

"Quinn, a reader?" Annie said as she pulled two plates from the cupboard and gathered up silverware and napkins. "No, no. I can't say that he is. Although, since he was a little boy, I have encouraged him to read. I bought him all the books I thought he would enjoy—the Hardy Boys series, Treasure Island, then the Jack London books."

Sam listened as Annie talked, but another part of her observed.

On the wall by the back door, there was a bulletin board crowded with post-cards. Someone had a lot of friends who traveled. Most likely Annie's friends, given the woman's nature. The cupboards were painted that pale green Sam remembered from a hospital stay when she had her taken tonsils out. A hand-made braided rug lay on the floor before the sink. The linoleum flooring had long ago lost its ability to sparkle, but it did gleam.

Annie set the plates on the table, folded the napkins, and aligned the knives and forks over them. The yellow nasturtiums on the plates were faded.

"As Quinn got older, I brought home a few science fiction titles like the *Dune* series, thinking that might stir his interest, but it didn't. I even tried to get him interested in fantasy like Stephen Donaldson." She chuckled as she went to the Kelvinator. From the freezer she pulled a small plastic bucket and spooned out ice cubes. They clinked against the inside of the tall glass.

Annie then took the few steps to the sink and turned on the faucet. "I loved *Thomas Covenant, the Unbeliever,*" she said, raising her voice over the sound of the running water, "but you do need a dictionary at hand to read Donaldson."

Annie set the glass before Sam, returned to the counter, slipped on a pair of yellow padded oven gloves, carried the coffee cake to the table, and placed it on a wooden trivet.

"Quinn was never a reader," she added, sounding regretful. "But then, he was always so clever with his hands. He could fix anything. More than once I found him in the back yard taking his bicycle apart and then trying to put it back together. He would tinker with old motors his father had in the garage. As he got older, people in the neighborhood would call him over to look at their cars or fix their lawnmowers." She beamed with pride. "He's very smart in that way."

Sam had to wonder if Quinn's natural proclivity with nuts and bolts included firearms.

Annie removed the padded gloves, poured herself a glass of orange juice, and finally settled in the chair opposite Sam. "May I cut you a piece?"

Sam nodded. "Yes, please do." *I won't have a brownie. I don't need a brownie.*

"It's still warm but it should cut okay." A generous slice landed on Sam's nasturtiums.

"Perhaps Quinn bought the books for me," Annie said as her eyes settled on the RiverRun bag. "I'm the reader, actually. In fact, I work at the library. As I said, I help youngsters who have difficulty reading."

"Oh, that's wonderful, Mrs. Stevens. Our world would be much poorer without books and people to read them."

The woman is definitely an Anne. The N's and the E in her name signify intelligence, curiosity, and a quick mind, certainly a necessary prerequisite for Donaldson readers. A knowing smile curled Sam's lips. *And she works in a library, how appropriate!*

Sam examined Anne Stevens. The round face and soft features gave the impression of a lamb. But in the surprisingly firm jaw and set of her shoulders Sam sensed a lion lay in wait. The leading A in her name showed that Annie Stevens had more gumption and backbone than one would expect from her appearance.

"I agree," Quinn's mother said. "I can't imagine a world without books." She reached across the table and patted Sam's hand. "Please. Call me Annie."

Sam was touched by the warm gesture. She could tell that *Annie* Stevens was one of those women who smiled through trial and tribulation, offering comfort to the sad, and hope to the lost. She could envision Annie's round bottom spilling over the edges of one of those tiny chairs in the children's room of the library, her arm curled protectively around a child, offering encouraging words and praise as the child struggled to read the large letters printed on colorful pages. Sam hoped there were many grandchildren in Annie Stevens' life.

A flush found root in the center of Sam's chest and began to work its way out and up toward her face.

How could she pull off this deception? She looked down at the warm coffee cake with the buttery nuts and cinnamon sprinkled over the top and forked a big piece into her mouth. It was to die for! Now she felt even worse.

But she had to squash her uneasiness. Her mission, and she had accepted it, was to ferret out some information about Quinn Stevens, one of the suspects on her list. If Quinn turned out to be innocent, Sam would make her apologies to Annie Stevens later. She'd make Annie a silken chocolate pie. Maybe she'd even reveal her secret recipe. Surely the woman would understand that Sam's friends were in trouble, and she had no choice.

Beads of moisture broke out along Sam's hairline.

"This is so good, Annie," she said through a mouthful of coffee cake.

"It's not too hot, is it?"

"No, no. It's perfect." Sam wiped a few crumbs from her lips. "Do you share your recipes?"

"Of course. Remind me before you leave and I'll copy it down for you."

One of the beads broke rank and began its descent to Sam's left eyebrow. She feigned a pass at a strand of hair, catching the errant trickle on the way. It wouldn't do to break out in a guilty sweat when you were about to interrogate a potential witness. The "witness" is supposed to sweat, she told herself.

"That's so nice of you, Annie. Thanks."

"Have another piece, dear."

Cutting a more modest triangular wedge of coffee cake with her fork, Sam said offhandedly, "You know. I always felt sorry for Quinn after what happened to Lynda. They dated for a short period, didn't they?"

Annie's eyes dropped to the table, the hand around her fork motionless. "Yes," she said, her voice full of what seemed regret, pain. Maybe fear? Sam wondered.

Annie regained her composure, looked at Sam and smiled. "Yes, they dated a few times." She took a small bite of her coffee cake and worked too hard at chewing it.

Sam vowed she would perform the ritual of self-flagellation tonight, but she had to go on.

"I know they broke up before the accident. Lynda started seeing another guy, as I recall."

Annie sat back in her chair and looked across the kitchen at the parallel lines on the pottery vase on the windowsill. She rubbed the curls at the nape of her neck. The sudden rigidity of Annie's body told Sam the truth. The mother feared for her son. Annie must have known about Richard Brennan, how he took Lynda away from Quinn. In Georgetown, the news, like Emily Dickinson's squirrels, had run over the grapevines.

Sam figured that, at this point, Annie knew where the conversation was heading, but she was probably trying to figure out who Sam really was and why she was involved.

Time to change the subject.

Sam motioned at the plastic bag on the table. "I noticed the books Quinn left behind are by Sandra Brown, who is a mystery-romance writer. Do you like her books?"

Annie looked at Sam, the wariness in her eyes apparent. She hesitated.

Then those eyes softened as she said, "Sandra Brown? That's interesting. I wonder why Quinn would buy those titles for me. I have access to almost any book at the library, and I'm not a book collector. It's more of a space problem than a lack of desire." She paused, casting a glance at the RiverRun bag. "Do you suppose these books are not Quinn's?"

"That's a possibility," Sam said, knowing that the two paperbacks were not Quinn's.

"Well, I'm sure he can tell us." Annie looked at the big clock on the wall over the kitchen table. "He should be here in about five minutes."

Sam practically swallowed her tongue. "Excuse me?"

"Quinn. He'll be here shortly. He's leaving work early so he can take me to the eye doctor. I'm getting drops in my eyes so I won't be able to drive myself home."

Sam's heart began to race. She didn't want to get caught in a sham in Annie Stevens' kitchen with Quinn Stevens blocking the exit. The Boston Patriot linebackers should be so big.

She stood quickly. "Oh, I didn't realize how late it is, Annie." She glanced at the clock as if to punctuate her statement. "I do have to run."

But it was too late. Sam could hear someone at the back door.

CHAPTER 27

❀

THURSDAY 2:45 PM

Hannibal had to do something, he couldn't just sit around and wait for the police to come knocking on his door. The board of the Second Puritan Church of Georgetown had overlooked the trouble at his last assignment, but could he expect their forbearance if, once again, he was involved in a homicide?

Trouble at his last assignment? He sighed. *Two connected murders, one in the basement of his church? That was more than trouble.*

Although the guilty party was arrested, Hannibal's connection to the incident was less than commendable. Thank God no one had found out about his obsession with that woman.

He sat in his office, at the back of the church on the north end of the Georgetown green, with the most recent copy of *Publick Occurrences* spread out on the desk before him. He had read the same sentence numerous times. The words seared into his brain:

> Richard Howard Brennan, accountant to recent suicide victim, Claudio Frazetta, was found shot to death at Pottle's Campground on Route 125 in Georgetown around three o'clock Monday morning.

Hannibal lowered his head into one hand and closed his eyes. *Think*, he told himself, *think. There must be something I can do.*

But he couldn't seem to focus on his current dilemma. Instead, his mind wandered over the past, over the years of his ministry at the last post. He couldn't believe what a weak man he had been. He'd had nothing to do with the two murders at that last church, but he *had* been guilty of the ungodly sins of lust and deceit. He recalled how he had tried to lure that woman into his office with the gift of a diamond chip necklace. His face still burned when he remembered how she had spurned his advances. He had sinned.

He rubbed his face hard with his hands.

And the nightmares; he was having them almost every night now. He didn't know how much longer he could handle the torment. He had to talk to Emmaline.

Emmaline.

Through her quiet acceptance and abiding love, she transformed him into a better man. She brought love and laughter and a higher calling into his life. Everything had meaning for him now. He couldn't lose her.

He met Emmaline Parker in the breakfast room at a bed-and-breakfast on the coast of Maine, on that second day after his arrival. And they had spent the subsequent six days of his vacation together, walking on the beach and through the town. Hannibal told her he was a man of the cloth. She had been startled at first, but relaxed as the days melted by. Their relationship had fit like a pair of old slippers.

That last night at the beach, under a bright moon, they sat on a stone bench by the ocean and watched the waves in their eternal embrace of the shore.

"I'd like nothing better than to hear your life's story," he told Emmaline. "I know you're an English teacher, but I'd love to know more about you."

She squeezed his hand gently, then let go.

"There may be things you wouldn't want to hear," she said, her smile slipping away.

"I've heard many strange stories in my career." Hannibal paused to push his glasses into place. "I have one or two stories myself."

"Yes, I suppose you have."

They reached for each other's hands and sat quietly for some time. Hannibal sensed something was troubling Emmaline, but he waited for her to speak, the silence between them softened by the susurrant murmur of waves on the sand.

"Hannibal?" Emmaline finally said. "I have something to tell you. I don't know how you'll take it but I think you should know."

His heart stopped.

Oh no! She's married. What would he do if he heard that? How could he covet another man's wife? What lonely years stretched ahead of him with only her memory? He couldn't lose her now.

Hannibal looked into her face, her lovely face with that creamy skin and one askew eyebrow. How he wanted to kiss that brow, her cheek, her lips. His voice was trembling when he said, "You can tell me anything, Emmaline."

Little worry lines popped up between her brows as she said, "I have a hobby."

He swallowed hard. *A hobby? How bad could it be? Gambling, prostitution, scamming tenth graders out of their lunch money?* He blinked, wondering where those thoughts came from.

"I've been doing it for a number of years, and it has helped many people. But it's not the kind of hobby of which you might approve."

She helps people. That's a good sign. Of what wouldn't I approve? Who am I to not approve, with what I have done in my life?

Rationalization was overtaking his train of thought.

He saw the distress on her lovely face, bathed in the light of the moon, and he wanted to relieve her worry, stroke her brow, kiss her sweet lips. "I can't imagine you doing anything of which I wouldn't approve," he answered softly.

"It's just that, being a minister, you might not approve."

"If you're helping people, then your hobby must be good. What is it, Emmaline?"

She sat very still. "I study palmistry."

Palmistry!

Hannibal closed his eyes.

He had seen the neon hands glowing in shabby store fronts in the city, garish signs along the road side advertising Madame Zelda, Palmistry, Tarot; cubicles at honky tonk beaches proclaiming love, fortune and fame through the lines of the hand. But his Emmaline, his sweet, educated, beautiful Emmaline—*a fortune teller?*

A part of him wanted to rise up with Bible in hand and pontificate about the evils of would be prophets, a part of him that was his father. His father would have grabbed his whip and taught the sinner a good lesson. But he was not his father, and who was he to cast the first stone? He had done unspeakable things.

Rationalization overtook him.

All he knew was that this woman beside him was good. She filled him with joy. If she were a sinner, so be it. He would happily tread down that path of good intentions, to hell if it must be, to walk by the side of Emmaline Parker.

He turned to face her full on, kissed her hand ever so gently, looked into her worried gray eyes, and heard his shaky voice uttering the second most important words in his life, "Emmaline, will you marry me?"

To his everlasting joy, she responded with the most important words he had heard in his life. "Yes, Hannibal, I will."

In his office, Hannibal fell to his knees beside his desk, folded his hands on his lap and began to rock. As he had almost every day since he'd met his wife, he thanked God for her love and prayed for forgiveness for all his past indiscretions. He knew he'd made bad choices after he'd left the Kansas farm and arrived a neophyte in New York City: the wild parties, the sex, the drugs— although he had only dabbled in that hazy world. The memory of the religious rantings of his crazed father, along with the sting of the whip, had embedded in his soul a deep fear of the hell and damnation he would face if he sunk too far into debauchery.

He rocked.

His weary mind could not stop the image of the baby from seeping into his consciousness. She was always there, on the fringes of his thoughts, waiting for an opportunity to creep into his brain cells and fill his head with her tiny red face and tight fisted hands. He wondered if she was still alive and, if she was, where she was and what kind of a life she had. Was she happy? Did she still have that distinctive heart-shaped birthmark on her shoulder? In the warmer months and upon those formal occasions when women dressed more skimpily, Hannibal found himself glancing at every young woman's shoulder, hoping one day he would find her. Praying he never would.

He moaned.

On the floor of his office, Hannibal rocked harder and began to sob. He thought his heart would break.

Finally, he gathered some of his senses, climbed back into his chair, and slowly calmed himself. He glanced at the newspaper on his desk, at the article about the murder. He wondered how the Frazetta family was holding up under this terrible burden and thought about paying them a call. He wasn't their pastor, but he'd met Mary on a number of occasions. Perhaps, in addition to offering solace to the grieving family, he might discover something about Richard Brennan that would lead to…what? Who killed the man? He wasn't a detective. He wasn't cut out for that sort of thing. He hoped Samantha Blackwell would use her considerable detecting skills to extricate him from the terrible dilemma in which he now found himself.

With his elbow on his desk, he chewed on his thumb. His eyes moved around the office and stopped at the framed painting of the praying hands of Jesus. He usually found solace in those translucent hands, but today he found none. He was bereft, lost, a lamb that had strayed from the flock.

He shut his eyes as if that simple act would block out the terrifying labyrinth into which Brennan's midnight call had plunged him. An unrelenting darkness gripped his heart. He buried his head in his hands and cried into that darkness, "Help me, oh Lord. Please, help me."

Hannibal closed his eyes.

The cool scent of daffodils, from the glass vase Emmaline had placed on the corner of his desk, filled his nostrils. She often brought him a bouquet of fresh flowers to brighten up his office. With that one breath, his wife's essence filled him as completely as it always did whenever he looked upon her. He felt her presence, as if she were really there beside him.

But when he opened his eyes, he didn't see Emmaline. What he saw was the stain on his sleeve. He would have to take this suit to the cleaners. He laughed, amazed at how such a mundane thought could intrude upon his mind when he was facing the possible extinction of everything about which he cared.

He rubbed his face hard, tried to focus, but his mind had a course of its own. It segued to Clarence Tuttle, the owner of Clean As A Hound's Tooth Cleaners, the establishment that sat to the south west of the church and across the town green from Samantha's home. Clarence had told him about an exchange at a recent dry-cleaners' convention in Manchester. The Frazetta's plight was the buzz through the weekend. Clarence heard that Richard Brennan had been like a family member to the Frazettas, and they were devastated when they heard he'd embezzled their funds. Now, the potential loss of their business, on top of the death of Claudio Frazetta, was almost too much for the family to bear.

In truth, Hannibal's heart went out to them, but his mind kept returning to his own dilemma. There had to be a way to handle the events that had unfolded since the night of that telephone call. He knew he should go to the police and tell them exactly what happened, starting with the midnight call from Richard Brennan. But before he did that, he had to talk with Emmaline.

On his desk, next to the worn Bible his mother had given him when he was six years old, stood the wedding photograph of he and Emmaline, posed on the rock strewn shore of Rockport, Massachusetts. She wore a simple white dress. The wind caught her long auburn hair just as the camera had caught her sweet mouth open in laughter. The memory of that silvery sound seemed to waft from the photograph and into his very soul. Hannibal stared at her face for a long time.

Finally, he took a deep breath, settled his shoulders, leaned back in his chair, and thought once again about the situation in which he now found himself. He had to face the inevitable, a talk with Emmaline—a conversation that would take every ounce of his strength. As a man of God, his faith, his future, his very purpose in life shouldn't depend upon another person's response. It shouldn't.

A shudder ran through him.

In the sepulchral sound of the office, he gazed down at his fingers. The silence filled his ears. He thought how strange it was that silence had a sound. It was as if the space that silence took up was crammed with tiny particles in a constant state of bombardment, a mute world of noisy chaos, mirroring his own existence.

Hannibal began to rock once again, as the enormity of his situation threatened to overwhelm him. His mind stumbled over the twisted black pathways into which Brennan's phone call had cast him, searching desperately for the way out of this underworld of horrors. He should go to the police, but then maybe he should wait for Samantha to get back to him. He also wondered if he should pay a visit to the Frazetta family before making any rash decisions.

He had to make a choice, do something. He couldn't continue to sit here and lament over his fate. Whatever he decided, one thing was certain. Either he would overcome the moral dilemma in which he now found himself and then return to his idyllic life, or he would suffer an excruciatingly painful demise.

As the furnace kicked in, the baseboard broke into his silent chaotic world with a cascade of ticks and pings before slowing to a trickle, and a final dry crackling.

The Frazettas.

The warmth of his office could not melt the icy fear, coiled in the pit of his stomach, as he contemplated the Frazetta's adopted redheaded daughter.

CHAPTER 28

❁

THURSDAY 3:15 PM

Relieved that the someone at Annie Stevens' door was a frail neighbor searching for her dog Fritz, Sam nevertheless hightailed it out of the kitchen. With a hastily wrapped, half-eaten slice of coffee cake and two brownies in a brown paper bag, she kept her eyes peeled in both directions as she slid into her Honda and took off, leaving a strip of rubber on the street.

Sam wondered if she was cut out for the sleuthing life. It was one thing to sit in the safety of her sun porch and work on codes, but the last few years had put her—and on one occasion, her daughters—in harm's way. Although she had nothing to do with the incidents that occurred, she and her daughters, nevertheless, became the victims of a crazed psychopath's obsession.

Instinctively, her hand slid under her sweatshirt to the round, fleshy scar on her left side. That trauma taught Sam that if she would ever be involved in the investigation of a crime again, even on the periphery, like now, she would never allow her family to be placed in danger. In one of his metaphoric moments, Nick had told Sam she was like Mother Moon, protectively encircling her earth family, using her own body to deflect and absorb would-be invaders into her world.

She glanced up at the blue sky, at a plump white cloud moving as with purpose toward the east, trailing thinner wisps behind it. Chris Thomas, the Channel 9 weatherman, had predicted gray skies and falling temperatures by late afternoon, followed by three to six inches of snow by morning. *Poor man's fertilizer*, Sam thought, remembering Nick's grandfather and his homespun wisdom.

On Interstate 93, heading for Route 101 South and the trip back home, she reached to turn on New Hampshire Public Radio when her hand stopped midstream. Through the windshield, a black motorcycle grew exponentially as it hurtled toward her Honda. She went rigid, gripped the steering wheel with both hands. In a teeth-jarring rumble, the Harley zoomed by, but not before Sam recognized the huge man straddling its back, and not before Quinn Stevens' eyes locked on Samantha Blackwell.

Sam walked toward her car in the Wal-Mart parking lot, bags in hand, her treasure hunt finished. Earlier, she had purchased a black wig and leather vest from a costume store in Portsmouth, and now she had just picked up black mascara and eyeliner, purple eye shadow, and Ruby Red lipstick and Fire Engine red nail polish. Since her wardrobe consisted of mostly sweats, she had also bought a pair of jeans. She glanced up at the gray sky that Chris Thomas had predicted. The air smelled like rain and, if it got much colder, it was bound to snow.

Great! She grimaced. All she needed was to wade through the woods in knee-high snow in the dark of night.

She climbed into her car and headed towards Georgetown.

At home, she shredded the knees and cuffs of the jeans, rolled them in the dirt in the asparagus garden in the back yard and left them outside to "season" overnight. In the basement, she found a pair of Sadie's black boots and one of her old tee shirts—white with black letting—that read: TOO MUCH GIRL FOR YOU. With the purchases she had made today, she had all the equipment she needed to ensure that not even her own mother would recognize her. She would tease the wig before making a grand entrance in the Pigpen on Saturday night.

She was ready. Or as ready as she'd ever be.

Sam glanced at the clock on the stove. 5:45.

"You almost ready, hon? We're going to be late for the movie."

"Be there in a minute," Nick called from the bedroom.

Sam always marveled at how long it took Nick to get ready to go anywhere. Everything had to match—socks, pants, belt, shirt, jacket, whatever. And you couldn't rush him. He'd just smile and say, "I'm almost ready," and proceed to move like a glacier. Over the years, Sam had tried to resign herself to his epochal movement, but sometimes it was hard.

"I taped the news and *Seinfeld*," she called out as she wandered into the back hall. He probably didn't hear her.

She sat on the bench, arms crossed over her sweatshirt, foot tapping on the floor. Then she felt it. The ankle that she had sprained badly a few years back twinged. *That's what I get for exercising*, she thought.

"Storm's coming," she said, a little louder. The twinge turned into a slight throb. "Probably a good one, too," she mumbled to herself as she reached down and massaged her ankle.

"Is that right?"

She looked up.

Nick stood in the doorway, gracing her with a sparkling smile. He was polished as bright as the schoolteacher's red apple. His dark curly hair was glistening and combed neatly in place, damp curls at the nape of his neck. He wore a brown woven belt and an earthy-toned Orvis print shirt over a yellow turtleneck, both tucked into freshly washed chinos. He smelled of spearmint toothpaste and that old reliable Old Spice, the same aftershave his father had worn. He liked tradition.

"Move your cute butt," he said, nudging Sam off the bench.

"What now?" Sam stood, arms akimbo. She glanced through the kitchen doorway at the digital readout on the stove. "We've got twenty-four minutes to make it to Newington before the movie starts. You know I won't go in if it's already started."

"Just a quick touch up on my shoes." He lifted the bench seat and pulled out a brush and proceeded to brush every microscopic inch of his brown loafers. When he was done, he examined his nails to be sure they were spotless.

Sam was so exasperated she felt like throttling him, but then he turned those eyes the color of blackbirds on her and said, "Are you ready, sweet thing?"

Caught in frustration between succumbing to his innate charm and shredding his L.L. Bean catalog that he kept in the bathroom, Sam was too speechless to answer. For a brief moment, she stared at him, wondering if he knew his catalog-shopping destiny hung in the balance.

"We're taking 95," she said, then turned and went out to his Toyota 4 Runner.

Fifteen minutes later, they were on Interstate 95 heading north.

Sam's ankle pulsed metronomically. She fiddled with the radio dial and caught the time—nine minutes before the movie started. She scowled.

"You okay, honey?" Nick asked. "You're awfully quiet."

"Fine." She was softening. "Please concentrate on your driving." Nick tended to drive slower when he talked.

The announcer went on, in a gleeful voice, to comment on the big snowstorm predicted to hit during the night. *Can you believe it, folks? At least five to six inches by morning.*

Sam sniffed. Like this never happened in New England. She wondered if the guy was a transplant from Arizona.

The snow won't last long, she thought, gazing out her window at the trees slipping by. *It had better not. I've got plans.*

Last spring she had set out four tomato plants in mid-May, and on the 17th, they'd had a major snowstorm. The plants didn't make it. Sam had learned first hand the old-timer's wisdom of waiting until after Memorial Day before planting tomatoes.

They pulled into the parking lot of the theater with two minutes to go before show time. Sam leaped out of the Toyota before Nick had shut off the ignition. "I'll get the tickets," she said.

They felt their way through the darkened theater and sat down just as the commercial finished and the previews were about to begin.

Sam settled back, breathing deeply to settle the knots in her stomach, and wondered how Nick managed to slip his routine between the cracks in time as tightly as the mortar cementing the blocks of the Great Pyramid. Even with his nonchalant unhurried manner, they had never been late to a movie. She was convinced he could charm more minutes on the clock.

"Well, what did you think?"

"I liked it," Sam said, yawning and leaning against the headrest. "What time is it?"

Nick examined his Rolex. "9:10."

"Keep your eyes on the road."

"How can I keep my eyes on the road and tell the time at the same time?"

Sam chuckled. "Good point. You ought to get that light behind your dash clock fixed."

"Yep. It's scheduled for Monday."

Going home from Newington, Sam usually took I95 to the Hampton toll-booth and onto Route 101 West because it was faster, and a straight shot home—no lights or twists and turns or leisurely drivers that held up lines of traffic. She wanted to get home. She had things to do.

Nick preferred to take Route 33 out of Portsmouth, through Greenland and Stratham, then cut off through Newfields onto old Route 101, to Pine and Middle Roads which led to Georgetown. Sam suspected taking this route was based on his innate love of countrified landscapes, plus his need to be aware of what was going on in the communities. When Nick was behind the wheel, his head swiveled as if he were watching a tennis match. In defense of life and limb, Sam had to drive from the passenger seat. She told herself it wasn't that she needed to be in control. If she didn't tell him when to turn and in what direction, he would drive straight through to who knows where, his mind so engrossed in what was going on in this field or that wetlands or the building site on that corner.

They were idling at the red light by the Buckhorn Restaurant in Greenland, while big rigs rumbled past them to turn left into the truck stop, when a motorcycle went blasting by the passenger side of the Toyota.

Sam jumped toward Nick. "Jeesum Crow!"

"Did you see that?" Nick said aghast. "That guy went right through the red light."

"See that? I think he took a layer of paint off my side of the truck." She let out a big puff. She was shaking.

"He's one lucky son-of-a-bitch. What if someone had been turning on the green light?"

"I don't want to think about it," Sam said, hugging her arms to her chest.

But she did think about it. She thought about Quinn Stevens on his big Harley. His mother had probably told him about Sam's visit that afternoon, and Quinn had probably recognized her when he zoomed past her on the highway after she left Annie Steven's house. Sam wasn't hard to find in the phone book, or on the Internet for that matter, as she well knew, having found Annie's address there.

Was Quinn Stevens following her? Was he trying to scare her? Maybe it wasn't him. But then again, maybe it was. Regardless, she would have to tell Charlie about this.

CHAPTER 29

❀

THURSDAY Midnight

He lay in bed thinking about the next nocturnal mission. He waited for these nights, his link to all that was meaningful.

He prayed for heavy clouds to blot out any light that would come from the last of the dying moon. He would be less visible then.

As usual, he would dress in black so that he would be invisible as he crept through the darkness and up the steps of the sagging back porch.

It had to be that way.

CHAPTER 30

❀

Friday 5:30 A.M.

As predicted by Chris Thomas, five inches of snow had fallen during the night. Sam knew this because she had taken a ruler and measured the inches on the back deck railing. That was just after she'd snuck out, at dawn's early light, to extract her newly shredded jeans from beneath the snow in the asparagus garden and tossed them into the dryer in the back hall, hoping they'd be done before Nick got up. Not that he ever looked in the dryer, and he certainly wouldn't question her laundry schedule. After all these years of marriage, nothing Sam did surprised him.

Now, sitting at the table with a glass of Silk chocolate soymilk and the carton, she looked out at the fresh white blanket and wondered if it would melt by tomorrow night. She hoped so.

With only the early morning light for illumination, Sam read from the side of the carton. "…Silk—its smooth, rich taste without any cholesterol—whole organic soybeans—…." She swallowed a few mouthfuls and peered at the tiny quotes.

Yogi Berra: "You can't think and hit at the same time." Sam smiled. On the surface that sounded like a Berra-ism, but in reality it was very Zen.

She read what Zen Master Shunryu Suzuki said: "If your mind is empty, it is always ready for anything."

Sometimes Sam wished that she could empty her mind for a little while, just for a rest, just to escape the constant whirlwind of thinking and analyzing and planning. But, since she had been old enough to remember, she swam in an ocean of sensory input—colors, sounds, smells, shapes, images, feelings. Sometimes her head got tired just thinking about what she was thinking about. She couldn't imagine an empty mind.

Suzuki went on to say: "In the beginner's mind there are many possibilities; in the expert's mind there are few."

That, to Sam, sounded like what Thomas Edison said. "Give me an uneducated man who doesn't know it can't be done and he'll go ahead and do it. But
if you give me an educated man, he'll give me a thousand reasons why it can't
be done."

Well, she certainly was an uneducated woman when it came to detecting,
but perhaps, in some ways, that was an edge.

She finished the milk, rose from the table, and put the empty glass in the
dishwasher and the milk carton back in the refrigerator. A package of Ring
Dings sat eye-level in her Amana. She closed the refrigerator door, hesitated,
pulled it open, eyed the Ring Dings, then, once again, firmly shut the door.

Minutes later, from the desk on her sun porch, as she stuffed the last few
crumbs of the second Ring Ding into her mouth, she watched two squirrels
chasing each other in the brilliant sunshine, tunneling into one side of a small
mound of snow by the pool and poking their heads out the other side. They
scampered and circled and rolled in a heap, rough-housing like a couple of
kids.

With a feeling of contentment, Sam watched their antics.

It was still early—5:45—but she'd had an idea for her column and she
wanted to get started on it before Nick got up and the phone started ringing.
She scratched her neck and gave her back a good arch. Her eyes fell on the Ring
Ding wrapper. She positioned it in her wastebasket under some of the numerous
advertisements that came in the mail every day.

Resting her hands on the split keyboard, she wondered how to present the
information in this column in an interesting way.

A corner of her mouth curled. *There's that word 'interesting' again.*

She typed ALHIM, then rested her chin in her hand and stared at the word.
It was the first of numerous names in the Old Testament that was applied to
God.

Historically, the names of God were placed in a circle reflecting the axiom:
God is a circle whose center is everywhere and circumference is nowhere.
Therefore, the circle became a symbol of the Creative Source.

Sam had learned that when the word ALHIM is examined in this manner,
the number values behind the letters of the name revealed a magical
number—3.1415. This important mathematical value, called Pi, is used to
determine the measurements of a circle. Its discovery is attributed to the Greek
mathematician Archimedes (280 BC), but it also lies hidden behind the first
name of God in the book of Genesis, the first chapter in the Christian Bible,
the writing of which supposedly began around 1200 B.C.—a thousand years
before Archimedes!

How did they know? Sam thought as she pulled the flowered scrunchie from the nape of her neck. She ran her hands through her hair to pick up the loose ends and secured the elastic once more.

She thought of all the hidden ways that numbers influenced life: the Golden Mean found in Greek temples; the Fibonacci sequence displayed in nature; the 'G' inside the Masonic triangle—God Geometrizes; the Great Pyramid called "Mathematics in Stone", the Chartres Cathedral whose precise angles lift the spirit and draw the soul through its archways; the identical mathematical angles found in the masters' paintings, woven into the design on the serapes of South American peasants, and carved into coins dug up in archaeological sites throughout the world.

She rubbed her mouth with the flat of her fingers.

There had been no Internet to spread these ideas. Somehow, these artisans tapped into knowledge, patterns, and truths that exist in the Universal Unconscious, in the mind of the Creator. Through the visual beauty of their works, these masters connected the viewer with the interlocking wonder of the world and the Source of all creation. The hidden connection was through mathematics, through the simplicity and elegance of the universal language of numbers.

Sam sat in awe of the enormity and sacredness of numbers and symbols and how they could evoke spiritual connectedness.

She drifted.

Then she found herself thinking about her plans for tomorrow night.

The tingles started. Each time the awareness of an unsettling situation arose, that scrambling little feeling—the flutterbys—started in the pit of her stomach and worked its way up through her chest, down her arms and out to her fingertips. She didn't want to think about tomorrow night, about wigs, and leather, and boots, and bikers, and the Pigpen, and belligerent drinkers. Martha Stewart wanted to focus on her salad: Sam wanted to concentrate on her column.

She leaned back in her chair and stared blankly at her monitor.

Maybe she should wash the kitchen counters down with bleach. She wrinkled her nose. Or bake some brownies. She tilted her head, raised her brows, then shook her head. No. She still had some pieces of apple pie left from the other day. Gad! She was even desperate enough to take a walk. Her cells were screaming for any physical activity that would release the tension building inside her.

She watched the squirrels romp, examined the L.L.Bean thermometer outside her window, and, for a few moments, listened to the birds chirping around the feeders. She thought about the trouble she might get into tomorrow night.

Martha Stewart got into a fine kettle of fish for fibbing about her stock sale, *if* that's what she did. Sam knew she could get into an equally unsavory stew for fibbing about her plans for tomorrow night, and that's what she *was* going to do.

Her head felt stuffed with cotton as she pondered the difference between an outright lie and a fib.

Strange word…fib.

The phone rang.

She reached for it and glanced at the wall clock. 6:05. It had to be Charlie. He knew she got up early.

"Sam."

"Oh, hi, Charlie. I'm glad you called." She was relieved to hear his voice, and not that of her mother or the girls. "Something happened last night."

"You're right about that. How did you hear about it?"

"Hear about what?" Sam frowned. "What are you talking about?"

"The Frazetta boys. They got into a fight, and Frank ended up in the hospital emergency room."

"No kidding! Is he badly hurt? Do you know what the fight was about?"

"He's okay, bruised ribs, maybe a sprained wrist. And no, I don't know what the fight was about. But you can bet your bottom dollar I'm going to find out. The Frazettas are persons of interest, as they say, in the Brennan homicide. This murder happened in my town and, even though it's been handed over to the State, I'm keeping tabs on it. Besides, I'm the State's discreet link to you."

Sam could understand the reluctance of the police to have a 'psychic', as they called her, working on the case. Even though she had explained numerous times that her profession was the study of numbers, patterns, and symbols, the appellation stuck.

"Maybe I should arrange a visit with Mary Frazetta and see what I can dig up," she told Charlie. "Mary's a friend of mom's so it won't seem odd if I tag along."

A thought stirred in her mind.

But first, I need some mulch for the garden. I think I'll take a ride to Manchester and visit Frazetta's Hardware store. She glanced at the clock, suddenly more alert. *Wonder if they're open at 7:00 A.M.?*

She hung up the phone, totally forgetting that she hadn't told Charlie about the maniac on the motorcycle who had nearly taken a layer of paint off the side of their Toyota, and who had almost stolen one of her nine lives.

CHAPTER 31

❀

Friday 6:30 AM

"I can't believe you two!" Mary Frazetta screamed as she paced back and forth, her arms flailing at the air like a mad woman. "As if we haven't got enough troubles, you two have to act like a couple of punks brawling on the street corner. What the hell am I going to do with you?" She didn't expect an answer.

Frank was leaning against the counter in his mother's kitchen, his ribs tightly taped and, the only outward sign of their fight, a small splint on his left wrist. He reached to scratch his elbow, then dropped his arm to his side. He shifted against the counter, working his jaw, the muscles bunching like bags of marbles.

CJ sat at the kitchen table, head down, scowling, arms folded lightly across the bruises on his upper body. He wanted to pull the rope from his pants pocket and make a hangman's noose. He wanted to wrap that noose around Frank's thick neck. He took a deep breath and winced. His hip was sore and he had a shiner that would require not a steak, but a whole side of beef.

"This is just great!" Mary went on, her fury building. "Now that you two are incapacitated, Rita and I are going to have to do the heavy work. How much more of this can I take? What more do I have to take responsibility for? It's not enough that your father committed suicide, and that weasel Brennan may have put us into bankruptcy, and gotten himself killed, which puts us all under suspicion, but you two have to fight. Look at yourselves! What the hell were you fighting about?"

CJ and Frank were struck by the intensity of their mother's anger. She'd always had a temper, but this was a side of her they'd never seen.

When neither one spoke, Mary grabbed CJ's shirt, bunched it under his chin, pushed him back into the chair, and screamed, "Answer me!"

CJ shrunk into himself, desperately wanting to get away, but fearful of moving, afraid he'd provoke his mother to further violence.

Frank enjoyed the brief moment. He hoped his mother would wind up and belt his brother in the other eye. His half-brother, he corrected himself, CJ, his mother's favorite son. So sensitive, Frank sneered. He wasn't the least bit sorry that he'd pummeled CJ. He just couldn't believe his own bad luck when he tripped over the bags of fertilizer in the back storeroom and fell on his hand. Recalling the excruciating pain as bolts of lightning shot up his arm, he reached over to cradle his wrist.

Mary abruptly let go of CJ's shirt, stepped back, and looked long and hard at both her sons. "I'll tell you what," she said, poised like a rattlesnake, "for the next week or so, you'll both take it easy. CJ, you'll cook the meals for Rita and Frank and me, and keep the house clean as best you can. Frank, you'll spend your time at the store, behind the register or in the office doing paperwork, whatever is needed most. *And if, if* I find there's been any trouble between you two…" her eyes shifted between them, "…you'll both end up in *body* casts!"

CJ and Frank didn't dare to speak or move. Mary was coiled to strike.

Then, as if two distinct personalities struggled for dominance, a strange looked passed over Mary's face. The winner of the battle dropped into the kitchen chair and stared at her hands.

Frank and CJ looked at each other, but neither one spoke.

CHAPTER 32

⚘

Friday 9:30 AM

It was dead.

Sam wondered if the suicide of Claudio Frazetta and the murder of Richard Brennan had frightened people away from Frazetta's Hardware Store because they believed that contact with anyone in the building would cast the evil eye in their direction. She had to admit that the Frazetta's had had a string of bad luck, and she wondered how people got through such trying times. One eyebrow lifted. *Maybe by knocking someone off?*

Nick had risen that morning before Sam was able to leave him an innocuous note and slip out of the house for her trip to Manchester and, maybe, encounters with one, or all four, of the Frazettas. Trapped, she cooked Nick a full breakfast. He lingered over his Dunkin' Donuts coffee while fondling his favorite mug, the moose mug with the hairline crack down the lip, and rambled on about a variety of topics: the orders lined up at his printing shop, the upcoming yard work—and would she please pick up bug bags so he could set them out by the raspberry bushes—, about calling his friend, John Tatone, for a day's hike, about the storm they'd just had, correctly predicted on the news and by Sam's throbbing ankle, and on, and on, until Sam had been ready to scream. He took a long hot shower, shaved, and dressed himself with glacial precision and, before leaving the house for work, made sure Sam had everything she needed. Frustrated at the pace at which he'd moved, and loving him for his sensitivity to her needs, she had surprised Nick with a long good-bye kiss at the doorway, thankful he was leaving and, at the same time, feeling guilty that she wanted him to leave, although she enjoyed the kiss. He had wonderfully soft lips.

The earthy smell of fertilizers and peat moss, from the large bags stacked by the entrance of Frazetta's Hardware Store, followed Sam into the building. Her eyes surveyed the place in one wide sweep. There was one main aisle, running the length of the store from front to back, with intersecting side aisles comprised of tall shelving. Signs at the ends of each side aisle identified the products to be found there. The wall to the left held the checkout counter. The front of the store was crowded with piles of small bags of grass seeds and fertilizers. Numerous racks held packages of flower and vegetable seeds, small garden tools, and gloves.

It was eerily quiet in the store, for the middle of a spring morning. Maybe the bulk of the hardware business came on Saturday and Sunday with the weekend warriors. Sam wondered which, if any, of the Frazettas would be here today. She'd gotten a thumbnail description of the four from her mother, and thought she'd probably recognize them. Frank would be more easily identified; she assumed he'd have some kind of splint on his wrist.

Sam wondered again if one of the Frazettas could have been so angry over the suicide of the elder Claudio, brought on by their embezzling accountant, that one or more of them would have taken a gun and shot the man to death. She tugged at the neck of her sweatshirt. She didn't dismiss the possibility that the murder was a family affair.

Then there was Quinn. Love propelled many a mild mannered man into acts of unspeakable violence. What could the loss of Lynda Johanssen have done to a big, bad, tattooed, lovesick biker?

The thought also crossed Sam's mind that if Brennan gambled, maybe he owed the wrong people too much money. *Money, the root of all evil. Well, not money per se*, she thought, *but what people will do to get it.*

Her thoughts were disturbed when two small boys bumped against the outside of the glass doors behind her. She turned to see the mother in harried pursuit. The young woman grabbed the children's wrists roughly, admonishing them about running through the parking lot without her. Pushing the door open with her hip, the woman entered the store, dragging the resisting kids with her, still scolding them roundly. Her long hair looked as if she had taken an eggbeater to it.

Every time Sam saw a parent struggling with a child, or even worse, a passel of them, relief washed over her. She was glad her girls were adults. She loved all the years when they were little, loved the sweet smell of their infant necks, the warmness of their little bodies against her chest, the wonder of their discovery of the world when everything was wondrous and new, and their trusting eyes as they looked to her for guidance, but there were times. She imagined that raising boys was very different, all that walking testosterone. Sam glanced at the young woman once again. Yes, taking very young children into public places was like pitting your David strength against their Goliath enthusiasms. You won, but sometimes you wondered if it was worth the effort.

Sam once again thought of the expression that drove her to the brink: a working mother. A mother *is* a working woman! In a government survey, the statistics were clear. The most stressful *job* in the country was the role of home-maker. A bit of responsibility there, she scowled, like having the lives of other human beings in your hands twenty-four/seven.

Okay, get off your soapbox. No one wants to hear it. Even though she knew, if the subject arose in the future, she would once again and forever put in her two cents worth.

Then she wondered where the expression 'two cents worth' came from.

She refocused her wandering mind, shifted her shoulders, and started slowly down the center aisle, tugging once more at the neck of the lime green US BOYS sweatshirt she had pulled out of Sadie's bag of clothes for the Salvation Army. She had attached a ten-dollar donation to the bag. She loved the color, but the sweatshirt was too tight against her throat. When she got home, the pinking shears would take care of that.

She stepped into a side aisle as the two boys barreled down the center of the store whooping like wild Huns, their mother in pursuit. At the opposite end of her aisle, Sam noticed a big man pass by, wearing a wrist splint and moving toward the front of the store. It had to be Frank Frazetta! Her heart took a leap, and that funny tingle started in her stomach. The flutterbys.

She needed time to calm down and think about her approach. And, in case there were elevated mirrors monitoring her progress, she feigned casualness as she wandered toward the back of the store. She stopped to examine a ratchet-type rubber-handled screwdriver, the kind that, with small twists of the wrist, got into tight corners—like the tight corners into which she often managed to get herself. Maybe she should carry one of these things in a holster on her hip. $5.95. Not bad.

As one of the squealing boys bounced around the corner and into her leg and then careened off down the aisle, Sam noticed the open door on the back wall and the sign above it—EMPLOYEES ONLY. Like a bee to honey, how could she resist? She discreetly scanned the ceiling—no mirror or camera that she could see pointing in her direction—and checked both ends of the aisle. Then, whistling, she meandered by the open office door, surely appearing as carefree as Tom Sawyer after he perpetrated one of the slickest cons in fiction by persuading Ben Rogers to paint Aunt Polly's fence so he could take off for greener pastures.

Sam's eyes swept the office—a metal desk, a chair…. But then she was past. She needed more time.

In the distance, a woman's voice reverberated through the store. "Steven! Cody!"

Sam looked ceilingward and said, "Goddess, bless her."

That's when she decided.

With one last furtive look around, she backed up and stepped into the office. Like a volcano about to erupt, the heat stirred in her chest and began to creep, lava-like, up toward her throat. She flapped her sweatshirt front and, with her bottom lip pulled in, blew a cooling stream of air down toward her chest.

I am not menopausal!

Still flapping, she quickly surveyed the small room: no windows, clutter on top of the filing cabinets, on the metal desk—more clutter, a nameplate, and a metal tray containing windowed envelopes—*probably bills,* a beat up Morris chair against one wall, flickering fluorescent lights overhead, dead bugs. *Yuck.* But something seemed odd. What was it?

She stopped flapping. The heat had passed.

The voice came from behind her. "Are you lost?"

CHAPTER 33

❀

Friday 3:30

He had to stop thinking about her. But his heart wouldn't let her go.

He remembered a line from somewhere—a movie, his mother quoting a book, he couldn't remember—that struck a chord deep within. Something like: when life is more terrible than death, the truest valor is to want to live. He wasn't quite at the point where he didn't want to live, but he understood the pain embedded in that writer's mind.

Quinn glanced at the greased-covered clock on the cement wall. *Another hour and I'm out of here,* he thought. He worked mechanically, almost without thought, as he'd done for the past two years, but the Harley would be perfect when he got through with it.

In the background he could hear the other guys cussing, bragging about the broads they had conquered and would in the future, about cars and speed, and about their plans for the upcoming weekend.

Quinn wasn't in the mood. He hadn't been in the mood for a long time. He wanted his own place where he could customize bikes, working alone or, maybe, with one other guy who wouldn't blabber all the time. Someday, maybe. At least it was something to look forward to, as long as the police didn't come sniffing around because of that scumbag Brennan's death. But why would they? His beef with Brennan had erupted over more than two years ago and, as far as anyone knew, he was over it. He'd never mentioned Brennan to his buddies or associated with him in public, although he did speak to him once in a while at the Pigpen, but that was the extent of it, and he made sure it appeared friendly to anyone watching. He had harbored his hatred, keeping it a secret thing, imprisoned inside his heart, fully fed and growing through his daily trips to his dark dungeon of pain.

Forty-five minutes to quitting time, then the weekend.

Tonight he'd have a few beers, read his motorcycle magazine, and go to bed early. Saturday, he'd help his mother with a few chores—the back window, through which the next door neighbor's seven year old had hit a home run, needed new glass, and the railing on the cellar stairway needed to be secured. He didn't want his mother tumbling down the steps. Then, he would be off to his regular Saturday night at the Pigpen. He'd sleep late Sunday morning, only to rise, maybe watch the Red Sox, and think about the midnight delivery. Those nocturnal visits were the only way he could ease his pain.

He wiped the sweat from his forehead, as his big hands moved over the Harley before him.

"Hey, Quinn," Rod called to him. "Going to the Pigpen tomorrow night?"

"Where else would I go?" he growled.

Rod ambled over, wiping his hands on a greasy rag. "Heard anymore about Brennan? About who killed the guy?"

Scotty looked up from the wheels he was adjusting. "Yeah, have they caught the guy?"

"How should I know?" Quinn responded. "I didn't know him any better than you did."

"Yeah," Rod said, "But you went out with Lynda before Brennan did. Thought you two might have had a few words."

"Yeah," Scotty laughed. "Thought you might have hired a hit man to take care of the creep after he stole your girl and then…."

His voice trailed off as Quinn spun on him, the muscles knotted in his huge arms, his eyes hard, cold and dark as black onyx, his beard bristling under a tightening jaw. As Quinn lifted a lip, the one gold tooth glinted in the afternoon light. "Don't even think about going there."

"Hey, just kidding. Sorry man." They both backed off.

When Quinn turned back to his work, Scotty mumbled to his buddy, "Christ! Whenever we mention that accident, he turns meaner than a junk yard dog with glass up his ass."

CHAPTER 34

❀

Friday 4:00 PM

After she had explained to Mary Frazetta that she was looking for a clerk—at first, Mary had not been convinced—and wishing she had bought that screwdriver for tight spots, Sam had finally eased out of the touchy situation by sliding into a half-truth. She was Elizabeth Blackwell's daughter, and Elizabeth was hoping that she and Mary could get together. Elizabeth hadn't been able to reach Mary by phone and she didn't like talking into an answering machine so, since Sam was in the neighborhood, she thought she'd stop by and see if she could leave a message at the store to let Mary know that Elizabeth was trying to reach her.

On the drive home, Sam replayed the scenario over and over in her head. She felt that Mary Frazetta had believed her and she was pleased with herself. She had extricated herself from that sticky wicket quite cleverly. She thought she was getting pretty good at this sort of thing.

A voice in her head said, 'Don't congratulate yourself on fibbing.' Duly chastened, she shifted in the seat, disappointed that nothing of import had come from her trip. Yet, just out of reach, there was something…

Upon arriving home, the first thing Sam did was to whip out the pinking shears and cut the band off the neck of her lime green sweatshirt. She slipped it back on. Much better. Maybe she'd start a fashion trend.

Then, she moved on to the business at hand.

As she proceeded to dress herself, a delicious tingle mingled with apprehension washed over her. She was out of her mind to even think about doing this. But, as the English war cry went, 'For God and country.' Although she did think 'Goddess.'

When she finished dressing and stood before the full-length mirror on the back of the bedroom door, she barely recognized herself: a strip of rawhide tied around the black curly wig, ragg socks crammed into her bra under Sadie's tight tee shirt, a leather vest, soiled jeans shredded at the knees, high black boots, and a face-full of makeup to rival Tammy Faye Baker.

She felt like a stuffed sausage with too many splits. But then, Queen Latifah and China were full-bodied women. Not that she was in their league, but she was passable. *In a dimly lit bar. With thick smoke. And myopic bikers.* She hoped that Quinn was near-sighted.

She turned sideways and sucked in her belly. Then sucked again. Defeated, she sighed and let it all hang out. At that point, Sam decided that she defied the scientific axiom that matter contains more space than solidity. If that were true, she'd be able to compress her body into a much thinner version of herself.

What the hell, she thought, as she stripped. *This is as good as it's going to get.*

She stashed the wig, boots, clothes, and makeup in her Christmas box that was tucked in the back of her closet next to the Mother's Day card and the five magnets she had bought at the Paper Patch. More than once she'd been relieved that she and Nick had separate closets. With a sigh, she retired to the bathroom to scrub the color off her face.

Stretched out on the sun porch couch, she chewed on her knuckle. Now—what to tell Nick? It wasn't like she could say to her husband—honey, I'm going to the Pigpen, dressed as a biker babe, and I hope Quinn Stevens is there so I can find out if he's a murderer. That wasn't going to work. She didn't want to lie to her husband, but maybe she could come up with a half-truth.

What can I tell him?

She stared up at the Siamese wooden angel hanging from the ceiling above the two rockers in the corner. It stirred slightly, as if in response. She drummed her fingers on her chest and wriggled her toes. She scowled at her feet, at the ragg socks turned inside out so the seams wouldn't irritate her toes. She scratched the center of her chest. She'd come up with something. She was good at that.

Her mind drifted to the code.

One, one, two, three…

It was hauntingly familiar. Like she should know it as well as her own name. It had to have been a message from the dying man. Bankes was so sure. Even the police thought there might be something to it. Why else would they have relayed the message through Charlie to suggest that she work on it?

Once again her mind was pulled toward the back yard. The bare tree branches wavered slightly against a pewter sky. The answer was in her back yard, she was sure of it. But she wouldn't tell the police that. They already thought she resided on the fringe of lunacy—she sniffed—but not so far into that wild realm that they wouldn't discreetly ask for her help. Charlie understood her. They'd been close since first grade, when she'd shared her lunches with her hungry friend. He knew about her mental movie screen, how she saw pictures in her mind. Her visions.

Well, somehow, since her visions about this code were riveted in her backyard, on the trees and plants, the answer lay there. She stretched her arms over her head, locked her hands behind her neck. She had to set aside her frustration and relax. The answer would come...

Sam finished the last bite of chop suey—made with soy scramble—and wiped her lips with a paper napkin. She looked over the pine table at Nick, braced herself, and said, "Nick. Have you heard about that mystery club that meets once a month in Manchester?"

"Nope," Nick said, sopping up the last of the tomato sauce on his plate with a piece of garlic-onion bread. "What's a mystery club? Do they discuss mysteries?"

"No. They invite experts to speak on their area of expertise on metaphysical subjects like ghost hauntings, ESP, psychometry, that sort of stuff. They're meeting tomorrow night at midnight."

Nick finished off his bread and wiped his mouth on his napkin. "Really? Seems like an odd time for a meeting."

"Well, it *is* a mystery club. Maybe the witching hour adds ambience to their meetings. I thought maybe I'd check it out."

His eyebrows went up. "You plan on attending?"

"I'm thinking about it. I might ride up, see where the meeting is held and how many people attend. If it looks okay, I might go in and listen to the lecture and, if it looks promising, contact the president to see if they'd be interested in having me as a speaker. It helps sell books, you know."

She *might* ride up.

"Maybe I should go with you," Nick offered. "I don't like the idea of you riding around at midnight by yourself."

"Come on, Nick. I'm a big girl."

She wondered if she was, planning on dressing up like it was Halloween and walking into the Pigpen on a Saturday night to confront a roomful of hard drinking men—and women. She thought about the tee shirt hidden in the Christmas box in her closet. She hoped its message—TOO MUCH GIRL FOR YOU—wouldn't provoke sexual responses from the patrons of the Pigpen. It would be very dark, and Nick was always telling her she looked at least ten years younger, and some men did like buxom women. She raised an eyebrow as she thought that that was a nice word for the thirty extra pounds she was carrying around.

"If I go, I'll take the cell phone," she said, looking down at the table as she straightened her soiled silverware. "Most of the streets in Manchester are well lit, and I'm not going to get out of the car unless the place looks safe."

If I go, Sam added to herself.

She allowed her eyes to drift back to Nick. "And besides, you're going hiking with Dr. John. And you said that, when you get back, you want to start watching *Lonesome Dove* over the weekend. So, if I go out, you won't be interrupted. Watching those videos will take you Saturday night and into Sunday, the movie's so long. You know I don't care for westerns. I was going to find something else to do anyway."

After cleaning up the supper dishes, and when Nick would be watching *Lonesome Dove*, she planned to slip the biker outfit into the trunk of her Honda. Around 10:30, she'd start the drive to Manchester, then change her mind, and head to the Pigpen, and park on a secluded back street. In the car, she'd slip into her biker babe outfit, apply her makeup and tease her wig. Considering the confines of the Honda, all of this ought to be a gymnastic challenge. Then she'd make her way through the woods behind the bar. Later, when she'd left the Pigpen, she would return to the car, change back into her sweats, and arrive home in the early morning. If Nick were as predictable as ever, he'd be snoring on the couch, with the television still going, or sound asleep in bed.

Hopefully.

All in all, it seemed like a good plan.

Sam swallowed dryly and smiled at her husband over the supper table.

"I hear the wheels spinning, Sam," Nick said, the crease between his dark brows deepening. "Why is it that I don't quite trust your intentions? It's like there are layers of meanings beneath your words."

"Layers?" She saucered her eyes and tried to look innocent. "Don't be silly, honey. There's only one layer, and it's really thin."

CHAPTER 35

❦

SATURDAY 10:45 P.M.

Ignatius "Iggy" Weathers was not a particularly imaginative man, but he'd had one moment of brilliant clarity in his life. However, naming his establishment "Iggy's" was not that one moment—he'd named the place after himself. The neon sign over his bar had pulsated his name in blood red letters for seventeen years. What he could not have foreseen, those many years ago, was what a few teenagers with more imaginative minds would do to unknowingly make Iggy's Den a destination.

On that spring night, fourteen years back, Willie Claxton and Tom Melvin had clambered up the back wall of the cinder block bar, snuck across the flat roof to the gaudy neon sign and duct-taped a large plywood P—which they'd cut out in woodworking shop—to the left of Iggy's name. Hence, the boys became legend and a tradition was born. For the first few years, Iggy had angrily removed the offending P, only to find a duplicate duct-taped to his sign a few nights later.

Iggy's moment of revelation had occurred in the fourth year of the legend, on an exceptionally hot spring day, when he was sweating on the roof of his bar attempting to extricate the latest addition from yards of duct tape. A beat-up Chevy Malibu had slowed and the driver had yelled out his window, "Hey, Iggy, love your P!" He'd laughed and taken off, his tires kicking up a spittle of pebbles and dust.

It was then, standing on the roof with his knife and scissors in hand, that Iggy had assessed the financial benefits the notoriety of the P had brought to his establishment. In that moment of enlightenment, he'd decided to leave the P attached to his sign.

PIGGY'S DEN. It had a certain ring.

In fact, as he'd stood in the sunshine that day, wiping his forehead with the back of his hand and staring at the sign, Iggy had become so enamored with the sound of PIGGY'S DEN that another idea had struck him. Suddenly he'd felt like Moses, exultant on the mountaintop, receiving the commandments that would alter the world. Iggy would redecorate his bar.

To the dismay of the more righteous Georgetown residents, he eventually did just that.

Over the ensuing fourteen years, not wanting to appear too receptive to the high school prank, and as a public gesture of disapproval, Iggy would complain to the police. Publick Occurrences, the town's newspaper, would make mention of the vandalism in the police log. The letter P would stay where it was and that would be the end of it until the following spring when the next graduating class would try to outdo their predecessors.

Each year, during those first few weeks of spring, the traffic down Wattles Road increased. Some drivers openly gawked and made lewd comments about the P on the pulsating red sign, others tossed the letter a casual glance as if they weren't really interested, while the more conservative cranky New Hampshirites appeared to stare straight ahead while their eyes slid surreptitiously toward the unkempt building where a six-foot-high pair of dancing pink piglets bracketed the doorway.

Somewhere down the line, the locals took to calling Iggy's Den the Pigpen.

Happily, this year's senior class had done its job well. The old P had been ripped down and replaced with another in the shape of a generously endowed woman, her arms curled to her waist, and her ample attributes scantily covered in sparkling sequins. Strands of purple fringe dangled from sensitive points.

The Pigpen was once again anointed.

Trussed up like a roasted piglet, Sam picked her way through the snowy woods behind the bar. *All I need is an apple in my mouth,* she thought grumpily.

It was ten o'clock, Saturday night. She had pulled her Honda into an abandoned dirt drive on a little-used back road that ran parallel to Wattles Road. She hoped no one would see it. She'd have a hard time explaining this one to Nick.

Gee, honey, I got lost driving the five miles from our house to Route 125 so I parked my car that had a full tank of gas on that side road so I could walk to find help and the only place that was open was the Pigpen. I didn't call on the cell phone because there was no signal.

That was about the thinnest layer she'd ever thought up. The obvious solution to this possible problem was, don't get caught.

An owl hooted somewhere in the tangle of branches above her. A lacework of white drifted to the snow-blotched ground. Some little critter rustled the bushes behind her. She hoped it was a little critter. Maybe this wasn't such a good idea after all.

Sam tugged at the ragg sock-stuffed bra that dug into the flesh under her breasts. She never could figure out how women could wear these things. Images of the pencil-thin models in Sadie's Victoria's Secret catalogs popped into her mind. Breasts pushed up and in like ripe melons. She sniffed. Once the camera clicked, they probably ripped the torture hammocks off and donned oversized sweatshirts.

A slight breeze whispered through the woods, nudging snowflakes off branches and leaves. Tendrils of mist drifted up from the carpet of snow and swirled around her ankles. The night air was damp, penetrating, and smelled of fecund matter that nourished the undergrowth and its abundance of living things. Creepy crawly living things. Sam's eyes cut to the wet white-patterned floor of the woods. Things with slimy green antennae, beady red eyes. Probably long pointed stingers.

She shivered.

Trying to convince herself there was nothing here in the dark that wasn't present in the light of day, she moved a bit faster, pushing branches out of her way. A twig caught in her wig, pulling it askew. She adjusted the wig as she kept forward, feeling the dampness on the nylon fibers under her fingers.

Slipping on the spongy ground down a small embankment, she came upon the small stream that meandered behind the Pigpen. A few feet to her left a rotted log formed a natural, if unstable, bridge. All she needed was to fall into the icy water and show up at the Pigpen bruised, bloody and wet. She managed a weak laugh. She'd probably fit right in. As she crossed the spongy log, she fanned the air with her arms to keep her balance.

Safely on the other side, she stepped into a depression in the mushy earth before scampering up the slippery slope and back into the thick of the white woods. Her boots squished as she worked her way through the underbrush. Water had seeped through the seam of Sadie's old boots and now her feet were wet and coated with a muddy layer of snow.

Fine. Just fine!

Uncertainty and fear joined forces and propelled her forward. Suddenly she was moving faster and faster, her arms thrashing at the thin switches of brambles and bushes that reached from out of deep shadows to grab at her legs. Her mind conjured up memories of every child's cellar monster who waited under the stairs for a shot at fresh flesh. Seconds seemed like long minutes as the fear grew in her fertile mind. She was waiting for the icy grip of a skeletal hand around her ankle, pulling her down into the tomb of the earth. Shades of *Carrie.*

With her heart thumping wildly, finally, up ahead, pulsating behind the trees, Sam could see the reddish glow of the Pigpen's neon sign. With more than a modicum of relief, she clawed up the embankment behind the bar and scurried between a rusted green dumpster and the cinder block wall. Her eyes darted to each side of the metal container. A great sigh escaped her. She was alone.

She fell against the cold wall to catch her breath, to slow the thumping in her chest. Against her back, the building seemed to throb as if it contained the heart of an angry beast.

CHAPTER 36

SATURDAY 11:00 P.M.

Hunched over his Bud, Quinn Stevens glanced up at the mirror that spanned the wall behind the bar. She stood just inside the entrance, hesitating, a woman with a mass of curly black hair and a black leather vest, squeezed into an eye-opening white tee shirt that read: TOO MUCH GIRL FOR YOU. Quinn automatically took inventory. Late thirties, early forties maybe, overweight, but with all the right curves. She was a lot of woman. Not beautiful, but sort of sexy in an unaffected kind of way. She seemed to be working too hard at making a casual entrance, which was impossible because everyone made an entrance into the Pigpen. Iggy's idea of grandeur was the eight-foot wide platform that led two steps down into the bar.

Quinn frowned into the mirror. The woman looked familiar. He couldn't quite place where he'd seen her. He scratched at his beard, rested his chin in one hand. Where had he seen her before? Under all that hair, the dark glasses, and makeup, she could have been his own mother and he wouldn't have recognized her, but there was something about the mouth, the curve of the chin, the way she stood. He wondered what she was hiding. Not that it made any difference. Everyone had a story.

He closed his eyes and slugged back a mouthful of Bud.

Sam stopped inside the doorway of the Pigpen, cold, wet, and uncertain. She needed to get her bearings, figure out what to do next. She resisted the impulse to tug at the damn bra.

Smoke was thick, permeating. The place was awash in leather and bandanas, beards and tattoos, and body odor. Her ears rang with competing sounds. Country music boomed from a jukebox somewhere in the back. An argument was in full swing around one of the two pool tables to her left. A couple in jeans and tee shirts jostled her from behind, nearly knocking her down the steps into the pen.

She bit at her bottom lip and looked around for a vacant seat. She sat at one of the few unoccupied tables clustered to her right, and glanced around nervously. She'd never been here before, but stories about the fabled bar ran rampant through her town.

Iggy had followed his bliss and decorated the interior walls of his bar with garishly painted cutouts of sows and hogs riding motorcycles, smoking cigarettes and drinking beer, and industriously engaged in porcine-reproducing acts. Small lights mounted beneath the porkers cast raggedy shadows on the ceiling. As told during a newspaper interview, Iggy had seen paintings lit that way on a TV cop show when the perp was chased into a museum. But those paintings were lit from the top. Iggy had mounted the lights underneath his artwork. He felt it displayed his personal touch of creativity. It also kept the stained and matted rug in the shadows, a fact he failed to mention to the reporter. All in all, Iggy felt that the lighting added a little class to his joint.

Sam glanced at the sign hanging over the long bar at the back of the room, the letters burned into the rough wood: THE TROUGH. Mounted over the racks of glasses was a Budweiser sign. The neon W in Budweiser flickered off and on. Sam could imagine the zzzt zzzt sound, like the horseflies that buzzed around her head on one of her infrequent exercise walks around the Loop. Images of the war in Iraq flashed across the television screen. The volume was either turned down or drowned out by the cacophony of noises bouncing off the walls. No one was watching it.

She wiggled her toes. Her feet were wet and cramped in Sadie's old boots. Her bra had a death grip on her chest. Her lungs felt thick with smoke. By now, she probably smelled like a dirty ashtray. Suddenly she felt claustrophobic. She desperately wanted to leave the Pigpen, but Hannibal and Emmaline were counting on her. And Charlie had asked for her help in deciphering that code. She couldn't let her friends down, and she was rather intrigued by the enigmatic tapping that Richard Brennan had left as his last message to this world.

Everything will be okay, she told herself. *Just be calm. Think of this as an adventure to tell my grandchildren—in about fifty years. By then, Nick will probably forgive me for fibbing to him. If I get caught.*

Fibbing.

Frown lines bracketed the bridge of her nose as she stared at the black plastic ashtray in front of her, momentarily unaware of the moving mass of humanity around her. Why did that word seem important?

CHAPTER 37

❀

SATURDAY 11:10 P.M.

The redhead who just walked through the door was gorgeous. Like every man in the bar, Quinn's eyes swept over the sweater that hung from her breasts and down the long blue-jeaned legs, but Quinn took no pleasure in women anymore. He'd been celibate for over two years. Not that he'd tell his buddies, but he hadn't been able to touch a woman since…

He felt the familiar stab in his heart.

Elbowing his buddy, he said in his slow honeyed voice, "Hey, asshole. Slide the pretzels over here. You going to chow them all down?"

Quinn had pulled on his dirty jeans, the ones he kept for appearances at the Pigpen. He wasn't about to make an entrance into this dive washed and polished like a ten year old in an Easter pageant. He had an image to uphold.

He glanced at the redhead again. Another woman who looked familiar. He shook his head. He'd been celibate too long.

Rita stood in the doorway of the Pigpen, her eyes searching through the milling bodies. She was a few minutes late and wondered if Randy Sturgis and his short-legged friend had already arrived. She couldn't see them anywhere, although the place was now so crowded it was hard to tell.

What the hell did they want from her? Her eyes narrowed. Like she didn't know. From the lascivious leers in the aisle of the hardware store Thursday morning, she had a pretty good idea. If it was just their hormones talking, that was one thing. But if they knew things that could cause trouble, that was another story. She'd do what she had to do, as she had always done, to protect her family from further pain and disgrace. And that was the only reason she had agreed to meet those two low lives here. She would take care of this problem. Somehow.

Suddenly, she felt very tired. The events of the last few weeks decided to take this moment to come crashing down on her like an avalanche. She felt overtaken with emotion and fear and crushed under uncertainty about the future of her mother and her two brothers and herself.

Rita pushed her way through the crowd and sat on the one available seat at the end of the bar. She ordered a Coors from the grinning bartender, took a sip, set her glass down, and lowered her head to massage the back of her neck. The noise decibel seemed to inch higher and higher, reverberating in her ears. She didn't know if she could deal with this now. She wanted to be whisked away to a tropical island like St. Lucia, lay on the silky white sand, and sip on those fruit drinks with the little brightly colored paper umbrellas.

Rita was startled out of her thoughts by a loud voice in her ear. "Hey, babe. Can I buy you a beer?"

The voice belonged to a skinny guy wearing a leather jacket, jeans, and a black belt in which was set a silver skull buckle with glittering ruby eyes. His sandy hair was oiled back into a skimpy ponytail.

Rita's nose wrinkled as she lifted one eyebrow. "Obviously, I already have a beer." The man smelled awful.

"My name's Al and I'd like to buy you the next one," Al said, his lids lowered to bedroom level. His breath was heavy with chili and onions. "A woman like you shouldn't sit alone."

Rita felt anger like a hot poker in her chest. She didn't need this. "Get lost!" she blurted out.

"Come on now, you don't mean that," he oozed, leaning closer. "You look like a woman who'd enjoy a good time, and I'm just the man who can give it to you." Al shifted on his skinny legs and hooked his thumbs in his belt, his long fingers pointed at his groin.

Rita steeled herself. "I guess you didn't get my drift. Read my lips," she said slowly. "Get lost."

Al grabbed her wrist in a surprisingly iron grip. "Listen, you bitch…"

She winced, but wasn't about to show any pain. Her eyes darted around for a weapon.

"Something wrong here?"

A hush moved out over the crowd radially. A space opened up.

Rita looked up at the sound of the menacingly low, but somehow mellifluous voice. A mountainous man with a black curly beard stood there, his thick tattooed arms hanging loosely by his sides, his head tilted, friendly-like, his eyes fixed on Al.

Al released her wrist, took a step back. "No, man. Ah, we was just having a friendly conversation."

Quinn nodded. "I see. Well, why don't you just take your friendly conversation over there to the pool tables where someone might really appreciate it."

"Sure, sure," Al said, backing away. He retreated toward the pool tables, scowling and glancing about as if to assess the number of witnesses to the ego bashing he'd just received. A few laughs and crude remarks followed him. When it was obvious a fight had been averted—to the disappointment of many—the noise level rose once again and things fell back to normal.

Rita stared into the biker's dark eyes. She wondered if one mean biker had been replaced by an even more dangerous one.

When the noise level in the Pigpen dropped to sepulchral level, Sam realized something was going on.

Through slivers of space, she glimpsed some commotion at the bar between the redhead and the skinny guy with the ponytail. She wasn't about to stand by and miss the action while the redheaded damsel was saved by the big-guy-to-the-rescue so, casting caution to the wind, she climbed up on her wobbly chair to peer over the heads of the quick-frozen crowd. Although she couldn't hear the actual words spoken between Ponytail and Quinn, she got the gist of the problem from the body language of the threesome at the Trough. What she didn't know was if Quinn was moving in on the redhead for his own purposes.

The redhead looked familiar.

Safely back in her chair, Sam flipped through the files in her memory cabinet, starting with the A's. She stopped when she got to F.

Oh, my God!

It finally sunk in. The redhead was Rita Frazetta. Both Charlie and Sam's mother had described the Frazetta family to her. Plus, there was that fuzzy photo in the newspaper.

How lucky can I be? Two suspects in the same place on the same night I chose to be here?

She ran her tongue over her dry front teeth while fiddling with the plastic ashtray on the table before her. She could barely hear her own thoughts over the roar in the room. She never liked loud noises and she fought to find a quiet place in her mind to think.

Is there a connection between Rita and Quinn? Or is it a coincidence they're both here tonight? What are the odds of that happening?

Sam recalled an old saying: many tributes are laid at the feet of the great god Coincidence but, if one goes back far enough, coincidence becomes inevitable.

"What'll you have?"

Startled, Sam looked up. "Excuse me?"

"Whaddya want?"

Pressed against the table was a weary-looking woman whose lined face seemed pasted in a cloud of bleached hair, teased in the old style of the Country-Western singers. She held a round plastic tray in one hand and an order pad and pen pressed on its surface with the other hand. The nail on her pinky finger was broken to the quick.

Sam winced. "Oh, um, ah, a beer."

"What kind?"

"Oh, whatever." Sam had no idea. She hated beer.

The waitress rolled her eyes as if to say it takes all kinds, then turned away and pushed back through the crowd toward the bar.

But Sam was too busy thinking to notice the eye roll. She arched her neck toward the crowded pool table area where Ponytail had scurried, wondering. She needed to talk to the guy. Obviously he was not a fan of Quinn Stevens now, not after he'd been embarrassed by the man in front of a roomful of roiling testosterone. And he probably harbored enough resentment, because of the perceived loss of his manhood that, if he knew anything about Quinn, or perhaps Quinn and Rita as a twosome, he would talk.

After the waitress returned with a Coors, Sam made up her mind. She would have to draw and draw hard upon her high school play acting skills. She reminded herself that she'd had the lead role in *Good-Bye My Fancy* and got a standing ovation at the final curtain. Surely she could carry off this little charade. That's if this final curtain didn't fall on a stuffed sausage with a knife in her gut.

For Hannibal and country, she thought, swallowing hard.

She rose, patted at her black wig, tugged at the bra strap over her left shoulder, then moved through the smoking, yelling, badgering, laughing, pushing, swearing, beer-swilling mass of sweating bodies toward the pool table area.

Slouched against the far wall, she saw him. Ponytail. Wearing a scowl that would frighten a posturing politician into a blubbering idiot. The scowl almost deterred her.

But she gathered her gumption and brushed past him, grimacing as she picked up an offensive odor. What was it? Chili, onions, and something else…God! the guy had B.O.! An eye-watering combination not to be found in any bottle on the supermarket shelf, unless it was labeled "bug repellent, toxic, do not consume". Not that the guy's odor was that noticeable in this place, but it would have won the Pigpen Smelliest Patron award. Girding herself, she turned back and coyly, she thought, pulled at one of the black locks that fell over her shoulder. "You look familiar," she said.

Oh, my God. What a weak line.

Ponytail just looked at her. Sam realized he hadn't heard her.

"Don't I know you?" she practically yelled as she blinked false black eyelashes and hoisted her chest an inch higher. If the damn bra didn't choke the life out of her, Ponytail's chili flavored B.O. would do the trick. Between that and the cigarette smoke, Sam was about comatose.

The guy's scowl faded as he looked Sam up and down. His gaze ended on her chest. As his eyes took in the rolling message, he smiled and said to her breasts, "Would you like to? Because, believe me, baby, you're not too much girl for me."

Sam cringed at her choice of Sadie's tee shirts, but it was too late to worry about that now. At least the guy was acting interested in her, even though she was second choice after Rita. Ponytail seemed willing to anchor his ship at any port in a storm.

Sam thought she smiled. She wasn't sure. "Actually, I think that big guy at the bar is an asshole." She winced at the use of the word. "He must think he's God's gift to women."

"You're right there, baby. I could've taken him easy, but didn't want to start trouble and get thrown outta here for nothin'."

"I could see that. He's all talk and no action."

"Right again." Ponytail hooked his thumbs over his black belt; his fingers curved around a silver skull buckle whose glittering ruby eyes seemed filled with malice, as if they contained prescient knowledge of Sam's fall into the depths of depravity. "But if you're lookin' for a man of action, you've found him." His close-set eyes bored into her like a vulture's focused stare as it circled over its dying prey.

What I'm looking for is information, and for God's sake, take a shower and brush your teeth, is what Sam wanted to say to him. She wondered what she had gotten herself into, but she was in so deep now, she had to swim or else sink.

"My name's Al. What's yours?"

"Alice." It just slipped out. Sam had no idea where that name came from—actually it was an easy slip from Al to Alice—but now that it was hers for the evening, she would have to remember it. "Want to join me for a drink over at my table?" She could only wonder what Nick would think of her now.

"Sure, baby." He rubbed a long hand over his oily hair and wiped it on his jeans.

Seated at the small table, his knees touching Sam's, he signaled the fluffy-haired waitress and ordered a Miller.

"What's that guy's name anyway?" Sam nodded toward the Trough. "The one with the redhead, at the bar."

Al snuffed. "Quinn Stevens, the asshole. You named him right, lady."

With her finger, Sam caught a drop of condensation as it dribbled down the side of her beer glass. She had left the glass unattended while she'd lured Ponytail to the table so she wasn't about to take another sip. "Wasn't he involved with that murdered guy's girlfriend once? I thought I heard something like that somewhere?"

"Yeah. He went out with her before Brennan took her away from him." It was obvious he took pleasure in the telling. "Shows you what a man he is. Couldn't even keep his woman."

Al took his beer from the waitress, paid her, adding a quarter tip, then slugged down half his beer.

"Wouldn't surprise me if he had killed the guy, knowing his temper." He wiped the foam from his mouth, and belched.

In some countries, a burp was a sign of respect for a fine dinner but, here in the Pigpen, it was just plain disgusting. "He has a temper?" Sam asked.

"Well, you saw him up at the bar, didn't you? All I did was ask the broad if she wanted a drink and he barged over like all hell had broken loose. Probably wants to dick her himself."

Sam closed her eyes. She wasn't used to this kind of coarse language, and she wanted no further conversation or contact with Mr. Al of the greasy Ponytail. She steeled herself.

"Who's the redhead?"

"Don't know. Never saw her in here before, and I'm here every weekend. I woulda remembered her if she'd been here."

Sam pursed her lips. It would seem this was Rita's first visit to the Pigpen. Why? And it was curious that she ends up talking with Quinn. Did it have something to do with the homicide?

"But Quinn," Al continued, "he's in here every weekend. And a few days before that Brennan guy was killed, they had a fight."

"Really?" Sam leaned forward, then pulled back quickly. "What happened?"

"Well," Al said, moving his knee against Sam's, "it wasn't a knock-down-drag-out fight. But it could have been. They had words."

"What were the words?"

"Hey? Why you so interested in Quinn?"

Sam shifted in her seat, discreetly pulled her knees closer to her side of the tiny table. "He doesn't interest me at all. I'm just the curious type. I was just wondering if he got in trouble with the police because he had a fight with the dead guy just before he was murdered."

Al smiled. It wasn't pretty. "I hope so. That asshole probably did kill him." His look suggested he hoped that Quinn had.

He took another swig of beer and belched again. He set the beer glass down and looked at Sam with lecherous intent. With both elbows on the table and one hand massaging the other, he leaned toward her. "But enough about them." His chili-onion-beer breath and curdling B.O. penetrated the billows of smoke swirling around Sam's head. He reached to take her hand. "Let's talk about us, sweet thing."

Before flesh could contact flesh, Sam stood abruptly. "Would you excuse me for a moment. I have to go to the ladies room." She barreled off through the crowd.

CHAPTER 38

❁

Saturday, 11:25 P.M.

"Jesus Christ, Vinnie! You work in a goddamn gas station. I'd think you could keep this clunker running."

They were on a lonely side road and the battered Buick had managed to sputter on to the damp shoulder and now lay deader than a necrophiliac's date. Neither of them had a cell phone and, given the remote possibility that someone did come along this back road, the chances were nil that anyone would stop to pick up two men in the middle of the night.

A muffled voice came from under the hood. "Sorry, Randy. I'm a clerk, not a mechanic."

"Then why've you got your head in the goddamn engine if you don't know what's wrong?"

"Thought it might be something simple," he muttered.

"Yeah?" Randy shifted from one leg to the other, "Well, if you can't fix it and we can't hitch a ride, we're going to miss Rita. She isn't going to wait forever." He pulled open the car door and, under the dome light, peered at his wristwatch. "We're already a half-hour late."

"What?"

Randy backed out of the car, slammed the door shut.

"We're late!"

Vinnie straightened up, wiping his hands on a dirty rag. He looked up at the dark sky as if expecting another catastrophe, like rain, or plague, or the thundering hoofs of the Apocalyptic steeds, although he wouldn't have put it quite that way. He just knew that he'd let Randy down. A sense of impending doom fell heavy on his shoulders. He tried to shake it off, but it clung to the nape of his neck like a mass of ticks, digging in and sucking at his blood. He rubbed his neck. The feeling of failure seemed out of whack with the reality of the situation. He guessed it was the look on Randy's face that set him off. He was disappointed, too. Rita the Redhead. He didn't want to miss that show.

He hung his head and, with apology in his voice, said, "I can't fix the damn thing."

Vinnie shivered. He felt bone cold. He wished he had worn a jacket over his tee shirt, but who expected snow in May, for Christ's sake.

When Randy didn't respond, Vinnie stuck his flashlight under the driver's seat along with the greasy rag he'd been wiping his hands on, and stood quietly by the side of his car, his fingers working the sides of his short-legged jeans. He waited for Randy to say something.

Gray shadows draped the woods and mounds of snow where the sun's fingers had not reached. From the stonewall behind him, Vinnie caught the smell of pine needles and dead leaves rotting in the cracks.

Finally, he looked down at his feet. "I guess we'll have to thumb."

Vinnie shrunk under the look of anger boiling in Randy's eyes. He watched as Randy talked himself down.

"Okay. Forget it," Randy shrugged. "It happens." Randy glanced at his watch once more. "Let's get moving and hope that someone will pick up two guys thumbing in the middle of the night. "Fat chance," he groused, as he started over the road winding toward Route 125.

Vinnie once again looked into the heavens. A lace cookie moon hung in the night sky, its delicate light crumbling into the mouth of night.

Vinnie shuddered, and then fell in step next to Randy.

CHAPTER 39

❀

SATURDAY 11:30 P.M.

Sam's big intake of breath was a mistake.

Under cloying clouds of what smelled like a toxic mix of perfumes and hairspray and some sweet weedy substance, the fluorescent pink SOWS bathroom also reeked of sweat and jaw-tingling disinfectant. She could only imagine the odor in the HOGS bathroom.

She excused her way to the sink, wondering if that made her an anomaly. Maybe she should have just pushed through the knots of raucous women but, then again, she didn't relish the idea of nudging the wrong woman. Catfights weren't her specialty.

At the two sinks wedged between jutting wall studs, she splashed cold water on her cheeks, carefully avoiding her heavily mascared eyelashes and layered lipstick. With a paper towel from the wall dispenser, she patted her face dry and tried to figure out her next move.

As her hands hovered above the counter—she certainly wouldn't put her hands on it—she stared at her reflection in the cracked mirror, shaking her head slowly at the painted floozy who stared back at her. She couldn't believe what she looked like. She wouldn't have recognized herself.

What was she was doing here in the Pigpen? Was she nuts? What would Nick say? He was easy-going, but this? She poked her tongue at the corner of her mouth then compressed her lips into a thin line. Her daughters would be appalled, but her mother...she smiled...independent Elizabeth Blackwell, a woman half-a-century before her time, would probably cheer her on.

Sam winced as she tugged the edge of the bra out from under her left breast. By the time she got home and released herself from this straight jacket, around her chest she'd have dents as deep as the Marianna Trench.

Attempting to shut out the bits of conversation that would embarrass a seasoned lumberjack, Sam assessed her situation.

168

Problem number one: Ponytail. She had to avoid him for the rest of the evening. That probably wouldn't be too hard, given the number of bodies in the bar and, especially, if she stayed in the vicinity of Quinn Stevens. Maybe Ponytail would give up and look for greener pastures.

Problem number two: finding out what was going on with Quinn and Rita. Were they here separately or were they a twosome? Should she lurk on the edges of their conversations trying to pick up information, or make an attempt to talk with them? The mental image of the tattooed and bulging biceped biker, leering down at her while she tried to discreetly question him about the murder, gave her pause.

From the corner of her eye, she noticed two biker babes giving her the once over. Their breasts challenged the laces in their leather vests. Sam dug into her jeans and pulled out a tube of lipstick, and made a pretense of touching up her lips. She wasn't sure if they knew she was a phony, or if they had noticed her polite entry into the SOWS pen, or if they were wondering why a woman would come to the bathroom by herself. She gave a private sigh of relief when they pushed through the door and left.

As she wound the lipstick back into the tube, an idea popped into her head. It was lame, but it was worth a try. She just hoped Al the Ponytail wouldn't see her.

"Men! They're nothing but heartache."

Rita's head moved a bare fraction to look up at Sam, who was leaning against the Trough and talking at the mirror behind the bar. Sam's gaze remained fixed on the rack of glasses, as if she saw nothing but what was troubling her mind.

Rita returned to her beer and continued to roll the glass between her palms.

Well, that's not going to work, Sam thought. She sighed heavily for effect. No response.

Maybe I should try tears. She started to sniff and rub at her nose.

Rita shuffled her shoulders and looked the other way.

Zzzzt, Zzzzzt.

Sam glanced at the flickering 'W' in the Budweiser sign on the wall next to the muted television. Even above the din, it was loud enough to be an irritant. Sam frowned. How could the bartender stand that constant buzzing? It was like the sound of Nick's metronomic snoring when she was trying to get to sleep at night.

She snuffled again.

"Hey, don't let it bother you."

Sam swung toward Rita. "But don't you hate that sound?"

"What sound? What are you talking about?"

Suddenly, Sam realized that Rita was referring to her comments about men and not the buzzing sign. "Oh, right. Don't mind me." She stumbled around for the right words. "My mind, it's…it's so messed up these days. I just found my boyfriend in the back hall with another girl, the creep. And to think I trusted him all these years."

Rita nodded. "Trust is hard to come by these days." Her eyes dropped to the beer glass between her fingers.

"You can say that again." Sam paused. "You sound like a woman who knows," she added.

Rita worked her mouth but she didn't speak. Her red hair billowed over her shoulders in enviable curls.

In my next life, Sam thought, patting at her black wig. "Who's the big guy who came to your rescue?"

Rita looked at her with a hint of suspicion lining her brow.

"Oh," Sam scratched at her cheek, "I saw that skinny guy giving you a hard time."

Rita shook her mane. "I have no idea. I've never seen him before."

"I thought that big guy was going to come on to you, too."

"Yeah. So did I. But he didn't."

Sam could see Rita's mental wheels spinning. Obviously Rita was used to having men approach her—as Erin Brokovitch had said, "It's the boobs," and Rita certainly had them—and she most likely wondered why Quinn didn't make a play for her, like every other man who orbited her planet.

Sam wondered the same thing.

"So, do you want to blow this joint and get a cup of coffee somewhere?" Sam was really getting into this lingo.

Rita shook her head. "I'm tempted, but I've got to meet a couple of creeps here." As if realizing she had said something she shouldn't have, Rita took a quick breath, and locked her lips.

From that point on, Sam tried all kinds of girl talk, but to no avail. Rita wasn't in the mood for conversation.

Sam was beginning to feel like Alice in Wonderland. The situation was becoming curiouser and curiouser. She chuckled. Maybe that's why she had told Ponytail her name was Alice.

Sam had just about had it.

And she felt uneasy in this milling, noisy and, she was convinced, dangerous crowd. She couldn't shake the feeling that eyes were following her. Eyes that knew exactly what she was doing and why. She shrugged it off.

Rita had clammed up. The woman wasn't about to engage in a discussion with a stranger in the Pigpen, about the homicide of the man who caused her father's suicide. And Sam couldn't figure out how to get in with Quinn.

Hmmm. That rhymed. Get in with Quinn.

Anyway, what with the smoke and the noise and the jostling and the evasive techniques she had to employ to avoid Ponytail, she was exhausted. She could only wonder what drove these people to spend their nights in a place like this.

For years, this sort of wild nightlife had been going on within the radius of her small world, and she'd never had a clue. It wasn't as if, from the clean-cut chirrupy newscasters with just the right dose of concern in their voices, she didn't hear nightly segments about bar fights and stabbings and murders, but that news came to her within the safe confines of her living room. The gritty truth didn't register as a reality unless you were smack dab in the middle of the noise and the smells and the raw testosterone.

There was that feeling again. Those fluttery little wings in her stomach, the flutterbys, as she had called them when she was a child. She sensed that some-one in the room knew who she was and what she was doing here. With all these people milling and jostling around her, there was no way of telling if her imag-ination was running wild or if there really was someone on her trail.

Her lungs were burning, and she was getting claustrophobic.

The clock over the bar read midnight. It was time to get out of the Pigpen. She'd have to catch up with Quinn at a later date. Maybe come back to the Pigpen another night, although that thought clutched at her gut.

She reasoned that, although her fictional mystery club was supposed to start at midnight, Nick would be asleep when she got back, so the time of her return wouldn't matter. She would creep into the house like Sandburg's fog, 'on little cat feet'. Not that she needed to…Nick could sleep through the sound of the hoofs of the great horse Silver thundering past his ear.

Sam worked her way through the sweating bodies, all the time on the lookout for Ponytail. Within two minutes, she was up the few stairs and out the door.

With a relieved exhalation, she stopped and rolled her shoulders as a line of perspiration trickled down from under her wig and tickled her ear. She wiped at it with the palm of her hand.

Even though the night air was chilly, it settled around her like a comforting blanket. She lifted her head and, to clear her lungs, inhaled deeply of the smoke-free night air. It tasted so sweet.

She looked up at the dark sky, enjoying a moment of quiet, the tension draining from her shoulders. A slight shiver registered down her neck.

Then she thought about the expedition back through the dank and very dark woods, with clutching branches and whispers of childhood witches waiting in the black shadows, and hesitated.

She wiggled her toes. Her boots were still wet and squishy from the trip over. She reached behind her, unhooked her bra, and reached under Sadie's tee shirt, wincing as she gently massaged the trench under her breasts.

At that moment, three drunken bikers weaved past her, pushing and jawing at each other. They managed to mount their Harleys and shoot out of the parking lot in plumes of pebbles and riotous laughter.

Charlie will earn his salary tonight, Sam thought.

Once again she looked up at the midnight sky. Even though the moon was in its last phase, there was more light on Wattles Road than in those scary woods, and it would take her only twenty minutes to walk that mile, if she hurried, maybe fifteen. And she could use the exercise. That's when she decided not to go through the woods. She'd walk the mile down Wattle's Road and around the block back to her car.

Another shiver, this time scrambling down her spine. She wished she was at home—curled up on the sofa, in her fuzzy flannels, and with a package of Ring Dings, a cup of hot chocolate, and James Lee Burke's latest book.

Only fifteen minutes, she told herself.

She stuffed the loose socks back in her bra, hooked up, and took off at a run.

A pair of eyes followed her.

CHAPTER 40

❀

SUNDAY 12:15 AM

A passing motorist called 911.

When the ambulance and police arrived at the scene, a trembling man stood huddled by the body of his friend on the shoulder of the two-lane road.

"It was deliberate, I'm telling you!" Randy shouted, his voice rising to near hysterical pitch as he watched his friend being gently lifted by two attendants. He looked away, his eyes searching the woods as if the driver of the death vehicle lay hidden in its depths.

The rotating lights splashed streaks of blood red and blue-white color on the woodsy canvas-like backdrop. The trees, painted by the flashing lights, seemed alive with glittering eyes that watched gleefully.

Randy looked away, away from the eyes in the woods, away from the blood-stained road.

He could hear the feet of the attendants shuffling as they eased the gurney into the back of the ambulance. Once again, his eyes focused on the body. A limp hand lay open beneath the strap across the sheet.

"The light was coming towards us," he rambled, his voice hovering on the edge of sanity. His body shook. "Vinnie was walking on the outside. I heard a noise and saw the light coming around the corner. It was coming right at us! I jumped into the woods. Vinnie didn't see it. He was looking at me, talking."

The blood was pounding in his veins, thundering in his ears. "The guy tried to kill us!"

"A man was driving?" the cop asked.

"What? What?" Randy looked puzzled, his eyes whirling pinwheels. "What man?"

The police officer held Randy's arm in support. "You said a *guy* tried to kill you."

"Yeah. I don't know. I think it was a guy. I don't know."

"What type of vehicle was the person driving?"

Randy blinked numerous times, shook his head. "I don't know. I just saw the light coming around the corner. It veered across the middle line and clipped Vinnie, then took off. I'm telling you it was no accident!"

Randy looked down at his open hands, at the bloody strobes sweeping across his palms. "There was nothing I could do! I couldn't help him!"

"Calm down, sir," the officer said.

"Is he going to be okay? Is he all right?"

"They're taking him to the hospital. They'll do the best they can. Now, please, sir, calm down and tell me again everything you remember. Exactly what happened?"

Randy's face crumpled in a sack of wrinkles when he heard it. He stooped down and, from under his foot, picked up the flattened package of Lucky Strikes.

CHAPTER 41

❀

SUNDAY 12:20 AM

The bloodless moon offered little assistance.

Sam's knees were about to buckle. She started out from the Pigpen at a brisk walk and, as the wind soughed in the woods and the bushes and trees metamorphosed into malignant specters, her pace picked up. Before she went a hundred yards, she broke into a lope, then a full out run.

Someone was behind her!

Her heart pounded in her chest as she pumped her arms and forced each leg forward. She felt the energy draining from her body. *Who runs faster?* she asked herself. *The rabbit or the wolf.*

The answer, she figured, was the rabbit because the rabbit has a lot more to lose. Unless that wolf was awful hungry. So she became the rabbit. She ran faster than she had ever thought possible.

She gulped for air and welcomed the breath of life even as it seared through her lungs and became a fire in her chest. She shelved the pain, and pushed faster, as if the Big Bad Wolf was slavering at her heels. She pushed out of her mind the thought about Nick and her daughters and her mother grieving at her graveside, and concentrated on becoming the rabbit, propelling herself forward on her powerful hind legs through a series of jumps, her speed increasing until she reached thirty-five miles an hour; her excellent eyesight giving her almost spherical vision, able to see in all directions without moving her head. She would have chuckled at the idea that she could have remembered all that data from a report Sadie had done in grade school, but she didn't have the available breath to do so.

And finally, there it was! Her car. Up ahead. Safety.

Sam slammed against the trunk of her Honda, felt the pain of the impact against her upper thighs, scrambled around to the driver's door, and struggled to get the car key out of her jeans pocket and into the door lock. Her hand shook so hard that she imagined the scratches on her car door would end up looking like the spikes on a fibber's lie detector readout.

As her mind commanded her body to stop trembling and as her body refused to obey, the word fibber swirled around in her head, but fear overcame that strange wandering word. Looking back over her shoulder, she finally willed herself to stop shaking.

There's no one out there.

She frowned as her heart slowed to a bumpety-bump in her chest.

There's nothing out there.

Only dark moving shadows...and slithery things, with leather wings and rancid breath and poisonous claws and teeth the size of...

Feeling the hairs on the back of her neck waving like red flags, she peered through the night at the tiny slot in her car door. Why couldn't she get the damn key in the lock? She swore that, after tonight, she'd get one of those flashlight key chains. Claws scrabbled at the base of her skull and pin-wheeled down her spinal column.

She couldn't believe she was such a fraidy dog. In her mind, "fraidy cat" was a slam against women; women preferred the companionship of cats, but men shun the independent felines and prefer obedient dogs.

She stood straighter, buoyed by the thought that she wasn't a fraidy dog. More calmly, she fit the key into the lock. When she finally got the door unlocked and open, she dove in and pressed the door lock button. The satisfying sound of all four locks engaging allowed her a sigh of relief. Once the key was in the ignition and the car was idling, she felt safer. At least now, if a headless body knocked on her side window, she could take off, as Gramp used to say, "like a bat out of hell". Maybe she wasn't a fraidy dog, but neither was she an idiot.

With both hands, she wiped the sweat from her face and glanced into the rear view mirror. She recoiled in horror at the hideous face that sneered back at her, eyes dripping black, blood smeared around the flesh eating mouth.

Then, realizing the face was her own, she closed her eyes and took a moment to calm herself. Sliding the seat back as far as it would go, she unhooked her bra first. Then off came the black wig and the boots and wet socks. She scrubbed at her scalp, and worked her hair back and into the scrunchie she'd left on the dashboard. Slipping out of the vest, she pulled her arms through the armholes of Sadie's tee shirt and fumbled underneath the thin material to slip the bra straps off her shoulders—as if anyone could see her sitting in her car in the inky night, but it wouldn't do to have a local cop come by at the moment she sat naked from the waist up on a heavily wooded back road. How would she explain that one?

A jumble of socks fell onto her lap.

Sam rubbed her shoulders and under her breasts where she could feel the valleys in her flesh.

With a sigh of relief, she put the socks and the remainder of her costume into a plastic bag, to be stored in the car trunk once she was safely home in her garage. No way was she getting out of the car on this back road to put the bag in the car's trunk. She's seen enough *Friday the 13th* movies to know better. After Nick was out of the house, she would transfer the damning evidence to its appropriate resting place.

She slipped into her sweatshirt and fell back against the seat.

Then she remembered where she was. It took a nanosecond for Sam to regain her strength.

She put the car in gear, did a U-turn and headed for home.

Three minutes later, on the dark two-lane road, Sam saw the light behind her, a single headlight, like on a motorcycle.

She lowered her window a few inches and listened. Yes. It was definitely a Harley—no other motorcycle made a noise quite like that. *Probably one of the Harleys that was parked in front of the Pigpen. Probably Quinn Steven's Harley. And most probably, with big bad Quinn on the back!*

Sam decided she was a fraidy dog, after all. She floored the gas pedal.

Rather than taking the desolate roads back to the Georgetown common and home, she decided to head the half-mile to Route 125 and then to Route 101, where there was a well-lit all-night gas and goodies mart right off exit 9. For sure there'd be people around on a Saturday night, even at this late hour.

Her eyes flicked to the rearview mirror again.

The light seemed to be getting closer. Her heart flapped and flung against her ribs until she thought she couldn't get her next breath. She was sure it was Quinn. The other day, he had seen her coming back from his mother's home and, most certainly, it had been his bike that almost skinned the paint of their truck as they had idled at the light by the Buckhorn after the movies.

By some miracle of astute observation, Quinn must have recognized her tonight at the Pigpen. If it was Quinn, what did he hope to prove by following her? Was he going to stop her and try to scare her into staying out of the homicide investigation? Or was he going to stop her and do something worse?

Sam shuddered. Her knuckles were white around the steering wheel, her teeth clenched tighter than a Victorian corset.

Hunched over the steering wheel, she pressed harder on the pedal. Fifty-five on these curving back roads was not a good idea. She prayed she didn't come upon some unsuspecting insomniac taking a nightly stroll, or an innocent animal crossing the road.

She looked back. She couldn't see the motorcycle.

Finally, up ahead, she saw the STOP sign at the intersection of Route 125. Fortunately, she had a clear view to her left. No cars. She slowed only minimally as she took the corner at a skid, leaving arcs of black marks on the hot top.

Back in control, she never realized that her speedometer had reached seventy.

Just a few miles to Route 101.

She glanced into the rearview again.

From the same side of the road, a vehicle had pulled out on Route 125. This one had two headlights, a car. It was coming in the same direction as she was driving.

She tried to lick her parched lips but no moisture was available. Thankfully, her heart rhythm was easing up. A car behind her was a good sign. She kept telling herself she'd be okay. She just had to get to that gas station.

Her eyes darted between the highway ahead and the rear view mirror. Then she saw it. A single headlight pulled out from the road she had just left. It turned in her direction and was now following the car behind her.

She glanced at the speedometer and eased the pedal down. Seventy-five. Even though this two-lane road was fairly straight, she didn't dare go much faster. The car behind her was not keeping up, but it was still close enough for her to feel some comfort. Unless the motorcycle passed on the double yellow line, the bike would eventually fall behind.

Another mile to Route 101.

Once there, she took the exit to 101 at fifty-five miles-an-hour, then gunned the Honda back to seventy-five. Two exits to go and she'd be at the all-night gas station.

A sprinkle of headlights on the opposite side of the four-lane highway cast long beams of increasing, then fading, light into the night. The sky seemed blacker than a hearse under the heavy clouds moving in.

Behind her were the single car and the motorcycle.

Eighty miles an hour.

Along the highway, the forest shadows morphed into a black tunnel, through which the sound whistled past her speeding car. She rode in the eye of the storm, her mind whirling with memories of passages from Ouspensky's *New Model of the Universe.* Here she was, sitting totally still, yet the car in which she rode was hurtling through space and time. Was this the fourth dimension? When she reached the end of the tunnel would she pass through some dark hole and emerge in another reality? The fifth dimension? Maybe even the second dimension, as in Edwin Abbott's *Flatland,* a book she adored.

She didn't know whether it was fear or menopause that caused the rivulets of perspiration to run down her forehead and into her eyes, and at this moment, it didn't matter. She was scared. All she wanted to do was get home, into her flannels and under the covers, spooned against the man she loved. She swiped at her eyes with the back of her left hand, then clutched at the steering wheel once again.

Finally, exit 9.

Sam slued to the right and screeched to a halt at the end of the ramp. Obliquely to her right sat the gas station, ablaze in light. With just a moment's hesitation, she jammed the pedal to the metal, darted across the road, and squealed to a halt before the well-illuminated building. Behind the bank of glass windows she saw the startled faces of the night clerk and a few customers.

She scrambled out of the Honda and into the store. Stepping to one side behind a potato chip display, her heart doing triple jackhammers, she watched the road.

The car that was traveling behind her passed by, heading toward Exeter.

Then she saw the headlight.

It *was* a Harley. The bike slowed and crept along the road. And there he was, astride the bike, a leather-clad Quinn Stevens. There was no mistaking that bushy black beard and muscular body. His head moved slightly back and forth. Sam could imagine his eyes sweeping the station, his gaze settling on the storefront.

The bike stopped.

Her heart stopped.

Quinn hesitated, one foot on the ground for balance, his motionless head directed straight at the fish-bowl building in which Sam trembled behind the potato chip display.

She was sure Quinn Stevens was staring straight at her.

He had to see her car. He had to know she was in there.

After a few terrifying moments, in a roar of mufflers and exhaust, Quinn turned his bike and shot off down the road in the direction from which he had come.

Before the disbelieving eyes of the night clerk and the few customers, Sam grabbed a package of Ring Dings from off a nearby rack, ripped off the cellophane, and, before she realized what she was doing, ate both chocolate-covered cakes.

CHAPTER 42

❀

SUNDAY 2:45 AM

Vinnie LaRoche hovered between this world and the next. He had a concussion, broken ribs, a fractured pelvis, two broken ankles, and internal injuries. If he made it, he had a long road of therapy ahead of him.

If he made it, and his chances weren't good.

As Randy Sturgis sat in the emergency room outside the ICU, he knew deep in his heart that the 'accident' was a deliberate attempt on Vinnie's life. And Randy knew who had done it. The guy who had killed Brennan, that's who. Vinnie must have seen the killer that night at the gas station, but Vinnie didn't know it. And the killer thought Vinnie could make him, so he figured he'd take care of loose ends.

Or maybe 'he' was a 'she'. Randy was becoming more and more convinced that the killer was Rita. She was the one who knew where they were going to be tonight, on their way to meet her. She had probably waited for them on the back road, knowing that was the route they would take from Portsmouth.

Randy could hear the sandpapery sound of his whiskers as he rubbed the back of his hand across the stubble on his chin. From down the hall, a bell rang. Two nurses hurried after the sound.

Randy clenched and unclenched the hand that didn't clutch Vinnie's pack of Luckies. Even though fear twisted the muscles of his body into tight strands, he could barely keep his eyes open. He leaned back against the padded seat and rested his head on the cushion. He closed his eyes. Just for a minute, he thought, flexing his hand one more time before letting it fall to into his lap.

The sounds: a squeal of wheels, not braking but increasing in speed; then the thump, whump. Vinnie never cried out. He just tumbled up into the air, a dark shadow of jeans and white tee shirt, flickering like one of those old black-and-white silent movies, up and over and down until he landed as an unmoving lump by the side of the road, arms and legs askew, head tilted at an odd angle.

All Randy remembered was stepping on Vinnie's Luckies, stopping to pick them up, and wondering if any had fallen out of the pack. Vinnie needed his cigarettes.

His Luckies.

In the chair in the hospital, Randy's lids flicked open. He blinked hard and sat up in the chair, rolled his shoulders and cleared his throat.

Vinnie hadn't been so lucky tonight.

He laughed, a little too loud, and looked around to see if anyone had heard. No one took notice of him. There were too many more important issues on this floor.

With the fingers of one hand, he combed his hair back and sighed deeply. *What a hell of a mess*, he thought. *Vinnie could be dying right now.*

His eyes canvassed the hallway. No one was coming toward him with that funny look, like, how do I tell you your friend is dead. So that was a good sign.

Randy got up and began to pace back and forth in front of the few chairs lined against the wall. His mind was a jumble of thoughts, but they always came back to the Redhead. Maybe Rita thought Vinnie had told him about that night, about seeing her at the gas station, which Vinnie didn't. Vinnie had talked about some woman with a flowerpot hat and dark coat, but he didn't get a good look at her face. But Rita didn't know that, so maybe she tried to get both of them in one swoop. She had missed Randy. He could still be on the woman's hit list. And maybe, unlike this attempt, next time she wouldn't miss.

He shuddered, leaned against the wall and tapped the fist holding the Lucky package against his mouth.

He heard someone groan and realized it was himself.

That's what I get for making decisions. And all because of that broad. I had to be a big shot and try to take charge. And see what it got me—nothin' but trouble.

He sank into the chair once again, his elbows on his knees. He wondered if he really was next. But maybe it was an accident and whoever was driving got scared and drove off. Hell, that's what he would have done. But Randy knew at some gut level that he was next.

He could hear his father's voice shouting at him, over and over, that he didn't have enough brains to get out of the rain. The old man had never hit Randy, but his constant belittling had crushed the spirit out of the little boy Randy had been. Randy grew up knowing he didn't have brains. He knew he was stupid. So why did he think he could make decisions and take charge of the broad who probably murdered that Brennan guy?

He'd always heard that redheads had tempers, so he should have known that Rita wasn't the type to fool around with. But, no, he had to walk in like Tarzan,

King of the Apes. He felt like an ape, a stupid, dumb, brainless ape trying to make decisions. His father had been right all along.

Randy's pitted face scrunched into wriggles of pain. He felt sick to his stomach. He was scared witless. If Rita deliberately drove down Vinnie, she would try to get him too, not only because he could identify her as the one who came to his motel looking for Brennan that night, but also because he was stupid enough to tell her at the hardware store that he and Vinnie knew something about Brennan's murder, when actually they knew zilch. Then he'd made the stupid decision to force her to meet him and Vinnie at the Pigpen. And look what happened. He ends up sitting in the waiting room of the hospital while his buddy lay near death in the ICU.

Every decision he'd made since he'd met that redheaded she-devil had backfired. Look where he was now.

His friend might die.

And sure as hell, he was in the crosshairs.

CHAPTER 43

❀

SUNDAY 3:03 AM

LIAR!

FIBBER!

FIBBER!!

Sam tossed, turned, thrashed out at the air in front of her.

DO IT NOW!

I can't. I don't know the answer.

She was surrounded, trapped in her college math classroom. A circle of crew-cut males pounded the floor with the eraser ends of their mechanical pencils, their glassy eyes glittering with malicious glee as they flung accusations and demands at her. Punctuating the taunts, maple trees beat their bare arms against the blackboards encompassing the room.

Sam knew she had to provide the correct answer to the mathematical problem scrawled across the boot of Italy on the map at her feet, or suffer the fires of hell and damnation.

She felt the heat and looked down. Yellow-blue flames licked at the edges of Italy's boot, lifting higher and higher, twisting and turning in angry tongues, threatening to engulf her in a fiery witches' death.

"LIAR!" the men shouted. "FIBBER!"

SOLVE THE PROBLEM!

SAVE YOUR FRIEND!

IT'S YOUR RESPONSIBILITY!

Sam shuddered as she drifted helplessly down onto a wooden chair that was attached to a lift top desk. Like the desk she'd had in first grade, when they had used real ink pens, this one had a circular cutout in the right hand corner for an inkwell. A black wooden pen with a metal tip wedged in the slit at its end rested in the horizontal groove at the top edge of the desk. A blank piece of paper lay before her.

As if through deep water, her hand moved toward the pen. Her fingers closed slowly around the shaft. She looked for the inkbottle but the hole was empty. How could she solve the math problem without ink?

She needed ink!

With more urgency, the men pounded the pencils on the floor, and the maple tree arms slapped at the blackboards. The sounds of the pounding and slapping burned into her brain.

Magically, the inkbottle appeared, twisting itself into the hole in the desk.

Sam dipped her pen into the ink and held her hand poised above the page. From the metal tip, one black drop fell on the blank page and spread like a wayward amoeba, in constant metamorphosis, searching for delineation. The ink drop seeped through the paper, rained to the floor, and smothered the flames that threatened Italy's geography.

Sam watched as the flames died and one word formed, Polaroid-like, on Italy's boot. Even as another part of her brain was thinking that the word was written using the Palmer method from her grade school days, the meaning of that one word jolted her into consciousness.

Her eyes snapped open.

My god! she thought. *Could it be?*

Oh, it be, a voice in her head said. Recalling a scene from *Seinfeld*, she almost laughed aloud.

Then Sam remembered where she had seen the word that had formed on Italy's boot in her dream, and how the word 'fib' and its variations had repeatedly crept into her awareness over the past week. Suddenly it all made sense to her.

It wasn't enough to convince the police, and certainly not enough to convict anyone. But she had made a pact with Charlie and, through him, with the police, that she'd report any information that she gleaned from the code. She was sure this was the right answer. The police could take it or leave it, but she prayed they would take it to heart. The happiness of her friends was at stake.

Quietly, she untangled herself from the covers, turned on her side, and fumbled for the water glass on the nightstand to lubricate her dry throat.

That one word on Italy's boot had solved the code left by the dying Richard Brennan. Even in his last moments, he'd had the presence of mind to leave a clue, albeit an obtuse one. But that was the way his mind worked. He was, after all, an accountant with a penchant for the beauty of mathematics.

Sam slipped out of bed and went to the phone on her desk. She wasn't going to tell Charlie about her adventures in the Pigpen because he'd ream her out worse than Nick would. But she had to tell him about the code. Time was of the essence, and even a few hours could make the difference, especially now.

Brun wouldn't wake up. She was used to her husband's police calls at all hours of the day and night.

A sleepy voice, "Burrows here."

"Charlie. It's Sam. I'm okay. I wanted to tell you I figured out the code."

Through throat clearings, Charlie listened as Sam explained what she had seen the past week and how she had come to this strange conclusion. When she had finished, Charlie didn't speak for so long that Sam thought he had fallen asleep.

Finally, he said, "Good work, Sam. We're going to need more than what you've given me, but with this code thing figured out, we can put a tail on this suspect and see what develops."

Sam had arrived home a few minutes before 1:00 Sunday morning, wet, flushed, sticky, exhausted, spent from fear, and feeling like she was going to throw up the Ring Dings she had downed at the all-night gas station.

After she closed the garage door and stored the trash bag in the trunk of the Honda, she tiptoed into the bedroom, past a sleeping Nick who was flat on his back blowing puffballs, and into the bathroom to remove her makeup and wash her face. Slipping out of her jeans, she noticed red streaks across the tops of her thighs where she had plowed into the trunk of the Honda. She knew she was in for some angry looking bruises. If Nick noticed, she'd have to come up with an explanation for that.

She then stuffed the few clothes she was wearing under the bed and crawled naked under the covers. With a hand lightly on Nick's warm back, she thanked the powers that be she was home safe with her man.

Almost immediately, Sam fell into a deep sleep only to be awakened two hours later with that revelatory dream.

She sighed now as she looked at Nick over the wooden bowl of freshly baked orange-cranberry nut muffins on the breakfast table.

"You look exhausted, Sam? How did it go last night?"

Sam pasted on a guilty smile.

Let's see, she thought, stirring her oatmeal. *How did it go? I dressed up like a biker mama, sloshed through a snowy marsh in the middle of the night, spent a couple hours in the toughest bar in southern New Hampshire, flirted with a sleeze ball, and then got chased a mile down a lonely back road by the Big Bad Wolf and was almost killed by the tattooed Harley biker in a car chase. What did you do last night, honey?*

What she said was, "I figured out the code, Nick. The one Brennan tapped on the side of the Bankes' motor home just before he died. The answer came to me in a dream this morning."

She told Nick the same story she had told Charlie at 3:00 that morning. When she was done, Nick shook his head and said, "That's pretty amazing, Sam. Are you sure that's what the code meant?"

Finally feeling the crash of the adrenaline high and the sleep deprived night, Sam slowly licked at her spoon. "Yes, I'm sure."

"It's not much to go on."

Sam placed her spoon in the bowl before her and crossed her arms, as if to shut out the memory of last night that lingered in her thoughts, while her mind wondered how to divert Nick when the difficult questions would, eventually, issue from his lips.

"I know that, Nick," she said. "But I also know that was what Brennan was trying to tell the world. It was a desperate attempt, but what else could he have done?"

"Does Charlie know?"

"I called him early this morning."

"What are the police going to do?"

"I don't know. Surveillance, I hope."

Nick stroked the side of his moose mug. Sam could hear the wheels spinning. He was going to question her about what time she got in last night.

"What time did you get in last night?"

"About one. Aren't you late for work?"

Nick studied her face. "It's Sunday, Sam, remember?"

"Oh, yeah, right."

Sam picked up her plate and stood, hoping that would motivate Nick to move and to forget to ask the next question.

Nick lowered his chin into his hand and looked up at her from under his dark brow. He had that knowing but helpless look in his eyes. He gave a barely perceptible shake of his head as a slight stream of air escaped his nostrils.

Sam pretended not to notice, hurried into the kitchen, and started moving around pots and dishes.

She could see him watching her. Finally, he took a last sip of his Dunkin' Donuts coffee, placed his moose mug on the kitchen counter, moved up behind her, slipped his arms around her waist, and kissed the top of her head.

Sam knew that he knew she had been up to something, but she also knew that this was one of those times he would wait for her to tell him what was afoot.

Well, he might wait.

Just to be sure she didn't get trapped into performing evasive maneuvers, while Nick was bending over to retrieve the Sunday paper from the stoop, Sam slid out behind him and called over her shoulder, "Going for a walk." She hurried down the driveway and out of earshot before Nick could say anything.

Now he'll know for sure something's going on, she thought, as she turned onto the sidewalk and jogged past her mother's Inn next door.

Out of breath thirty seconds later, she slowed to a fast walk. Her leg muscles were stiff and achy from her marathon run after leaving the Pigpen.

She figured she'd take a walk around the Loop, then stop and see her mother for a few minutes, and visit with Selket, *if* the plump tabby could tear herself away from her food bowl.

She smiled as she thought about the shorthaired orange cat she had picked up at the SPCA a few years back, and who had decided to live with her mother at the Inn, but who did share some of her time with Sam.

She slowed her pace. No sense hurrying. She wanted to give Nick time to get involved in something else.

CHAPTER 44

❀

SUNDAY 10:00 AM

When Sam returned home over an hour later, after visiting with her mother and Selket, Nick was waiting by the door, hands on his hips, a scowl on his face. Charlie had dropped by to see her, mad as a wet hen that she had gone to the Pigpen, on her own and disguised as some floozy, and could have gotten herself into a peck of trouble.

In a small town, the "news like squirrels ran", and the little critters invariably stored their nuts in Charlie Burrows back yard. What Charlie didn't know about the goings-on in his town, Clarence Tuttle cheerily supplemented. There wasn't much that Clarence missed from the vantage of his catbird's seat above his business, Clean As A Hound's Tooth, situated on the town green. Sherlock Holmes in his many disguises could not outwit this duo.

"I said I *might* go to the mystery club," Sam said. "I didn't say I *was* going."

A thundercloud hovered over Nick's brow. "What would happen to me and the girls and your mother if something happened to you?"

"What could I do Nick? People I care about are in trouble."

"What people?"

Sam looked deep into Nick's eyes as if searching for a way to answer that question. She thought about her friends, Hannibal and Emmaline, and about the sanctity of their discussions with her. She made her lips into a thin line as her own eyes dropped to her hands where her thumbs were involved in a marathon massage. "I can't tell you that."

Nick stood silent, thunder on his brows, anger in his eyes. Then, slowly, his shoulders slumped. "Don't you know you're the reason I breathe?"

He turned on his heel, picked up his L.L. Bean catalog and disappeared into the bathroom. The door shut quietly behind him.

Sam just stood there, biting her lip.

A few hours later, Sam lay on the sun porch sofa in her gray sweats, a leg up over the back cushions, when she heard a knock on the breezeway door and a gruff voice yelling, "You home?"

"I'm on the porch, Charlie, come on in."

She pulled herself up, eased the scrunchie out of her hair and rubbed her fingers vigorously over her scalp. Stimulating the little gray cells. In preparation? She wondered.

Charlie paused in the doorway and gave Sam a measured stare.

Sam raised her palms in surrender. "I know, I know. Nick has already chewed me out for it. You don't have to say anything."

But her protestations were to no avail. Charlie railed at her for a good ten minutes, citing the numerous horrible things that could have befallen her, and of which he was intimately familiar in his line of work. When he had exhausted his repertoire, Sam rose and said, "How about an orange-cranberry nut muffin, Charlie? Maybe two?"

Music has charms to soothe the savage breast but food was the charm for Charlie Burrows. Sam felt a little guilty using that ploy as she thought about her friend's years of childhood deprivation. Their deep and abiding bond had started in grade school. She had sensed his hunger and one spring day, sitting at a picnic bench on the playground, had hesitantly offered to share a brownie from her lunch bag. Over the ensuing months, that offer had grown into sandwiches and chips that her mom had packed in double doses.

She had also been there the day he walked silently into their grade school classroom with his head swathed in bandages. She stayed close by him after that, alert and watchful. The resulting spaghetti-like scar which ran across his forehead and onto his left cheek, left marks deeper than that rubbery white ripple on his face.

His anger suddenly spent, Charlie unzipped his Red Sox jacket and dropped into the red rocker opposite Sam. "Yeah. Two would be fine. Plenty of butter."

Minutes later, Charlie was involved with his muffins when Sam said, "Do you mind if I turn on the news. I'd like to catch the weather."

Charlie managed a nod, catching with his tongue, a river of butter that trickled down his wrist.

It was a few minutes after twelve when Sam turned on WMUR, the New Hampshire news station. The broadcaster was in the middle of a news story about a hit-and-run. A Vincent LaRouche had been struck while walking with his companion on a side road after their car had broken down sometime around midnight. The pair was on their way to Iggy's Den, a bar off Route 125 popularly known as the Pigpen. LaRouche, an employee of the Route 125 Fill and Food, was transported to the hospital in critical condition. His companion,

Randy Sturgis, was unhurt but, because of darkness and the suddenness of the accident, Sturgis couldn't identify the type of vehicle or the driver. It was no accident, Sturgis told reporters, the driver meant to run them down.

Huh, Sam thought with a shudder, recalling her close call with Quinn Stevens. She rubbed her lips with the flat of her fingers. The two men were on their way to the Pigpen. Quinn Stevens on his Harley loomed large in her mind. Could Quinn have been the mystery driver? Would he do that? Why would he do that?

Sam fingered the mute button on the remote. "Charlie. Did you hear that?" She tipped her head toward the small television nestled in the greenery against the wall by the doorway.

Charlie had heard it. He had even stopped eating. They regarded each other for several moments. Sam knew they were both wondering if the gas station attendant had seen something, the night of Brennan's murder, which had placed him in the killer's sight.

That's when Sam decided, even though Charlie was liable to start in on her again, that she had to tell him about how Quinn had followed her when she'd left the Pigpen shortly after midnight. And how Quinn had stopped on the street and scoped out the gas station where she had stood huddled behind the potato chip display, before he'd taken off in a roar of muffler and exhaust fumes.

When she finished her story, to her surprise, Charlie did not speak. His chocolate-colored eyes, normally warm and friendly, now held forth an old pain, as if he were looking into a past he never wanted to remember. Except for the slight lifting and falling of his shoulders as he breathed, he could have been an exhibit in Madame Tousseau's Wax Museum.

Sam wanted to wrap her arms around the little boy inside Charlie and tell him that he was okay, that no one would ever hurt him again.

As the talons of Charlie's past tore loose from the flesh of his present, he said, in the softest voice she had ever heard emanating from her old friend, "I can't tell you how I'd feel if something happened to you, Sam." He looked away for a second, then returned his narrowed gaze. "Please don't ever do something like that again."

Sam clenched her lips against the trembling of her mouth. She felt terrible about hurting the two men she loved most in the world.

Charlie set aside his second muffin, sat more erect, and wiped his hands.

"I'm going to make a few calls. I need to have a talk with Quinn Stevens. And I think we need to question this Sturgis fellow." He paused. "I've also got a gut feeling LaRouche may need police protection."

Sam never questioned Charlie's gut feelings.

Sam managed to survive the emotional encounter with Charlie, although she didn't want to think about what Nick would he say if he knew that a leather-clad Quinn Stevens had chased her, on his souped-up Harley, over the back roads and highways of southern New Hampshire in the middle of the night. She could only imagine what he would have to say if she added the encounter with Mr. Ponytail to the tale of her wild escapades at the Pigpen.

She rolled her shoulders as she gazed out the sun porch windows, her eyes roaming across the expanse of her back yard, over the pool and towards the woods surrounding their lot. Shadows fell across the patches of snow and dead leaves at the feet of the trees.

She nodded.

Tonight she'd don her little black dress, splash on the *Wind Song*, set the table for a candle-lit dinner, put on her Beethoven CD, and serve Nick his favorite pasta dinner followed by a freshly made chocolate silken pie.

Just in case the squirrels ran again.

CHAPTER 45

❀

SUNDAY After Midnight

Clouds had moved in and covered the last fingernail of moon.

Dressed in black, Quinn Stevens kept a low profile as he crept through an ebony night, illuminated only by the dim yellow cones of light from widely spaced streetlights. He wondered if he should have dressed in lighter colors to blend with the traces of snow left from the surprise storm of a few days ago. But the snow was mostly gone now. The May sun had been warm and had melted all but the most protected areas.

As usual, Quinn parked his Harley a few blocks away, so as not to alert that light sleeper or insomniac who was still up at this hour and who would hear the roar of his Harley as he rode down this slumbering street. On previous trips, he occasionally saw one of them—standing fully illuminated in the kitchen, foraging for food, with one hand on the open refrigerator door, or laying in a recliner in front of the television and channel surfing, watching a late night movie, or reading a book. If the insomniac did look out the window, and if he did see Quinn, he might have mistaken that hulking form for a bush disturbed by nocturnal creatures.

Quinn moved over the sidewalks as silently as fog. The air felt damp and smelled of ozone. The old oaks and maples painted dark shadows on the sidewalk, across picket fences, and over hot-topped driveways.

Without warning, a vein of lightning tore the sky. Seconds later, thunder rolled across the heavens, seeming to shake the very earth beneath the sidewalk and well-tended yards.

Quinn shuddered at the suddenness of the noise as he thought, *five seconds to a mile. Lightning's close.* He welcomed the heavy clouds and storm-threatening night. It meant darkness, the cloak he needed to render his mission invisible. He quickened his pace, taking care not to trip over the roots of the old trees that had lifted and cracked the sidewalk at his feet.

He knew these streets well.

The neighborhood was old but prideful. Porches wore the fresh faces of spring paint. Mountain laurel and rhododendrons and arborvitae had shed their winter corsets, and plant beds had been stripped of leaves and winter covers. Homeowners had been at their yards and, mingled with the ozone, the night air smelled of newly spaded earth, and bark mulch, and freshly mowed grass.

Another flash tore the sky, limning the houses and trees in electric brilliance as the lightning traveled sixty thousand miles a second from the heavens to the ground. One second later, the throat of the storm let out a thunderous roar. The fury was upon him.

Quinn's fingers tightened around the bag in his hand. He was almost there.

A pair of headlights swung around the corner, their yellow beams cutting the night like a lighthouse beacon. Quinn scrambled behind a thick maple. He backed against the rough bark, held his breath. Had he been seen? If he had, did he make it worse by hiding? Well, it was too late to change that. His body tensed, his heart at double time. He waited.

The car passed him, turned at the opposite end of the street and disappeared from sight.

Quinn wiped a hand over his beard. Gathering his resolve, he stepped out from behind the maple and proceeded the few feet to the end of the driveway.

The house was modest. A small garrison with a single car garage and a hedge of thick lilacs that grew around its three sides. In the summer, colorful annuals would drip from the two front window boxes, and in the fall pots of yellow and orange chrysanthemums would grace the front steps, to be replaced later by spruce bows and holly and merry red Christmas bows on the front door and below the two front windows.

Quinn knew these things. He also knew there was a porch off the back of the house.

Keeping deep in the shadows of the lilac border, he slipped around the side of the house and into the back yard. Even though the night air was cool, he felt perspiration breaking out on his forehead and on his palms. He moved the bag to his other hand, wincing at the crackling sound of plastic as if it were a cannon's roar announcing the presence of the enemy. Crouching even lower, he scrambled from the lilac hedge to the back porch and hunkered down beside the sway-backed wooden steps and the wheelchair ramp.

He waited.

The house was dark, except for the faint glow cast by a plug-in nightlight over the kitchen counter. Only nocturnal whisperings and threatening rumbles from the belly of heaven broke the silent night.

Quinn placed a foot on the outer edge of the stoop where there was more support. On his first visit, he had made the mistake of stepping directly on the center of the tread, and the screak had carried through the night air like the cry of a cat in heat.

With measured movement, he took the few steps to the back door, bent down, and placed the sealed plastic bag on the rubber mat.

He relaxed as he turned away. It was on his retreat, when he set his foot back on the first step that the door behind him creaked open.

Quinn spun back.

As if scripted by heaven, a bolt of lightning revealed his outline and an ear-shattering thunder announced his presence. He stared into the kitchen at the figure silhouetted against the shadowy nightlight.

That's when the heavens opened up and Biblical rains let loose upon the earth.

Chapter 46

❀

MONDAY 12:35 AM

Lightning flashed in the sky and strobe-lit the statue of William Hornblower Coldbath, on the Georgetown common, setting in high resolution the stony face and proffered cowberry garland in his hand. In the flickering light, the old man seemed to move, his granite coat appeared to flutter in the strengthening storm.

The storm didn't disturb Hannibal Loveless as he sat in his favorite high-backed chair in the parsonage living room. But when he felt his wife's hands on his temple, he looked up, startled from his reverie. "Oh, Emmaline, dear. I hope I didn't wake you."

He had risen an hour ago, donned his black wool robe, and had been sitting there thinking. His eyes felt tired, his brain was mush.

Emmaline stroked his black hair back off his forehead. "What's the matter, Hannibal? Can't you sleep?"

Hannibal knew his restless nights had her deeply concerned. He laid his head back, closed his eyes, and allowed his wife's soft hands to allay some of the tightness banding his temple.

"It's nothing, my darling." His hand went up to take hers. He brought it to his lips and kissed it tenderly. Had it only been five years? It seemed as if she had been in his life forever, as if his sordid past belonged to someone else. How he wished that were true.

His mind drifted back to the day he'd found that body in the basement of his church. He had wondered then if his father had been right after all, that hell and damnation would follow his sinful soul throughout his pitiful life. But then he'd met Emmaline. That she could love him had proven to him, once and for all, that there was a heaven and it was populated with angels.

"I'm so sorry I've been distant, my darling," he said. "I know I've been preoccupied and have neglected you. This past week has been most difficult."

His lips tightened for a moment. "I just don't know what to do." He struggled to hold back a sob.

Emmaline moved around and knelt by his side. "What is it, Hannibal? Perhaps if we talk about it, we can solve the problem together."

Her hair fell in waves over one shoulder, her skin glowed the color of translucent ocean-washed shells. Hannibal wanted to wade into her liquid gray eyes, baptize himself in their cooling depths, and wash away his sins.

In that perfect instant, everything in Hannibal's consciousness dissolved. His disgraceful past, the long kept secrets, the homicide of Richard Brennan, his ministry, God, his very breath itself. There was only Emmaline.

He fell to his knees and embraced her. He wished he could die at this blissful moment so as not to inflict pain on this precious woman, to die now and not have to suffer her possible rejection.

Hannibal knew this was the moment. He had to tell Emmaline everything.

And so the story unfolded.

CHAPTER 47

❀

MONDAY 12:40 A.M.

"Please, Quinn. Come in. My neighbors are probably asleep at this time of the night, but in case one of them is up, we wouldn't want to start a scandal, now, would we?"

She wore a powder blue robe and white bunny slippers. Her golden hair haloed in the glow from the kitchen nightlight, Lynda Johanssen smiled from under a stray lock that fell across her forehead as she backed up in order to pull open the door a few inches more. The rubber on her wheel chair tires squeaked against the linoleum flooring.

Quinn couldn't move. He couldn't speak. To hear her voice, to be this close to her after the past two years of loneliness and heartache was almost more than he could bear. He didn't know what to say or do. He stood crystallized, as if he, like Lot's pillar-of-salt wife, had looked into a forbidden past.

A part of his brain still managed to function. He saw a slim body that would be confined to a rubber and metal chair for the rest of her life and he wondered how she dealt with her immobility every day. He knew that he would gladly deal with her immobility every day for the rest of his life. He would give up everything to take care of her.

"Quinn?" Lynda said softly.

The next crash in the heavens shattered his paralysis. He rubbed his hands over the sides of his jeans. He thought he said "okay," but he wasn't sure. He heard the word inside his head but his lips felt numb. He took a step forward.

Lynda nodded at the bag on the back porch. "Did you want to bring that in with you?"

What was she talking about? Bring what in?

At the puzzled look on his face, Lynda laughed softly. She tipped her head. "The bag on the porch behind you, Quinn. I wondered who was leaving all those books. For some reason, I thought it might be you. You are very thoughtful."

Quinn finally found his voice. "I know you like to read." He picked up the bag and stepped inside the kitchen.

Lynda reached up and flipped on the overhead kitchen light. "Would you like coffee or juice?"

What Quinn wanted was Lynda. He wanted to scoop her up in his arms, carry her off to a home of their own, and love her forever. For now, he would settle for orange juice.

"Juice," he managed to say, and wondered if he should offer to help. What was the appropriate behavior in a case like this? Would she be offended if he offered his assistance? Would she feel less of a person?

She seemed to sense his unease and solved the problem by saying, "Please sit down, Quinn. I can manage. I've learned how to take care of myself these past two years."

Amazing, he thought. There wasn't a trace of bitterness in her voice. He lowered himself into a chair and placed the bag on the table. Next to a bowl of fruit in the center of the table, sat a small fuzzy white duck with black button eyes, a yellow bill and yellow webbed feet, sporting a blue kerchief imprinted with the white lettering *Aflac* tied about its neck.

Quinn felt a smile inside him. White bunny slippers, a fuzzy white duck. Soft things, soft and warm like Lynda. "Aflac," Quinn said. Startled by his own voice, he wondered why he had spoken aloud. Maybe to fill the silence? Maybe to assure himself that he could continue to find his voice?

Lynda pulled open the refrigerator door and said, "A salesman from Alflac came into my dad's office. The duck is a promotional item. Isn't he cute? Press on his back."

Quinn did, and the duck squawked, "Aflac, Aflac, Aflaaack!"

In spite of his nervousness, Quinn chuckled. Lynda laughed too, a laugh that Quinn had always thought seemed too small to hold the joy she held inside.

She set the orange juice carton on the table. "I squeeze that little duck first thing every morning. He starts my day off right." Her blue eyes danced as she glanced at Quinn. She turned away quickly to get two glasses from a set resting on the edge of the kitchen counter.

Quinn watched as she set the glasses on her lap and maneuvered back to the table. She poured the juice.

He could smell flowers and soap and the musky smell of sleep. Her tousled hair shone in the overhead light. He took a swallow of orange juice before his dry throat closed and shut off the flow of air to his aching chest.

"Good juice," he nodded. And kept nodding, looking into the glass he held in his hands. Noticing the grease under his nails, he quickly withdrew his hands and stuffed them in his lap.

"Thank you so much for the books you've left for me. They have filled many hours. As Emily Dickinson wrote, 'this bequest of wings was but a book. What liberty a loosened spirit brings.'"

He nodded again. A loosened spirit. He'd heard that somewhere.

"Remember when we first talked on the town green at the Cowberry Fair a few years ago?" Lynda said, as if picking up his thoughts. "Elizabeth Blackwell owns an inn there called The Loosened Spirit. She named it after Emily Dickinson's poem."

He remembered. He remembered every little detail of that day, the day he had asked her out for the first time and she had said yes.

"Right." It was all he could think of to say and he had to stop nodding. What could he talk about? His eyes darted around the kitchen.

The silence that followed was almost painful to him.

Finally, Lynda spoke. "I'm sorry if I hurt you, Quinn. It was not my intention. I made a bad choice. Not that Richard was a bad person, but he had serious problems. And I began to realize that I didn't care for him as much as I first did. I knew our relationship had to end. Strangely enough, the day of the accident I was planning on telling him it was over between us." She glanced down at her legs and sniffed at the irony. "I never got the chance."

Quinn bit hard at his lip.

She sighed and looked over at Quinn. "And then, after the accident, he visited me once in the hospital. When he learned I would be paralyzed, he never came again. He said he couldn't deal with my being in a wheelchair, because of his mother. She had a crippling disease and Richard spent his childhood caring for her. He said he couldn't face it again. I told him that I had planned to end our relationship that night anyway, but I don't think he believed me."

Quinn felt a flicker of pity for the man. Not only because he had lost the most precious woman in the world, but also for the past that had been thrust upon him. Then the flicker wavered and sputtered out.

"But if he really loved you…" Quinn stopped. He didn't want his words to hurt her anymore than she'd already been hurt.

Lynda shrugged, then said, "I was reading when I heard you on the back porch. I often read late at night."

"Really? I never see any lights on." As the words left his mouth, he realized what they might imply, that for the past two years he'd been sneaking around her house in the dark. But, of course, she already knew that. He had been leaving books on her back porch ever since her accident.

Suddenly he felt ashamed at his inability to face her in the light of day. At any time since the accident, he could have called her, knocked on her *front* door, or made an effort to find out where she went and then he could have planned an 'accidental' meeting. But, no, he'd been a coward, too afraid that his last glimmer of hope would be dashed against the rock of her rejection. He should have known she was too much of a lady to treat him badly. Even so, he wanted more than her friendship, although he knew that if he had to settle for just her friendship, for being near her and basking in the light that emanated from her being, that it would be enough.

Lynda's lips lifted into a smile.

"After the accident, my parents decided I should have a space of my own. They turned the dining room into my bedroom, and the laundry room, off the kitchen here, into my personal library. It has no windows, which explains why you didn't see a light."

Quinn glanced toward the living room door.

"My parents are asleep upstairs. And besides, they would be pleased that you've come to visit." She grinned at him. "Even at this hour."

"Come see." She reached across the corner of the table and took his hand. Hers felt soft and warm and so small. Quinn swallowed hard, then stood abruptly. Lynda released his hand, backed up and wheeled toward a doorway beside the refrigerator.

The walls were buttercup yellow and the floor polished pine. Two of the walls were lined with floor to ceiling honey-colored pine shelves, filled with books. More volumes were packed into a waist high freestanding bookcase against a third wall. A computer desk held a small laptop and Lexmark printer. The room shone in the soft light from the floor lamp next to the desk.

"I think your mother would like my library," Lynda said, looking up shyly.

Quinn recalled how the two women hovered, over Annie's kitchen table, discussing this author and that novel. Although they'd only met that once, his mother had been very disappointed when Lynda had stopped seeing her son.

Mom would love this room, Quinn thought. *And she loves you. And so do I. More than you'll ever know.*

Quinn looked down at Lynda's bunny slippers and thought he was going to lose it.

CHAPTER 48

❀

MONDAY 12:45 AM

He took it from the very beginning.

Through tears and regrets and self-recriminations, and cups of hot coffee, and ear shattering lightning and deep throaty growls of thunder that threatened to silence the earth, Hannibal talked.

Although, early in his relationship with Emmaline, he had outlined his early days on the farm and the lashings he received from his father, and sketchily related his life in New York, his calling to the ministry, and the homicides at his last post, now he knew he had to tell his life's story from the beginning, in it's horrifying entirety, and pray that she would still love him.

He told her that he wondered if he would ever erase the memories of Billy Bob Meaney and Johnny Benson pelting him with rocks as he raced home, desperately trying to dodge the flying missiles. Occasionally one would hit him and cut into his skin, and the blood would pool on his white shirt.

Billy Bob and Johnny would chant, "Here comes Hannibal with the honker. Honk, Hannibal, honk." And then would come that boisterous sick laughter as they had lumbered after him.

He still had nightmares about being chased.

But he had been thin and fast on his feet, and had always managed to outrun his flabby taunters. He'd arrive home exhausted and sometimes bleeding. More often that not, his father would be waiting on the sagging weathered steps of the old clapboard house, his heavy black brows twisted over flashing cold eyes, clutching the buggy whip in his muscular fist, and he would start bellowing. "Fight back, you little coward. An eye for an eye and a tooth for a tooth."

And then the whipping would begin.

Hannibal told how he had rubbed his knuckles sore more than once trying to remove the blood stains from his white shirts. However, the cruel chanting of his classmates could not be excoriated. Many silent nights, those words had ricocheted in his head like the tiny metal spheres in the pin ball machines at Chubby's Pool Hall where Billy Bob and Johnny's wasted fathers got drunk and played away their meager salaries and lives.

The lash scars on Hannibal's back were "gifts" from his austere Kansas father who beat his only son as regularly as he quoted scripture. The mental scarring had crouched in the black hole of Hannibal's dreams. But he'd kept his counsel, waiting for the day he knew would come. And it had.

Hannibal had left that abusive home. He was 16, right off the farm, and totally unprepared for city life. He had managed to save enough money for bus fare to New York City. He didn't know what he was going to do when he got there but anything was better than the way he had been living.

He arrived in the city in the month of July. It was hotter than he'd ever experienced on the farm in Kansas. All those tall buildings seemed almost smothering. He fell in with the wrong crowd.

"I'm not excusing my behavior," he told Emmaline, "just explaining it."

He hesitated before he told her the most difficult part, the part she had never heard.

"A world of alcohol and drugs followed. I never took hard drugs or stole to support my habits, like some of my friends. I managed to keep a job, washing dishes at a small restaurant. My father's preaching must have sunk in."

He laughed bitterly.

"Then one day…"

He choked up. His breath came in short spurts.

Emmaline spoke to him from the loveseat on his right. "Please, Hannibal. Go on." She sat very still, her graceful fingers folded on her blue robe.

He nodded, sucked in a breath as he tried to find his voice. How could he tell her this? How could he hurt this woman he so dearly cherished. But he had to go on. She deserved the truth.

He settled his shoulders and looked straight into her eyes.

"I met a woman. Trudy Collins. She was a friend of one of the group at the time, and into drugs like the rest of us. We had an affair. Four months into our liaison she became pregnant." He choked, closed his eyes and began to rock. He found he couldn't look at his wife.

Finally, a shudder silenced his motion. "When I realized I was going to be a father," he said, as an ache in his chest almost took his breath away, "my world changed. I didn't want my child to have to suffer the way I had. I asked Trudy to marry me, to get away from the hollowness of our existence. She said she would think about it. For many months I pressed her but to no avail."

Hannibal felt his throat closing up, but he had to go on. He owed it to Emmaline to finally tell the whole truth.

"I managed to keep her off drugs during the pregnancy, but it was a struggle. Her mother died from an overdose and she never knew her father. She had been brought up on the streets. It's not a pretty story.

"The day finally came, her water broke. It was late at night. I called a taxi but we didn't make it to the hospital. She delivered the child in the taxicab, with the help of the driver and a passing policeman. It was a girl."

His hands were knotted in prayer.

"When the child was born, I noticed she had a birthmark on her shoulder, in the shape of a heart. I remember thinking how unusual it was. The policeman remarked on it as well.

"We finally arrived at the hospital, where Trudy and the child were taken away."

A wrenching sob caught in his chest. He cleared his throat to cover it.

"I went back to the hospital the next morning to see them but Trudy was gone. She had slipped out with our daughter. None of the nurses or doctors and administrators knew when she had left or where she had gone. I told them I was the father and, if they heard from her I wanted know. I went back every day, pleading with them, until the day they told me they had contacted Trudy. She had sent our daughter to an adoption agency. She probably wanted me to know that she hadn't left the baby in a trashcan or done something even worse. The hospital wouldn't tell me where she was."

He blinked repeatedly to erase the pinpoints of light that danced before his eyes. His gaze dropped to his open hands. Spots of red dotted his palms where his nails had dug in. One part of his brain screamed warnings—to go on was suicide.

He glanced at his wife. She seemed comatose. Every ounce of his strength seemed to drain from his body. But it was too late now. He had to finish. He had to trust in God. He had to trust in Emmaline.

He dragged his tongue over his dry lips.

"I was so distraught that I made a terrible scene at the hospital and they had to bodily remove me. That desperate act ensured that I would never be told where my daughter went."

He rushed to his destruction. He had to cleanse his soul. "Every time I see a young woman who is about the right age, I wonder if she could be my daughter. I find my self looking at her shoulder for that birthmark." He swallowed hard. "Trudy had red hair."

His clenched his lips into a hard line.

"If there had been DNA tests back then, I could have proven my paternity." A 'V' formed between his brows. "Rita Frazetta is the right age. She was adopted. And she has red hair."

He let that realization sink in.

"But I can't go up to every redheaded woman of the correct age and ask to look at her shoulder for a heart-shaped birthmark. Even if I found her, do I have to right to interrupt a young woman's life, a woman who may be perfectly happy with her adopted parents. She might not even know she was adopted. Do I have that right?"

For a moment, Hannibal hovered on the edge of his chair, then he fell back in a rumpled heap, drained, his throat raw from the telling.

In counterpoint to the silence in the room, the rain thrashed against the windowpanes like skeletal fingers desperate to get in.

Hannibal finally looked into Emmaline's eyes and saw the world of hurt, and wondered who it was who said that confession was good for the soul. God! He had said it to the suffering in his own flock. How little he knew.

He saw the answer in Emmaline's face.

His world dropped from under him. His life was over. He had lost her.

In the living room of the Georgetown parsonage, a jagged flash of lightning tore through the black sky and thunder banged the bottom of the heavens.

Emmaline sat quiet for a very long time.

Finally she spoke. "So many secrets, Hannibal."

CHAPTER 49

✿

TUESDAY 2:50 A.M.

Charlie huddled behind a white screen in the ICU cubicle, his second night since he had talked with Sam. If she was right, the murderer could very well try to silence this potential witness and would do so, most likely at night, when the hospital was quiet and sleeping.

Vinnie LaRoche was still unconscious. He lay still as death under the white sheet on the hospital bed, connected to life saving equipment with a variety of tubes, his elevated legs encased in plaster casts, his head and arms swathed in bandages.

Charlie stared at the bandages on the poor bugger's head as his lids drooped and his mind drifted back to the February day that had changed his life. He settled his back against the wall, folded his arms across his chest, and fell into that light alpha stage of consciousness that hovers between waking and sleeping.

It was night and ten-year-old Charlie was cold and hungry, huddled, under a blanket on the threadbare couch, with his mother and younger sister.

Tanker Burrows was drunk as usual and bellowing. He staggered across the room of the pathetic cabin they called home, toward the small television sitting on a wooden crate beside the wood stove. The flickering lines and static on the screen had driven him into a rage.

The wood stove sat cold. His father hadn't cut any wood that week, hadn't done much of anything that week except drink—he always seemed to find money for the cheap gin he bought with regularity—and the family had shared one large can of cold B&M baked beans for supper.

Tanker Burrows swayed before the television, staring down at it as if it were the seat of all the despair and frustration and evil in his world. His lips pulled back into a snarl and he swung his burly leg back and let go at the set. The screen shattered, blue-white sparks shot from its insides, and shards of glass flew into the room.

Not satisfied and unable to vent the rage that had taken root inside him many years ago, he turned toward his family, blood in his eyes.

He had taken one step when Charlie leaped off the couch, every muscle in his body quivering with fear...

Charlie flinched, then raised his hand to trace the rubbery white scar on his face.

He shook off the drowsiness. He had to stay awake.

Peering through the slit in the screen, Charlie could see Vinnie LaRoche's still body, the only sign of life the beeping of the machines and the barely perceptible rising and falling of the man's chest.

A man hanging on to the edge of life.

What did he see? Charlie wondered. *Did the man really hold the answer to the murder of Richard Brennan at Pottle's Pond?*

From what Charlie had found out about LaRoche, he didn't have many friends and had no relatives in the area, just a few cousins down Maine, in the boonies. LaRoche's buddy, Randy Sturgis, was so incoherent that first night that he barely remembered his own name. And since the accident report, Sturgis had clammed up tighter than the lacings on the Red Sox's cleats. That he was afraid of something or someone had led Charlie to believe that LaRoche had seen something that night at the gas station and had told his buddy.

It was almost three in the morning and Charlie knew he couldn't keep this up much longer. He blinked his eyes repeatedly, then wiped his hand across his face.

The hospital floor was tomblike, except for the ping of a machine here and there and the quiet murmur of voices down the corridor and around the corner at the nurses' station. The place smelled of disinfectant and flowers and dead air. Charlie rubbed hard at his eyes. If this were going down, it would happen soon. The cracker wouldn't wait until LaRoche had regained consciousness and could talk.

Footsteps.

The hair on the back of Charlie's neck stood up like thousands of miniature antennae.

The footsteps were heavier and sounded slicker on the floor, as if the soles were leather. The nurses' rubber-like footwear tended to squeak. Of course it could be a doctor, but all of Charlie's instincts told him that the person out there didn't belong here.

He dared not move. He slowed his breathing so he could hear better. He listened.

Seconds slipped by.

Charlie's ears strained to pick up the slightest indication that something was amiss. He felt, more than heard, a presence. He listened harder. A second breathing, very slight, but distinctly not LaRoche's. That's when he heard the swish of sheet on sheet.

He tipped slightly to his right and squinted around the edge of the screen. There was the cracker, outlined against the muted light of ICU, pressing a pillow down over the face of the unconscious Vincent LaRoche.

CHAPTER 50

❀

DAYS LATER

"Gonna be warm the next few days," Charlie said.

"That's what they say."

They sat on the sun porch and rocked slowly while Nick sipped from his moose mug and Charlie eyed the warm oatmeal raisin cookies on the corner table between them. He'd already had three.

Morning light streamed through the sun porch windows, hinting at the promise of the heat wave predicted by Chris Thomas on the early morning weather forecast. Today, in the sixties; the weekend, high eighties into the nineties. New Englanders took the mercurial fluctuations with considerable aplomb, secretly enjoying the dips and rises in their thermometers while they complained to their neighbors. From snow in July to heat waves in December, they'd seen it all and were ready to tell their stories quicker than the flick of a horse's tail.

Charlie set his cup down and, ignoring the paper napkin on the table beside him, wiped his hands on his pants leg and reached for another cookie. He examined the cookie, then looked over at Sam on the couch. "So, Sam. Explain to me again how you came up with Frank Bonacci?"

Nick laughed. "You're a glutton for punishment, Charlie."

"Yeah, I know." Charlie giggled, that high-pitched sound that had sent Sam into peals of laughter in grade school and was responsible for her only dismissal.

"Blame it on that Italian mathematician," Sam said from the couch. She tugged off her ragg socks, tossed them on the floor, and wiggled her toes.

"Fibonacci. Yeah, I got that much."

"Right. You know, when I heard Earle Bankes describe the tapping that night at Pottle's Pond, I knew I had read about that sequence somewhere. It was so familiar, but I couldn't quite get it. Even if I did, at that time it wouldn't have meant anything to me—not until I snuck into the office at Frazetta's Hardware store. Frank's nameplate was on the desk in big white capital letters. Bonacci.

"And then the word 'fib' kept popping into my vocabulary and my mind for no apparent reason. I mean, it's a word I rarely use."

"But practice," Nick interjected.

Sam continued unfazed. "And then there were the trees."

"You mean, trees like in forest trees," Charlie added helpfully.

Sam nodded.

Nick sat back with a subtle smile on his face, watching Sam and Charlie work their routine.

"Well, more correctly, branches," she corrected.

Charlie rubbed his rubbery nose and slouched back in his chair. "We're not in an interrogation room, Sam. Come on. Tell the story. I want to hear all the little details again, not like the broad outline you gave me over the phone."

"Well." Sam paused, as if ordering the story in her mind. "I shall begin where all good stories begin."

"Once upon a time there was an Italian Mathematician named Leonardo Fibonacci. He was also known was Leonardo Pisano, or Leonardo of Pisa, because he was born in Pisa, Italy, around 1180."

"Oh, boy," Charlie sighed. Resignation clouded his eyes. "We're going to get the long version."

Sam eyeballed him. "You wanted the details. It's important to know the background, the history."

"Yeah, I know. Or we're doomed to repeat it."

"Accept the inevitable," Nick piped in.

"I have to tell it from the beginning," she countered.

Obsessed with the concept of orderly progression, Sam read every intro-ductory page, including the publishing data and acknowledgements, before beginning a book. She wasn't about to miss one iota of information.

"Not much is known about Leonardo Fibonacci," she said, leaning forward to massage her toes. "He traveled throughout the Mediterranean and studied the mathematics of every country he visited. One of his books on the number systems and algebra of the East brought about the end of the abacus and counting boards, and introduced the numerals and decimal system that was eventually adopted by Europe. In fact, this book and others that he wrote on geometry and advanced algebra were the basic texts for many hundreds of years."

Charlie grabbed two more cookies. "So, when do we get to the tapping?"

Ignoring the question, Sam continued. "He discovered a sequence of numbers that was named after him—0,1,1,2,3,5,8,13, and so forth—where each number is the sum of the preceding two."

"And the big deal with those numbers again?" Charlie wanted to know.

"Well," Sam said, "the Fibonacci series represents an harmonious progression. For instance, you find it in the keyboard of the piano. There are two black keys, then three black keys, for a total of 5 black keys, and there are eight white keys. 2,3,5,8.

"The Fibonacci series is also a basic pattern reflected in the harmony of nature. It is found repeated in the spirals on the sunflower's face, in the growth of shells, like the abalone. Wait here a minute."

She jumped up, padded barefoot to the bookcase under the windows and pulled out a well-fingered paperback book. Settling down on the couch, Lotus-style, she laid the book on her folded legs, checked the index and thumbed to the correct page.

"Let me read you this. It's from *The Power of Limits* by Doczi. Here on page 52 he's writing about the Fibonacci numbers. 'Since this sharing…' he means the Fibonacci numbers '…is universally present in musical sound, color, light and weight, patterns of plant growth…'

"Remember, Charlie, how I told you about the branches in the back yard, how they kept calling to me?"

Charlie nodded.

Sam continued, running a finger under the sentence on the page. "So, the Fibonacci numbers are also present in those things I just mentioned, as well as in the ocean tides, rhythms of the calendar, plus, as he says here, in our own biorhythms, breathing, and heartbeat. He says, 'we can speak of it as a basic pattern-forming process.'"

She looked up from the page. "The Fibonacci series is connected to the Golden Mean, which is the measure of the most beautiful architecture in the world." She closed the book and held it lovingly to her chest. "So, you see, there is a cosmic order, a basic pattern that underlies what we know and observe, and numbers are the language of that order."

Charlie fiddled with the zipper on his Red Sox jacket. Nick tipped his head and gazed lovingly at his wife.

"So," Nick finally said, "you made the quantum leap from Bonnaci to Fibonnaci."

"Well, yes. I know it was a long leap, but according to Brennan's background report, he was deeply into mathematics. He had to have known about the Fibonacci series. Surely he made the connection between Frank's last name,

Bonacci, and Leonardo Fibonacci. He may have even joked with Frank about his last name. Who knows? Maybe you could find out, Charlie?"

"Yeah, maybe. Anyway, Frank confessed pretty quickly. Pretty hard to explain yourself when you're caught pressing a pillow over an unconscious guy's face in the hospital. It didn't take much pressure after that to get Frank to talk. He was smarter than most crackers though. Investigators found a few distinctive footprints by Pottle's store that matched C.J.'s shoes. Most prints had been washed away by the rain earlier that evening but these were fresh. And Pottle said no one had been in the store after 11:00 that night."

"CJ has a limp, right, Charlie?" Sam said.

"Right. The shoes were made special because of C.J.'s leg injury. Seems Frank wore his brother's shoes to implicate him. But the weight distribution was even and deeper than what would have been found had C.J. worn them. Then Frank took his brother's car when C.J. was passed out drunk in his apartment that night. The cracker even laced his mother's coffee with sleeping pills. Funny how the fates step in sometimes."

"How's that, Charlie?"

Charlie looked at Nick. "Normally CJ kept his gas tank full, had some quirk about running out of gas. But on the night Frank took his car, CJ hadn't filled it. He'd planned on selling it and wasn't going to spend the extra money. The tank was almost empty and that's why Frank had to stop to get gas at the station where Vincent LaRoche works." He snorted, shook his head. "And to top it all off, LaRoche never even remembered him. So Frank didn't have to try to kill him after all."

"Frank must have some issues with his brother," Nick said.

"His half-brother." Charlie ran a mitt through his thinning acorn-colored hair. "Frank hated CJ. Seems CJ was constantly reminding Frank that he wasn't Claudio's real son. He wasn't a Frazetta. He was a Bonnaci. Frank idolized his stepfather and the old man evidently loved Frank like he was his own son."

Sam looked at her lap and shook her head. "It's so sad."

"Yeah. And, according to Frank, his mother didn't help, the way she favored CJ."

"So, why did he do it? Kill Brennan?" Nick wondered.

"He figured he'd get rid of two problems with one murder. The man who caused his stepfather's death would be dead and CJ would be convicted. Then Frank would get his mother's attention. Oh, and Frank happened to be stocking a shelf in the hardware store when he overheard Sturgis and LaRoche talking to his sister, Rita. They were threatening to implicate her in the murder if she didn't meet them at the PigPen on Saturday night. That's why Frank was following the two of them that night."

"But Frank knew she didn't do it," Nick said.

"Right. But he thought they were just using what they did know to get her in a compromising position. That just added more fuel to his fire. So that, plus thinking Randy Sturgis and Vinnie LaRoche knew more than they did, Frank figured he'd get the two guys on the road on the way to the PigPen. If they hadn't broken down, he would have found a way to run them off the road, so he says."

"So that's why Rita was at the PigPen," Sam said.

Nick snuffed. "Frank went to extreme lengths for the love of his father and mother and to protect his sister."

"What about Quinn following me that night after I left the Pigpen?" Sam asked Charlie.

"I talked to Quinn about that. Seems he saw some guy leave the bar right after you did, a sleaze he knows who tries to pick up women and never seems to get anywhere. By that time he had figured out who you were. He didn't know why you were there, but wanted to make sure you were all right. The biker with the heart of gold."

Charlie giggled again.

The phone rang and Sam jumped up to answer it.

"Oh, hi, Emmaline."

Sam listened, her eyes focused on her fingers fiddling with the pen on her desk. She nodded a few times.

"You're entirely welcome. What are friends for? And give my best to Hannibal."

CHAPTER 51

❀

ONE EVENING, DAYS LATER

"Why are you smiling like the Cheshire cat, Sam?" Nick scowled. "Are you up to something?"

"Who? Me?"

Nick's eyes narrowed as he tipped his head.

Sam softened. "Everything's just fine. I'm happy, that's all."

"And why is that?"

Seinfeld had just finished and Sam turned off the television and settled back into the sofa cushions, pulling the afghan over her feet. The day was flickering out and the evening almost upon them. Through the picture window, the sky was layered in pink and gray and bruised purple.

Sam rubbed her hands gently back and forth over her thighs, over the purple and yellow bruises hidden beneath her sweat pants. Another few days and Nick would never know.

"Because I've figured out why you're so handsome," she said.

A little smile formed at the corner of Nick's lip. "Really. And why's that?"

"I was rummaging through some old Discover Magazines and came upon this article called "Beauty Secret", by Eric Haseltine. It seems research has shown that if a person's face and body are divided into proportions that equate to what the ancient Greeks called the Golden Ratio, that person is considered beautiful, or handsome, as in your case."

"Is that right? And just how did you deduce my facial and body measurements?"

"After years of exploration, I do know them pretty well, my darling, but to prove my suspicions, when you were sleeping last night, I got out my cloth tape measure and measured you from head to toe. You fit the Golden Ratio, just like the ancient Greek temples."

Incredulity spread over Nick's face.

"What?" Sam said. "I didn't do anything wrong."

"Violating my body while I sleep?" Nick said.

"Usually you like that."

"Woman, what am I going to do with you?" It was a question that he had asked since the day they'd met, and he didn't expect an answer.

"Oh, by the way," Sam said, gracefully changing the subject. "I just had a long talk with Annie Stevens," she said. "I drove up to Manchester to apologize to her about that visit I told you about. She is such a sweetie. And she is so happy now that Lynda and Quinn are together. They're planning on getting married, you know."

"That happened fast," Nick said, recrossing his feet on the hassock and reaching for his book, *Not Without Peril.* He was one-third into it, what with all the interruptions these past few weeks.

Sam had a dreamy look in her eyes. "Love happens fast sometimes, Nick. Remember when we met. I was ready to marry you that first day. I knew you were the right one."

Nick pulled the bookmark from between the pages. He looked over at Sam and smiled. "And besides, you hate to shop."

"You've got that right."

"By the way," Nick said, "I saw Quinn a few days ago. He's cut his beard. Looks like he's cleaned himself up. He was driving a beat up '47 Chevy, kind of maroon colored. Wonder where he got that old thing? Looks like it needs a lot of work."

"Really. I wonder if that's the old car I saw in Annie's back yard, covered with vines."

Sam wondered if there was a story there. Then she pushed the thought aside to concentrate on telling Nick the good news.

"Guess what, Nick?"

"God, Sam. You scare me when you say that."

"No, this is a good 'guess what.'"

"Okay. Lay it on me."

"Quinn and Lynda are planning on having a big family."

"Is that possible, given her condition?"

"Well, her doctor says her paralysis won't interfere with her having children. Of course, they will have to monitor her more carefully."

"Won't it be hard for her to take care of children from a wheelchair?"

"She'll have plenty of help. They're planning on a Christmas wedding. Quinn has a piece of land here in Georgetown that his grandfather left him. Can you believe it? And he's going to build an in-law apartment for Annie. She's ecstatic. She always wanted a houseful of grandchildren. And she and

Lynda just love each other. Plus, there's Lynda's parents…Lynda and Quinn will have plenty of help."

Nick chuckled. "You do like happy endings, woman."

Sam gazed at her husband, her eyes suddenly moist. "I got one."

"Don't start," he said, lowering his head into the book.

"I think I'm in love."

It was a half-hour later and Nick looked up from his book. "I hope it's with me."

"Well, you too," Sam said.

She had been sprawled on the couch, letting her mind wander through the events since the night of their camping trip to Pottle's Pond and then on to the everyday routine of the past week. The most recent thought was about another man. "This guy's name is Josh. Josh Groban."

"Is that the young singer you were talking about, the one you saw on Oprah recently?"

"Yup. I turned on the TV for the 5:00 news and caught the end of her show, and there was this young guy. He's 21, I think, slender, rather bashful, curly black hair. And when he opened his mouth to sing, I couldn't believe the voice. You would have thought he'd been singing for twenty years, his voice was so mature. He just blew me away. So I bought his CD."

"You what?"

"You heard me."

"You actually bought something besides Presley, Beethoven, and Bach?"

"Right. And just when you thought you had me pegged."

"Woman, you are a mystery."

"That's me. A mystery wrapped in a Ring Ding. Speaking of which…do I have any left?"

"Don't we still have left-over apple pie and chocolate pie and chocolate chip cookies? Seems like you've been baking up a storm the past few weeks."

"Yeah. But it's not the same."

Sam scurried into the kitchen to check her stash before McCutty's Market, on the other side of the town green, closed.

THE END

Addendum

Dear Reader,

You've come this far, so please journey with me through the next few pages. I think you will find the trip most "interesting".

The ancient adepts used geometry and numbers to search for and understand the fundamental relationship between Heaven and Earth.

The circle has historically symbolized the Creative Source, i.e.: Goddess, God, Allah, the Great Spirit, the Force. The horizontal line (and its extensions, the square and the cube) represented Matter, i.e.: all things that had form such as the earth and living creatures.

As synchronicity would have it, while I was working on this Addendum, I was also reading a novel, *The Genesis Code*, by John Case, in which one of the characters had written a book on the origins of relic worship and icon cults. In the novel, the character's book contrasted the ancient Greek culture with the Judaic and Islamic cultures.

Greece was a polytheistic society who depicted their many Goddesses and Gods through representational art, i.e.: icons, portraits, and statues.

By contrast, the Judaic and Islamic cultures were monotheistic and, because their beliefs forbade depictions of their Creator, they expressed their religious concepts linguistically, through the word. Therefore the early Christians, considered a Jewish sect at the time, produced no religious art.

However, as time went on, the Judeo/Christian sect became increasingly connected to icons, and pictures of Christ began to appear around 325 A.D.

But the ancient practice of secretly addressing their Creator through the power of names and numbers lived on.

I know your eyes are glazing over but hang in there.

In the Middle Ages, a group of Jewish scholars, know as Cabalists, claimed that much of the Old Testament was written in code. Remember, the Jews were religiously bound to express their Creator linguistically, therefore, they would have recorded their truths in words. The Cabalists believed that when the Hebrew code was broken, the confusion inherent in the Scriptures made sense, and divine truths were revealed. The chief method of decryption, in which a name or word or phrase was converted into numbers thus revealing the hidden message, was known as gematria.

In the Bible, there are different names for the Creator depending upon its function in that passage.

We find an example of gematria in the first sentence of the Bible: 'In the beginning, God created the heaven and the earth.'

In this first sentence, the Hebraic name for the Creator is ALHIM. The ancients portrayed this Being as a circle.

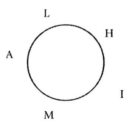

In gematria, the constant value behind these letters is:

A = 1, L = 30, H = 5, I = 10, and M = 40

If we start with the letter 'L' and go counterclockwise around the circle, we arrive at 30-1-40-10-5. In numerology, we reduce numbers by adding them. The zero does not change the sum. So, 30-1-40-10-5 becomes 31415, or the value of Pi!

Shades of high school math, I know. I used to feel the same way. If only my teachers had taught the symbolic side of numbers and geometry, I would have been glued to the blackboard instead of gazing at the cute guy in the third seat in the next row. But wait, the mystery unfolds.

The great Greek mathematician and inventor, Archimedes, supposedly discovered pi, the value used to determine the relationship between the diameter of a circle and its circumference, around 250 B.C. However, this value is found in the first sentence of the Old Testament written, according to some sources, around 1,000 B.C.!

I'm getting to the point. Honest!

We can read this first sentence in the Bible—'In the beginning God created the heaven and the earth'—in at least two ways.

First, as depicted on the ceiling of the Sistine Chapel, we could see God as floating in a cloud and reaching out to touch the hand of the first man. If we use representational art as the Greeks did, we could imagine the Goddesses and Gods as omnipotent beings stationed on Mt. Olympus with frequent weekend passes. Both images imply separateness, a space between the Creator and us.

Secondly, since the Old Testament was written in Hebrew, we can read that first sentence in the Bible linguistically, as the Cabalists did, to find the message hidden behind the words. I.e.: God, ALHIM or 31415, Pi, created the heaven, represented by the circle, and the earth, the horizontal line.

Since Pi is the value used to determine the relationship between the circumference of a circle and its diameter, this Pi version of the Creator defines the first act of creation as the geometrical relationship between Spirit, the circle, and Matter, the horizontal line. (In this view, we have matter, the horizontal line, enclosed within Spirit, the circle. There is no separation.)

The ancient Hebrew scholars wrapped their beliefs in words, in story, parable and myth, for the general public. But hidden behind the Word were mathematical truths that ruled out a chaotic universe.

The reason the linguisitic view of ALHIM was important to the ancients (and resonates with me) is that through mathematical constructs, such as the Fibonacci Sequence, the existence of our Creator was proven.

For example: in the Fibonacci Sequence, each number is the sum of the preceding two. This string of numbers is a numerical principle that occurs not only in the structure of living organisms but in the heavens as well. This unique pattern can be seen from the spiral formation of our own Milky Way Galaxy down to the arrangement of the soft pads of a kitten's paws; from the swirl in a seashell to the concentric rings in the center of a sunflower; from the soaring beauty of a Greek temple to the delicate patterns of a butterfly's wings; and in our DNA and fingerprints. The repetition of this sequence, built into such diverse elements as galaxies and butterfly wings, is far beyond the realm of coincidence!

That a specific principle, that could be measured mathematically, was inherent in the structure of life proved to the ancient scholars that the universe was not chaotic. There had to be an underlying Intelligence, a Great Architect, a Geometer at work.

We could lay these proofs at the feet of the great god, Coincidence, but, as an old saying goes, if one goes back far enough, coincidence becomes inevitable.

The ancient scholars believed that the Creator revealed the truth of Her/His existence and the essence of the universe through the mathematical and geometrical patterns hidden within creation. These geometrical patterns were incorporated into seemingly simple things as well as in the soaring temples and churches of antiquity, in the masters' paintings, in great poetry, and even in textile designs in the poorest of villages.

The fundamental patterns that rule the universe and life on our small planet can be read through the sacred language of Numbers and Geometry. The 'G' in the center of the Masonic symbol says it succinctly: God Geometrizes.

And yet,

> 'We dance around in a ring and suppose,
> But the Secret sits in the middle and knows.'

This elegant verse, written by the great American Poet Robert Frost, says it all.

Each one of us is the center of our own universe. Everything we know is around us, therefore we sit in the center of the circle of our specific view of life. It's all about perspective. Yet we search outside ourselves for fulfillment. We look into the circles of others, hoping to find truth and happiness and material comfort.

Someday, when we get that Hummer, or when Viggo Mortensen falls in love with us, or when we are chief CEO of L.L. Bean (now, Nick might be happy there), or when we have that plastic surgery and emerge looking like Angelina Jolie, then we will be happy.

According to philosophical teachings, fulfillment comes when we realize there is no separation between the Creator and us. WE are the Secret in the middle of Robert Frost's ring. WE sit in the center of the circle, in the heart of the Creator, the Great Geometer.

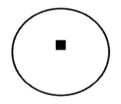

0-595-32735-4